AMOROUS LIAISONS

As the cage began its ascent up the Eiffel Tower, the Commissaire swung towards Annette and wrapped his arms around her pliant body. One hand cupped the swell of her bottom, the middle finger pressing the thin stuff of her dress into the crack between the two opulently rounded cheeks. The other hand slid round from between her shoulderblades until the palm cradled the weight of a large warm breast. He crushed her against his body and below the basque of her corset she could feel the hard pressure of his maleness jammed against her belly.

Also available from Headline

Eros in the Country
Eros in the Town
Eros on the Grand Tour
Eros in the New World
Eros in the Far East
Eros in High Places

By Faye Rossignol

Sweet Fanny
Sweet Fanny's Diary
Lord Hornington's Academy of Love
A Victorian Lover of Women
Ffrench Pleasures

Venus in Paris
A Lady of Quality
The Love Pagoda
The Education of a Maiden
Maid's Night In
Lena's Story
Cremorne Gardens
The Lusts of the Borgias
States of Ecstasy
Wanton Pleasures
The Secret Diary of Mata Hari
The Pleasures of Women
The Secrets of Women
Sweet Sins
The Carefree Courtesan
Love Italian Style
Body and Soul
The Complete Eveline
Sweet Sensations
Lascivious Ladies

Amorous Liaisons

Anonymous

HEADLINE

First published in 1991
by HEADLINE BOOK PUBLISHING PLC

10 9 8 7 6 5 4 3 2 1

ISBN 0 7472 3619 4

Typeset by Medcalf Type Ltd, Bicester, Oxon

Printed and bound by
Collins Manufacturing, Glasgow

HEADLINE BOOK PUBLISHING PLC
Headline House
79 Great Titchfield Street
London W1P 7FN

Amorous
Liaisons

Paris – April, 1900

Part One

Annette

CHAPTER ONE

The man waiting outside the stage door of the Moulin Rouge wore a black frock coat, a tall hat and a pale grey silk cravat beneath his starched wing collar. A gold-knobbed cane dangled from between the fingers of his gloved left hand.

The alley that led to the stage door skirted the famous Montmartre dance-hall's garden and passed behind a huge stucco and plaster elephant bought at the end of a World Fair in Paris eleven years before. A tiny stage was built into the body of the animal, but Zelaska, the oriental belly dancer who contrived thrice nightly to avoid exposing her pubic hair, had already gone home and the few whores left sitting at the lamplit garden tables were without clients.

The man with the cane was not interested in the whores, or in their better-dressed sisters crowding the vast *promenoir* behind the auditorium of the Folies Bergère lower down the hill. He intended to pay no more than the price of a brasserie snack for his pleasure that night. The full-breasted dancer in the back line of the Moulin Rouge chorus would do very nicely, thank you. And he wouldn't have to wait long. Already a burst of cheering and a blare of music from the thirty piece orchestra announced the climax of the final quadrille on the far side of the stage door.

The orchestra, installed in a gallery at one end of the

enormous dance floor, surged into the crescendo of Jacques Offenbach's can-can speciality. The girls, screaming excitedly, swept into the centre of the floor in a swirl of white lace.

They danced in four groups of four, knees raised and skirts frothing. Then they linked arms to form a single line, high-kicking with their daring, dangling, black-stockinged legs. . .separating into two files of eight as the tempo increased and the music became louder, wilder.

The dancers in the back row kicked again, spinning on their points while each lifted ankle was grasped and held high. The front rank girls shrieked and then dived, one after the other, into the splits, plunging into a surf of white petticoats as those behind turned to flip the many-layered undergarments up over their haunches in time with the final crashing chord of the dance.

The men crowded around the floor cheered again. Beneath vaulted colonnades on either side, customers drinking at small round tables rose to their feet to applaud the girls as they ran out through the stage exit on the left of the bandstand. There was laughter and badinage from unattached youths standing six deep inside the hall's mahogany and glass entrance doors. Above the stage exit, the theatre critic of *Figaro* leaned over the balustrade railing off the gallery, craning to watch the last girl disappear. He ran the tip of his tongue over his lower lip, then sat down again at his table and took a notebook from an inside pocket.

'The quadrille,' he wrote, 'has lost nothing of its salacity in the five years since La Goulue hitched up her notorious skirts for the last time and left the Moulin Rouge. Such blunt and unfeminine suggestiveness as is provoked by the dancers of today is made the more outrageous by a glimpse of naked skin deliberately permitted between garter and the first fold of the petticoat each time the dancer lifts her leg. Then, having inflamed the desires of the spectators by a lewd use of midriff and loins, the shameless performers perpetrate a last audacity when, bending double the better to stress their intentions, they insolently fling back these garments to make a display of their behinds.'

The critic licked the point of his pencil, thought for a moment, and added: 'Visitors to our city's Universal Exposition would be well advised to avoid this particular "entertainment".'

He looked up, trying to attract the attention of a waiter, but the electrified lamps on the panel below the conductor's podium had already spelled out the words *Galop Final*, and the crowd was fanning out over the floor from all sides. There was a roll of drums from the percussionist, and the orchestra blared into a military twostep. Beneath the coloured shields and flags of all nations that hung from the pillars of the colonnade, the dancers capered, stamped and galloped.

Most of the men already wore headgear. Silk hats, bowlers, cloth caps and straws moved among the draped velvets and flower-covered boaters of the ladies, for nobody wanted to wait in line outside the cloakroom when the last dance was over — especially tonight.

Zidler, the impresario who had opened the Moulin Rouge in 1889, had instituted a shuttle service of three-horse omnibuses to take his customers down to the Champs Elysées after the show, so that they could watch his dancers again (and hopefully spend more money) doubling the late-night performance at the outdoor Jardin de Paris. His partners, Joseph and Anton Oller, who had bought him out in 1894, still carried on the custom. And there was a particular reason not to be late and miss the free ride tonight: the Universal Exposition, fourth of the great World Fairs held in Paris since the middle of the

previous century, had been inaugurated that very
afternoon, and there were sure to be out-of-the-ordinary
attractions staged in the city spread out below
Montmartre.

The theatre critic was about to start another sentence
when a shadow fell across the page of his notebook. He
raised his head. Two men stood by his table, a heavy,
thickset fellow of about fifty, with a red face and mutton-
chop whiskers, and a younger man who was slim and very
tall. The writer stumbled to his feet and held out his hand
towards the older man, who was in evening dress.

'Forgive me. . .I did not see. . .Monsieur le
Directeur . . .'

Anton Oller shook hands and smiled. He removed a
cigar from his mouth. 'M'sieu,' he said politely. 'Permit
me to present a fellow writer: Doctor Lionel Giotto, of
Boston, in the United States of America. This gentleman,
Doctor, is Felix Romero; you may have seen his
entertainment column in *Figaro*.'

Romero shook hands with the American. 'Delighted,
Monsieur.'

'Doctor Giotto hopes that you may be able to assist
him in a journalistic task he has undertaken.'

The critic looked at the young man again. His eyes were
blue beneath a thatch of straw-coloured hair. The soft
tweed Norfolk suit he wore had obviously been expensive.
'Naturally, Monsieur Oller. Anything I can do, but I fear
that medicine is not my —'

'Not medicine. Philosophy. It's just a university title.'
Giotto smiled, wide mouth opening to reveal even, rather
large teeth. 'Since I was doing the exhibition anyway,
a magazine asked me to write a series of articles on the
Paris underworld. You know — how crime will be
affected by the influx of foreigners staying in the capital.'
His French was correct, but heavily accented, though it

lacked the nasal twang so often associated with transatlantic visitors.

Romero said, 'Of course. As I said.' And then, dubiously, 'But crime is not really my province either. Nevertheless, I do come into contact with the vice squad from time to time. Some of the lesser known music-hall artists, you understand . . .'

He paused and then went on, 'I could introduce you to Morand, the commissaire in charge. And perhaps some of the journalists who deal in. . .the more sordid aspects of life.'

'I should be grateful for any help at all,' Giotto said gravely.

Oller pulled out two chairs from the table, flicked cigar ash from his starched shirt-front, and motioned his guest to sit down. He raised one hand and clicked his fingers. A waiter appeared at once. 'A bottle of the Cliquot '87,' the impresario ordered.

'Bien, m'sieu. Immediately.' The man hurried away.

'It is very kind of you,' Romero began. 'But as a matter of fact I was rather hoping. . .if I could get away early. . .there was an interview I wished to. . .one of the quadrille girls . . .'

'It can wait,' Oller said brusquely. He saw the notebook lying open on the table and picked it up. 'Ah. The copy for tomorrow's column?'

Romero nodded as the impresario scanned the neat lines of script. Finally Oller's face softened. 'Admirable,' he said. 'My brother will approve. You see?' He handed the book to Giotto.

The American read the text with a puzzled frown. 'But. . .*you* approve of this? Yet it is extremely critical. It suggests – '

Oller's chuckle cut him short. 'You should remember the maxim of one of your own vaudeville chiefs: the surest way to sell seats is to have the show banned by the Purity League!'

'I beg your pardon?' The music was drowning their voices as the end of the dance approached.

'Nothing attracts a crowd so much as the advice to stay away lest they be shocked,' Oller said loudly. The waiter reappeared with a silver ice bucket, opened the bottle of champagne expertly, and poured three glasses. 'To your very good health – and a fruitful collaboration,' the showman toasted.

The last dance ended with a thunder of tympani and a crash of cymbals. Applause pattered up from below, and then there was the sound of many feet hurrying across the dance floor. The crowd was streaming out towards the waiting omnibuses. At the table above the stage exit, the bottle was still half full and Romero was trying unsuccessfully to conceal his impatience. At last Oller relented. 'Let me have your cloakroom ticket,' he said, signalling for the waiter. 'Pierre can bring your hat and coat straight here and save you time if this. . .interview. . .is so important.'

The critic flushed. He arranged a meeting with Giotto at the Café de la Paix the following morning and rose awkwardly to his feet. From the inside pocket of his topcoat, when it was brought, the tip of a plain brown envelope protruded. Romero's eyes registered it at once and he flicked a quick glance at Oller. The impresario nodded. 'We are grateful to you, as always,' he said, 'even though the report is laced with – ah – disapproval.' A small smile; the ash tipped from the cigar; and then, drily, 'A fine word, and a useful one – salacity!'

On the floor below, the critic ducked into the men's room to check the number of banknotes in the brown envelope, peeled two from the top of the sheaf, and stuffed them into his trouser pocket. Then, replacing the envelope in his topcoat, he hurried to the backstage area.

In the foyer, the girls hired to present the semi-nude 'plastic poses' had gone home, showcases exhibiting the waxworks and the three-legged man were shuttered, and attendants in uniform had started to bar the row of doors beneath the red windmill at the garden entrance. Romero passed brightly coloured Steinlen, Lautrec and Bonnard posters advertizing music-halls in which the Ollers had an interest – the Olympia and Les Ambassadeurs. He shouldered his way past the men crammed into the passage that led to the dressing rooms.

The smoke-laden air between the flaring gas lamps was heavy with female smells: greasepaint, sweat and cheap scent mingled with the dusty odour of much-used costumes and a rich tang of absinthe and port wine. 'Mademoiselle de Vervialle?' the critic said to the harassed dresser. 'From *Figaro*. . .I should like a word with Annette de Vervialle.'

The woman turned, shouldered open a door that was ajar, and shouted into the bright light beyond: 'Mademoiselle Annette! The scribbler is here again! The gentleman from *Figaro* requests an audience!'

'Oh, *merde*!'

The expletive came from behind a complex of bare backs, a machinery of naked arms lacing, unlacing, tugging off costumes, combing hair. And at once there was a chorus of shrill voices.

'Annette is going to be famous!'

'We shall see her name in lights – or under them!'

'Our Annette has a beau!'

'Yes,' another voice jeered, 'but the beau comes with a fiddle!'

Shouts of laughter. More ribald remarks. A young

11

woman edged her way through the press of dancers and came to the door. She was of medium height, voluptuously built, with the long, straight nose, the short upper lip and the deep chin typical of the period. Her hair was a deep lustrous copper colour. At that moment her large violet eyes were narrowed in a frown and there was an expression of irritation, almost of anger, on her face. 'What is it? What do you want?' she asked impatiently.

'Just a few minutes of your time, Mademoiselle.' Romero's gaze lingered on the soft triangle of flesh visible between the edges of the peignoir she was fastening about her waist.

'I have no time. I have to change my costume and get to the Jardin de Paris. You must know that.'

'Of course, of course. I did not mean now, tonight. If we could perhaps make a rendezvous? Outside in the garden, perhaps, before the performance tomorrow night?' The journalist cleared his throat. 'We could have a drink and – '

'I have no wish to have a drink with you, tomorrow night or any other night. I thought I had already made that clear, Monsieur Romero.' The top of a scarlet and black corset had now appeared in the gap at the front of her robe. Seeing that he was still staring at the swell of her generous breasts, the girl angrily wrapped the garment more tightly around her waist.

'I admire your dancing. I would like to make a mention . . . An article in a newspaper, a paper as important as mine, would help to further your career,' Romero persisted. 'With my recommendation, perhaps a famous director . . .?'

'I already work for a famous director,' Annette snapped.

'Yes. In the chorus. But not as a featured artist. I could

12

help you make the change.' Romero glanced over his shoulder. Several of the stage-door johnnies were crowding close, listening. One or two openly sniggered. 'Just a short interview,' he pleaded. 'All I need are a few personal details.'

'I know. Like whether or not I am prepared to go to a sleazy hotel in the Rue Lepic, and how quickly I can take off my clothes. Your reputation precedes you, Monsieur. Thank you: if my career is to be advanced, it will be on merit — and not on my back.' She stared at him contemptuously and added: 'If you cannot find yourself a sleeping partner without offering bribes, why not go out into the garden now? Some of the cheaper whores may still be available.'

Romero's face darkened with fury. 'You will regret this. . .this insolence!' he shouted. 'I am not without influence and I warn you, impudent hussy that you are: I shall make sure that you never — '

But the girl had already turned her back. 'Close the door, Marthe,' she said to the dresser. 'There is an ill wind blowing.'

Romero strode away, followed by the unkind laughter of the waiting men.

The streets were crowded when Annette de Vervialle and her fellow performers came out ten minutes later. A line of cabs waited between the trees in the centre of the Boulevard de Clichy, and there were still two of Oller's omnibuses drawn up outside the famous *Bal*. Across the road, waiters moved swiftly and expertly among swarms of people sitting at the sidewalk cafés. Somewhere up the steep hill leading to the Sacré Coeur an accordion was playing.

The frock-coated man with the gold-knobbed cane materialized from the shadows as Annette passed beneath the lamp over the stage door.

'Permit me, Mademoiselle . . .' He raised the tall hat politely. 'Comte Gustav de la Férérière, at your service.' He handed her a small gilt-edged card.

She looked at it dubiously in the light from the lamp. 'Monsieur le Comte? I am afraid I do not quite . . .?'

'I represent a consortium of showmen connected with the exhibition,' De la Férérière said smoothly. 'Gentlemen of some means who are on the lookout for talented entertainers, especially dancers. Your own artistry in that direction has been drawn to my attention, and I fancy a little chat might prove fruitful for us both.'

Frowning, Annette said, 'In what way? What kind of entertainment? What have your. . .principals. . .in mind?'

'Something that would bring you before a more sophisticated audience than the rustics who cavort here.' He waved the cane contemptuously at the red windmill. 'Something that would certainly pay better and probably set your feet on the ladder of success. You would in any case be featured in what the profession terms a solo spot.'

She hesitated, staring at the man. She saw a suave, sallow face with glittering black eyes, a neatly trimmed beard. The offer certainly sounded tempting. On the other hand . . .

'In any case,' she said, 'I cannot discuss it now. I am already late for another – '

'Precisely,' the Comte interrupted. 'I am aware that you have to be at the Jardin de Paris – where I hope to enjoy your performance after the *tour-de-chant* of Mademoiselle Jane Avril. My carriage is waiting.' He gestured toward the boulevard. 'If you would allow me to escort you to the Champs Elysées, we would arrive well before Monsieur Oller's omnibus, and we could. . .that is to say, I could explain the project in more detail on the way.'

14

'Very well.' Annette made up her mind and nodded briskly.

He led her to a closed landau with a coat of arms on the door and a liveried coachman waiting to hand her into the interior.

'Drive past La Trinité and then take the Boulevard Haussman and the Avenue d'Iéna,' he instructed the servant. 'There will be less traffic that way, and we can go past the Trocadero.'

'I really must not be late,' Annette warned.

He sank back on the cushions beside her. 'Do not worry, my dear. You shall see: this will prove to be your lucky night.'

The carriage pulled out to pass the crowd of hatless prostitutes, touts, vendors of postcards and hot chestnut sellers jostling the customers still milling around the omnibuses. In the garish light of a naphtha flare above a barrow piled with tubs of oysters, mussels and clams, De la Férérière cast a sly glance at the young woman beside him. The olive green dress that she wore was fashioned with a three-tiered skirt and a swathed peplum of the same colour. An ivory shawl triangled over her shoulders and fastened in front with a brooch below the scooped-out neck of the garment. There was ivory net veiling the cartwheel hat on her head, but although the ensemble was chic enough at a distance, he could see now that the clothes were a little shabby. The cheap velvet of the skirt was plushed, the egrets at one side of the big hat drooped, there were cracks in the worn and scuffed leather of her buttoned ankle boots.

Excellent, he thought to himself, painting an intriguing picture for the monied men whose private entertainment he was hired to arrange. He already knew that the girl lived in an unheated attic six floors above the street in an unsalubrious quarter near the Gare St Lazare. She was

15

fleshy and well-formed. She was poor. She cherished, no doubt, dreams of stardom and riches as a reward for her talent.

The formula, he reflected, was perfect.

It was not until they were rattling down the cobbled slope of the Rue de Clichy that he revealed the exact nature of the entertainment expected by the gentlemen connected with the exhibition.

The fact that it would be in private, before small selected audiences at discreet soirées, had called for a certain amount of smooth talking. But it was the nature of the dancing, plus the fact that the 'discreet' audiences would consist entirely of men − or, occasionally, only of women − that aroused the girl's suspicions.

'Monsieur le Comte,' she said, 'you have already told me that the exact *type* of costume is "unimportant". Now you are telling me that the garments themselves are less important than the body they clothe.'

'But of course. Especially as they would be visible for such a small part of the performance. It is the body of the artist −'

'Monsieur! Do I understand you? If so,' Annette said angrily, 'let me say at once that I am not prepared to exhibit myself naked for the titillation of lascivious gentlemen − however well connected − at that kind of private party.'

'My dear young lady! Be your age, as they say, which I imagine to be well over that of consent. There is nothing shameful in a naked body, particularly one as beautiful as yours. Think of the Romans, the Greeks and their statues, the Etruscan −'

'There *is* something shameful in a group of lechers, probably old ones at that, lusting after it!' the girl cried. Biting her lip, she stared out of the window, her eyes glistening with tears. So once again it was the old story:

16

the promises were worthless, no more than a cover for the usual indecent proposition.

Beyond the great dome of Garnier's new opera house, fireworks from the exhibition crackled over the roofs, sending bursts of red, white and blue stars exploding into the sky. Why, she asked herself furiously, did the bright sparks of hope extinguish themselves always as swiftly as those artificial stars?

The carriage rounded a corner into a side street, throwing De la Férérière momentarily against her. Instinctively, he shot out an arm to steady himself, the palm of his hand landing in her lap. He murmured an apology. . .but as the landau settled back on its springs and he was able to straighten himself, the hand remained where it lay. she could feel it as an unwelcome warmth and weight against the top of her thighs, an alien presence that was both distasteful and disturbing. She shifted herself further along the seat.

The hand twisted. She could feel hot fingers gripping her flesh through the stuff of her skirt.

She opened her mouth to protest, but he was already out of his own seat, hurling himself at her, wrenching up the skirt to scrabble in the froth of underclothes beneath, his other arm clamped around her waist.

Winey breath spiced with cigar smoke played over her face as his wet lips, bristly with beard, sucked on her neck and then slid downwards to gobble at the smooth slopes of flesh sculpting the bosom thrusting out the scooped neckline of her bodice.

'Come on,' he muttered hoarsely. 'Enough of this prudish nonsense! You want it, you little bitch, don't you? You know you want it! You're just aching to feel my big, hot . . .'

Annette screamed, squirming frenziedly in an attempt to fend him off, to free herself from his crushing weight, from the obscene explorations of his hands. 'Let me go, you monster!' she panted, flailing ineffectually at his chest with her fists. 'Take your vile fingers away from my . . .'

She screamed again. The probing hand had ripped aside layers of cotton and lace to touch her in that secret place whose sudden stimulation, she knew, could send shivers of forbidden pleasure flaming through her loins.

By this time the Comte was on his knees, his free hand tearing at the lacing of her bodice.

Annette raked her nails across the sallow flesh between the beard and his left eye. At the same time she drew up one foot and, with a superhuman effort, planted the sole of her boot against the man's chest and thrust him violently away from her.

De la Férérière's cry of pain and rage was drowned by a shout from the coachman as he pulled up the horses at a busy intersection.

As the carriage rocked almost to a halt, the girl seized her opportunity. She reached for the gilded loop of the landau's door handle, twisted it, and shoved with all her strength.

The shallow door sprang open.

While her would-be violator was still sprawled back on his heels, Annette stumbled out of the carriage, over the high step, and on to the cobbles below. She picked herself up and began to run.

CHAPTER TWO

Still sobbing with rage and humiliation, Annette de Vervialle ran down the entire broad length of the Avenue de l'Opéra. The roadway was crowded with cabs and carriages, victorias and broughams, dogcarts and coupés and *urbaines*, all on their way to the exhibition. But it was too late for an omnibus, there were no fiacres waiting at any of the cab stands, and all those she hailed were already occupied.

There was nothing for it: she would have to go the whole way on foot. And — she glanced at the clock in the tower above the arched entrance to the Louvre courtyard — she was due there in less than fifteen minutes. Hitching up her skirt, she turned into the Rue de Rivoli and sprinted between the astonished strollers beneath the colonnades.

The Jardin de Paris was an open-air café-concert with tables and chairs set out in the lamplight beneath the trees shading the lower end of the Champs Elysées. The entrance to the roofed pavilion housing the small stage and the orchestra was down a side street. Annette, panting and out of breath, was halfway there when a disturbance broke out on the far side of the iron railings bounding the place. In the garden, every seat was taken and there was an air of excitement and gaiety among the crowded tables that was almost tangible. On the stage, Jane Avril was singing. Beyond the trees on the far side of the avenue, the sky pulsated with reflections from the exhibition entrance on the river bank, and the roar of the crowd, punctuated occasionally by bursts of hurdy-gurdy music, swelled every now and then to swamp the small orchestra on stage. More evident still was the noise from a group of men sitting near the railings.

They had become engaged in a rowdy altercation with a dozen foreigners at a nearby table. From what Annette could hear, the foreigners — they looked as though they could be Dutchmen or Germans — were accused of making insulting suggestions to the young women with the Parisians. Both parties seemed to be the worse for drink.

As she hurried past, the argument flared into violence. A table overturned with a crash of breaking glass. Men shouted, women screamed, and the next moment blows were exchanged and a fight had started.

Waiters in long white aprons converged on the scuffling customers; other clients ran to the aid of the outnumbered Frenchmen; a gate in the railings was opened and a concerted effort to eject the drunken visitors began. Before she realized what was happening, Annette was surrounded by punching, kicking, swearing men.

Her cartwheel hat was knocked off and rolled away toward the pavilion. As she ran, bent forwards to retrieve it, a waiter struggling with two of the Dutchmen fell to the ground in front of her, rolling in the gutter to trip her up. At the same time there was a shout from the far end of the street, followed by a rush of feet. Compatriots of the foreigners had seen what was happening and were running to the rescue. Soon the battle was raging all over the narrow street and Annette, picking herself up, found that she was cut off from the side door to the pavilion. Hastily, she took refuge on the opposite sidewalk.

Police whistles shrilled in the distance. She could hear

the rumble of heavy wheels over the sounds of the combat.

Backed against the wall of a house, she looked desperately to right and left. The antagonists surrounded her more closely than ever. A man with blood streaming from his nose lurched against her shoulder and almost knocked her off her feet again. She felt a violent blow in the small of the back. From below, hands groped obscenely for her ankle, her thigh. Then a dishevelled giant extricated himself from the fray and lurched towards her with a drunken leer on his face.

'Why bother with the damned frogs when there's a pretty frog-ess ripe for the picking,' the Dutchman mumbled. He shot out a ham-like fist and seized the front of her bodice, tearing it downwards with a savage jerk. The lacing, already loosened by the pawing hands of the Comte de la Férérière, burst open and the green material ripped down to the waist, spilling out one naked breast above the busks of her red corset.

The attacker uttered a shout of triumph. He grabbed the quivering mound of flesh in one grimed hand and wrapped his other arm around her waist, crushing her to his sweating body in a bear hug.

Annette butted his nose with the top of her head as hard as she could and brought one knee sharply up into his crotch. The Dutchman staggered back with a yell of rage, jack-knifing to ease the pain clawing his loins. The girl, abandoning any hope of reaching the café-concert, turned and fled through an archway that pierced the wall of the building a few yards to her left.

She found herself in a cobbled courtyard. Gas lamps flared softly in the four corners but the place seemed deserted. At the far end, three steps led up to double doors which opened on to a hallway with a concierge's office at one side. Annette ran across the courtyard and up into the hall. The glassed-in, mahogany and brass office was empty. Beyond it, a dark passage curved around the stone staircase and disappeared towards the back of the building. She raced through, her footsteps echoing between the walls and the flagged floor.

There was another door at the end of the passageway. Cautiously, she opened it a crack and peered through. She breathed a sigh of relief. The door was at the top of a short flight of stairs that dipped down to another street.

She hesitated halfway down. There were a lot of people in the street: it seemed almost as crowded as the one she had left. She saw women walking dogs, women with outrageous hats and immodest décolletages, hatless girls with impudent smiles. She heard brusque male and angry female voices. She saw the newly installed electrical street lighting glint on brass buttons and buckles, recognized the dark shape of police uniforms, and then – as her eyes registered the presence of wire-netted black marias blocking off each end of the thoroughfare – she realized that the whistles and the wheels she had heard had been directed at this street and not the one where the fighting raged.

She remembered reading a newspaper article quoting the Prefect of Police. In the coming weeks, he had announced, there would be a concerted drive by the vice squad and other units to 'clean up' Paris, so that visitors to the great exhibition would not be offended by the sight of prostitutes openly soliciting on the streets of the capital. Clearly it was a phase of this operation that she was witnessing. She turned, wondering whether she dared after all go back through the courtyard and try to reach the café-concert by a roundabout route, or whether it would be wiser to wait where she was until the police roundup was over.

Before she could make up her mind, her arm was seized in a rough grip and a voice growled, 'Letting the punters enjoy a touch of window-shopping, are we? So the boys can have a preview of what they're paying for?'

She swung around. A tall *agent* in képi and night cape; a shorter man standing close by. 'Whatever do you mean?' she snapped. 'Let go of my arm.'

The tall man indicated the torn dress and her exposed breast. 'All right, sweetie,' he said. 'Come along with us and we'll give you a nice ride.'

Colour flamed in Annette's cheeks. 'Take your hands off me at once!' she stormed. 'What do you think I am?'

The shorter policeman chuckled. 'We know what you are,' he said. 'The question is: are you going to come quietly, or do we have to carry you?'

Her eyes suddenly widened in understanding. 'But . . .? Surely you cannot think . . .? You mean you are mistaking me for one of these unfortunate . . .? But you must be *mad!*' She choked on her words and gestured helplessly at the arguing women in the street.

'Why not spare us the injured innocent formula and come quietly?' the tall policeman said. 'You're coming anyway, so spare your breath – and ours.'

'How dare you! How can you be so stupid! How . . .' Annette was incoherent with rage. 'I was simply waiting on this step, when –'

'Oh, sure,' the short man interrupted. 'You were expecting a friend; you were seeing if it was safe to take the little dog for walkies; you were waiting for an omnibus.' He shook his head, sighed, and wiped the back of his hand across his heavy moustache. 'We heard it twenty times tonight already. Now come on: we have to finish here and do the whole of the Rue de la Boétie before dawn, and it's getting late.'

'But I tell you –'

23

'Tell it to the desk sergeant,' the first man said gruffly. He nodded to his companion and they stepped forwards. Protesting vehemently, Annette was grasped by the arms and hustled towards the end of the street.

Two minutes later she was pushed up the steps and into the back of one of the caged, horse-drawn patrol wagons known in Paris as 'salad baskets'. Then, with two dozen abusive, shrieking prostitutes, she was driven away to the station house.

CHAPTER THREE

The police headquarters of the VIIIth Arrondissement formed one side of a small square surrounding a public garden. It was a squat Second Empire building with dusty wooden floors and inside walls from which the plaster was already flaking. The night-duty sergeant sat high up behind a tall desk and peered down over the edge at the women lined up in the charge room. He was a thin-faced man with centre-parted hair and pince-nez which he wore slightly askew. Apart from his uniform collar, which had reddened loose folds of flesh beneath his jaw, he looked more like a notary or a pharmacist than a policeman.

As each prostitute was summoned to the desk, her name was called out by the arresting officer and a clerk at the back of the room consulted a card index, handing the relevant slip of pasteboard up to the sergeant as soon as he located it. The officer then took out his notebook and read his evidence in a rapid monotone; the woman — sometimes defiantly, sometimes mechanically, occasionally angrily — pleaded guilty; a fine of twenty or thirty francs was levied; and finally, having been cautioned not to solicit in the street, she was allowed to leave.

Still seething with indignation because she had been taken for one of these 'ladies of easy virtue', and angrier still because she had missed the performance at the Jardin de Paris, Annette de Vervialle waited impatiently for her turn to come. She had tried several times to capture the attention of the desk sergeant (surely, once she had explained the idiotic mistake his men had made, he would apologise and send her home?), but there had been such an outcry each time from the other women, and such uncouth behaviour from the policemen who had 'arrested' her, that she had at last decided, at least for the moment, to play the game their way.

She was standing next to a dark-eyed, hollow-cheeked girl whose clothes, gaudy and a little *démodé*, looked as though they had been handed down by an elder sister. 'Just who do we think we are then?' this girl asked after Annette's final attempt. 'Haven't you been on the game long enough to know that it's best to let the *flics* call the tune?'

Although she was furious at being mistaken for a prostitute, Annette was quite free of the normal bourgeois contempt for 'fallen women': there were too many whores living near the railway terminus in her neighbourhood for her to feel snobbish about them as people. And so she answered civilly enough: 'That's just the point. I am not on the game, as you call it, at all. That's what I am trying to get these fools to realize.'

'Oh, come on!' chided the dark girl. 'Keep that story for the beak — though it's you that's the fool if you think he'll fall for it. You've got a nerve anyway, trying to work our pitch. Who's your Jules?'

'I wish I could make *somebody* understand!' said Annette in exasperation. 'I do not have a. . .Jules?. . .if by that you mean a man who looks after me, a. . .a ponce.'

'Working on your own, are you? All the more reason to know – '

'I. . .am. . .not. . .*working* at all, not in the sense you mean,' Annette stormed. 'I am telling you the truth. If

26

you must know, I am a dancer at the Moulin Rouge.'

'Oh me! Oh my! A *dancer* at the Moulin *Rouge*! Do forgive my common *ignorance*!' Mimicking Annette's accent, the girl uttered a raucous laugh which ended in a fit of coughing. 'Hoity-toity, aren't we?' she choked. 'Here, Milady, meet someone after your own crooked heart!'

A tall woman of about thirty, who was standing just in front of them, turned around with a haughty stare. She was pigeon-breasted, with a tiny waist and billowy hips over which her pink-and-white striped dress fell in graceful folds. Her honey-coloured hair was piled on top of her head, and she was carrying a parasol edged with white lace. 'Were you addressing me?' she enquired.

'Nobody else,' the dark girl said. 'Here's another innocent who has no Jules. . .indeed she's far too pure to be on the game at all!' She coughed again, her thin body racked beneath the ill-fitting clothes.

Annette was aware that she was being scrutinized by a surprisingly shrewd pair of eyes – large, slightly prominent amber eyes with heavy lids and long curling lashes. 'Greetings! One does so relish an encounter with a person of one's own class,' the woman drawled, the eyes registering every detail of Annette's torn but relatively sober dress. 'Really, it taxes one's forbearance to the utmost, waiting for these incompetent morons to acknowledge their mistakes.'

'That is exactly what I have been saying myself.'

'I, of course,' the tall woman said a little later, 'have no place amongst this *racaille*. Confidentially, I am in fact of noble blood – a descendant of the Delannoys of Honfleur. It is only because of some wretched lawyers' quibble that one finds oneself in this humiliating position today.' The effect was only slightly spoiled by the fact that the husky voice spoke with a Marseille dockside accent. It was with some surprise therefore that Annette observed her, shortly afterwards, entering a brisk plea of guilty, handing over her fine, and sweeping out of the charge room.

'De Vervialle, Annette, address unknown,' the policeman who had arrested her called out.

'This is absurd,' Annette said to the desk sergeant. 'Surely – '

'No card,' the clerk interrupted.

The sergeant sighed, drawing a ledger towards him and picking up a steel-nibbed pen. 'Names and professions of parents?' he asked wearily.

'I insist that you allow me to explain. This has gone on far too long – '

'Your parents' names and what they did?'

She compressed her lips. 'Armand and Marie-Thérèse Durand. De Vervialle is my stage name. My father was a silversmith; my mother went to rich folks' houses to help sometimes with the laundry. They both died when I was thirteen.' Annette paused. 'I cannot see what this has to do with . . .I demand that you stop this nonsense at once.'

The sergeant looked sternly over his pince-nez as some of the girls behind Annette began to giggle. 'Your mother's maiden name?'

'Oh, for goodness' sake!. . .Fournier. Marie-Thérèse Fournier.'

'Evidence of arrest?' the sergeant said to the taller of the two *agents* who had brought her in.

'Acting on orders received, we were flushing out the Rue Rudolphe Laporte, off the Champs Elysées. She was loitering in a darkened doorway – exposing her body to passers-by.'

'That's not true!' Annette shouted. 'My dress was torn in a street brawl by the Jardin de – '

'Silence!' The sergeant was busy writing. He dipped his pen in an inkwell. 'What number in the Rue Laporte?'

'Number Fourteen.'

'And the street number, was it the usual size? Was it illuminated?'

Like most Parisians, Annette knew that licensed brothels had illuminated street numbers above their doors, and the figures of these numbers were larger than those of the houses in the rest of the street. For the first time a shiver of doubt tremored through her.

'The normal size,' the policeman was saying. 'There was no light behind it.'

'That is a very serious offence,' the sergeant said severely, 'operating from unlicensed premises. Especially when it is coupled with open soliciting on the street. And even worse when that is accompanied by a lewd display of the person.' He turned to the clerk. 'Fourteen Rue Rudolphe Laporte — that is not on the list, is it?'

The clerk was leafing through a file. 'Not as far as I can see.'

'What is all this about unlicensed brothels?' a harsh voice grated from the doorway leading to the street.

Annette and the remaining women swung around. A short, bulky man with a red face and bristling side whiskers was standing there. He wore a hard hat with a curly brim, a check suit and highly polished black boots. 'Who is that?' Annette whispered to the girl with the cough.

'Hervé Rochard, the inspector who's assistant to the vice squad chief. Watch out: he's a right bastard.'

'Where is this unlicensed house?' Rochard demanded.

'In the Rue Rudolphe Laporte, sir.' The sergeant was deferential. 'This woman was caught soliciting outside the door.'

'That's a lie!' Annette yelled. 'I was not soliciting, or

anything like it. I was simply coming out of the door —
it's the rear entrance of a house in the next street — and
I paused because I saw —'

'Be quiet!' the sergeant ordered. 'Speak when you're
spoken to.'

'I will *not* be quiet. It's time this comedy stopped. I
tried to tell you three times already: I am a dancer at the
Moulin Rouge.'

'A likely story,' Rochard sneered.

'It's true! And I can prove it!' She pointed at the brass
and ebonite apparatus of a telephone perched on its
wooden box. 'Just wind up that machine and ask the
operator —'

'Silence!'

Annette bit her lip. Fear, a sudden wave of it,
temporarily submerged her indignation. Rochard had
approached the desk. 'It's bad enough that we have to
suffer this pollution, this filth, in establishments licensed
and approved by the state,' he growled. 'But when it
comes to clandestine houses, the situation is
insupportable. Send a squad around to the Rue Laporte
to investigate this *bordel* at once.' His face was flushed
a deep red above his high celluloid collar.

'Why is he so *angry*?' Annette murmured to the dark
girl.

'First because he's a damned prude; more importantly
because he gets a rake-off from the licensed houses —
to make sure he won't oppose the renewal of the license
when it comes up. A wildcat house means a loss of money
to Rochard.' She giggled at her own unintentional word
play, then doubled over with another fit of coughing.
'Wild *cat*-house — that's not bad, eh?' she spluttered.

'Stop talking, you cheap sluts,' Rochard snapped. He
strutted towards Annette with his thumbs hooked into the
pockets of the waistcoat strained over his ample paunch.

'Very well, you. What have you got to say for yourself?'

Annette decided that charm might be a better weapon than protest with this kind of man. 'Inspector,' she said with her most winning smile, 'I am sure that a person of your intelligence will see at once that an unfortunate mistake — understandable but unfortunate — has been made by your men. As I have already explained, I was escaping from a street brawl when I happened to be caught up in your. . .in your operation against these misguided women.'

'Oh, God! Another Milady!' somebody behind Annette muttered.

Rochard was standing in front of her, his feet planted astride, his fingers drumming on the gold watch-chain looped across his belly. 'Go on,' he said.

'I am, as I told you, a dancer. I work for the Ollers at the Moulin Rouge and the Jardin de Paris.'

'Then why were you not at the caf'-conc' with the other artists?'

'I came down separately, with a friend in a carriage. It was after I. . .after I left him that the brawl — '

'Ah! A man friend! So you do have a Jules!' the sergeant exclaimed. 'His name and address?'

Annette thought quickly. The Comte could only confirm the first part of her story. And, important though he might be, he was unlikely to say anything in her favour after the way she had left him! She cursed herself for having mentioned the carriage. 'I don't know his name or address,' she said lamely. 'He was. . .just somebody I met at the stage door.'

'I see. A pick-up,' Rochard nodded. 'And when he wouldn't pay your price, you decided to try your luck with the other girls in the Rue Rudolphe Laporte?'

'*No!*' Annette stamped her foot impotently. 'Why would I be picking up somebody, as you call it, when

31

I had to be on stage, dancing, in less than thirty minutes? And I *am* a dancer. Telephone Anton Oller and he will confirm it.'

The police inspector fished a large gold watch out of his waistcoat pocket and sprung open the lid. 'I am certainly not going to disturb Monsieur Oller, or anyone else, at three o'clock in the morning,' he observed. He snapped shut the watch and dropped it back in his pocket. 'I can ask him to verify – or deny – that in the morning. In any case, even if you were a dancer, that's no proof that you don't do a little whoring on the side. I know how little a dancer earns, and –'

'I *am* a dancer; I am *not* a whore!' Annette cried.

Rochard seemed suddenly to tire of the exchange. 'Of course you are a whore,' he said, turning his back on her. 'If you weren't, you wouldn't have been in that street and my men wouldn't have run you in, would they?'

To this example of male logic, Annette could find no immediate answer.

The desk sergeant raised an enquiring eyebrow. Rochard nodded. 'Very well,' the sergeant said. 'Fifty francs.'

'Even if I was what you say I am, and even if I was prepared to pay it,' she said in a choked voice, 'why fifty for me when the others were all twenty or thirty?'

'Ah, well. . .they didn't make any trouble, did they?'

'I don't have that much money with me,' Annette lied.

The sergeant drew a blank card towards him. 'Then you will spend the night in the cells,' he said, writing. 'And you will stay there,' Rochard put in, 'until you can arrange for someone to bring the money down for you.'

The tears blinding Annette's eyes as she was led below by a uniformed gaoler were provoked as much by rage as by the unjustness of the accusation against her and the humiliation of her position.

* * *

By the time she was brought up into the charge room again at ten o'clock the following morning, Annette had plenty of time to reflect on the inequalities of the social system in France — especially as applied at the beginning of what had been widely hailed as a century of progress. Progressive it might be so far as men and their machines were concerned, but the more she though about it, the more she raged at the rôle she and her sex were still required to play.

It was, she thought, typical that because of a geographical accident it was necessarily assumed that she must be engaged in some clandestine sexual activity. At the exhibition which had indirectly been the cause of her plight, great emphasis was laid — so she had read — on the so-called feminine aspects of France. There was even a Palais de la Femme glorifying female achievements. Paris itself was publicized as a city oriented towards the female: from the society salons of the Comtesse Greffulhe to the *demi-mondaines* of Maxim's, the Parisienne was held up as the epitome of allure. Even the drooping curves and voluptuous swells of the art-nouveau style revolutionizing design hinted at eroticism and the caress.

And that was just the trouble — Annette fumed, pushing away the grey bread and watery coffee left in the cell at 6 a.m. — Paris might be a woman; it was permissible to glorify her. . .but only if she kept her place. And that place was in bed.

She was still seething with rage when she confronted the day-duty desk sergeant — a younger man with brilliantined hair and a wide moustache. And her temper was not improved when, picking a sheet of paper from a wire basket by his elbow, he told her that Monsieur Oller had refused to come to the police station to speak for her or bail her out. He had nevertheless confirmed

over the telephone that a dancer named Annette de
Vervialle had been in his employ.

'*Had* been?' the girl echoed. 'But I don't . . .?'

She had been dismissed the previous evening, the
sergeant said, for failing to appear at a performance
scheduled for the Jardin de Paris. 'And now we
understand why you joined the tarts in the Rue Laporte,'
he said not unkindly. 'You had lost your job. Perhaps
you needed money to pay the rent. Those bastards that
run the music-halls don't give anything away, do they?
You'd have got nothing in lieu of notice, I'll bet. So why
didn't you come clean last night? Maybe you'd have got
off with a lighter fine, even with Inspector Rochard here.'

Faced with this further confirmation of official
prejudice, Annette gave up. Suddenly it was all too much
for her: all she wanted was to get out of there. 'Fifty
francs, was it not?' she said wearily, fumbling in her
purse.

'But. . .if you had the money all the time, why did you
not say so?' The young sergeant was bewildered. 'You
could have saved yourself an uncomfortable night and
slept in your own bed.'

She shook her head. It was too difficult to explain. And
if she told him that paying the fine last night would have
seemed to her as if she was accepting herself at *their*
valuation, he probably wouldn't understand anyway.
Eyes smarting with tiredness and with tears, she stumbled
towards the door.

A tall man in uniform was standing on the far side of
it, at the top of the steps leading to the street. He turned
as the door banged open and shut, and she saw that he
had darkly curling hair, thick eyebrows and an unusually
handsome face. His eyes were a very bright blue. . .and
they were staring at her now beneath a forehead
corrugated with concern.

'Mademoiselle, you look both exhausted and distressed,' said he. 'Is there anything I can do to help?'

Annette halted. 'Who are you?' she said suspiciously.

'Commissaire Morand,' he replied, the voice deep and reassuring. And then again, 'Can I help you?'

The warmth in that voice, the hint of friendliness in his manner, were more than the girl, in her overwrought state, could bear. To her intense exasperation, she burst into tears and began blurting out the whole sad story.

Morand was at once sympathetic. 'Of course I believe you,' he soothed. 'Clearly some kind of mistake has been made. Now calm down, stop crying, and you shall tell me all about it.' He placed a comforting hand under her elbow. 'There is a small garden in the centre of the square outside. It is already quite warm. We will sit on a bench there and discuss the situation in private.'

As Annette clutched together the torn edges of her dress, he steered her out into the sunlight.

CHAPTER FOUR

Commissaire Bruno Morand was head of the Paris 'Brigade of Morals', more popularly known as the vice squad. Although his work brought him into contact with prostitutes, pimps, drug traffickers, extortionists, brothels and their keepers and cut-throats of various kinds, he was more concerned with the application of the law in general and the broad decisions this required than the mechanics of police raids in red light districts and suchlike. He listened sympathetically nevertheless to Annette's story.

Through no fault of her own, it seemed, she had been by a singularly malign stroke of ill fortune *fichée*, booked, registered in the police files as a common prostitute, convicted, imprisoned and fined. And she had lost her job into the bargain. It was, he agreed, intolerable. He would see what he could do to put matters right.

'Meanwhile' — he glanced at her tear-stained face — 'when, my dear young woman, did you last eat?'

'Y-y-yesterday m-morning,' Annette confessed.

'Then the first thing we must do,' Morand said, 'is buy you a meal. After that we can see about your damaged dress and I will drive you home.'

The torn dress was sewn together, at the Commissaire's expense, by the owner of a small draper's shop near the Trocadero Palace — but not before Morand had taken her to a brasserie and insisted that she eat oysters, a steak

37

and salad, and share a bottle of champagne with him.

'I have to take a brief stroll through the exhibition grounds,' he told her when they had finished. 'To see that my fellows posted there are doing their duty, you know. After that I shall take you home.'

Annette had never been inside the exhibition, which stretched, on both sides of the river, from the Place de la Concorde to the Eiffel Tower — which had been built, like the Trocadero, to grace a previous World's Fair in 1889. Slightly tipsy from the champagne, she was now in a mood to be dazzled by everything. The humiliations of the night were speedily forgotten as they walked slowly down the 100-yard-wide flight of steps leading from the palace to the riverside gardens. She marvelled at the medley of pavilions overlooking the Seine — Moorish minarets that rose above Polynesian huts, temples and pagodas from Indo-China, a reconstructed Algerian casbah. 'We will cross the river,' Morand said, gesturing towards the bridge, 'and then take the left bank as far as the Boul' Mich', where we can pick up a cab.'

He *was* handsome, Annette thought as they passed oriental dancers and African musicians performing among the cafés and sideshows on the far side of the water. The high-necked uniform and képi went well with his generous sideburns, firm mouth and those clear blue eyes. And the body beneath the uniform was lean, muscular and. . .she could not help noticing. . .very well endowed. Wasn't that what the other girls at the Moulin Rouge said when a man . . .?

She put the thought from her head. They were traversing the exhibition's Quai des Nations, where the wealthier exhibitors had each built an architectural display typical of their country. The English contribution was a Tudor manor house made from real stone, the American an office block that resembled a giant wedding cake. Sunlight filtering .through the riverside trees splashed dappled shadow across Morand's scissoring thighs as he strode purposefully toward the Place St Michel. 'My home from home,' he said, nodding across the water at the tall grey facades rising above the island that divided the Seine. 'The Quai des Orfèvres. You shall come one night to visit my office.'

She stared past a pleasure boat crammed with sightseers. 'One night?'

'Less formal; more. . .intimate.' Morand's hand tightened on her arm.

Despite herself, Annette felt her breath quicken. The tight blue trousers with their red stripe drew her eyes again. Could she be mistaken. . .really she must *not* allow herself to keep on glancing that way!. . .or was the obtrusive bulge at the upper limit of his thighs bigger, somehow harder, stiffer-looking than it had been before?

The boat passed beneath the low arch of the Pont St Michel, its paddle wheels churning the water into white froth. Morand was hailing a fiacre. He jerked open the door and bundled her into the dark interior.

The dusty, deep-buttoned upholstery smelled faintly of cigar smoke. He gave the cabbie an address in the Rue Notre Dame de Lorette, and dropped into the seat opposite her.

'But. . .my lodgings are in the Rue Halévy, on the other side of Montmartre,' Annette protested. She was surprised to hear that her words were a little slurred.

'We shall have a drink first at a little place I know,' the commissaire said firmly. He was sitting with his feet planted apart, and — yes, there was no doubt about it — that part of him expressly designed to stand upright was as rigid as the flagstaffs they were passing in front of Notre Dame cathedral. There was even, at the summit of this prominence, a small patch of material that was darker than the rest. He pulled down blinds to cover the cab's windows. 'Come over here,' he ordered.

'I am quite comfortable here, thank you.'

'We didn't hire this rattletrap for comfort,' Morand said, his voice suddenly rough. 'Come.'

To her own astonishment, Annette instantly obeyed. Her cheeks felt flushed and there was a curious tremor in her loins that reminded her, irresistibly, of the bubbles in a glass of champagne — only this time the tiny pleasure *bulles* were floating down rather than up.

She was sitting unaccountably on one of the Commissaire's wide-spread knees, her body at right-angles to his broad chest, her hands clasped demurely over her stomach. One of his hands rested casually on Annette's knee, the one nearest him. His other arm supported her around the waist.

'Come, *ma poule*, it is time for us to get to know each other, to get friendly,' Morand said. The hand on her knee tightened, drawing that leg towards him. The cab lurched, rounding a corner, throwing her off balance so that the outside of her thigh brushed his groin. And this time there could be no mistake whatever: through the thick stuff of her olive green dress she felt the pressure of a staff as hard as the bone and flesh of the thigh on which she was perched. Morand's heavy breathing was now audible over the clip-clop of the cab horse's hooves on the cobbles.

A little dazedly, the girl recalled her feelings of outrage when, less than twenty-four hours previously, she had been thrown together in a similar way with a man — in the Comte's landau. Why did she not experience the same sense of physical disgust, the same loathing at the effrontery of this police officer, with his forced intimacies and his invading grasp? Was it only because he had treated her — at least at first — as another human being rather than a plaything, that he had believed her story, acted in a warm and friendly way? Was she in fact reacting like a cat, that purrs because it is stroked? Or was there a hint of something deeper, something more profound, in her ambiguous reaction to his proximity?

She had no time to pursue the reflection, because the hand on her knee plunged suddenly to seize the hem of her skirt and whisk it, together with the two white petticoats beneath, up to knee level. Then the palm resumed its former position on her leg. . .but resting this time on the black stocking that sheathed her limb above one calf-length button boot.

The arm around her waist tightened. The leg was drawn closer to the Commissaire's crotch, spreading the young woman's feet further apart; the fingers of the hand on her knee slid down the inside of her thigh.

Annette, opening her mouth to protest, found her own breath quickening again. The subtle tingling at the base of her belly had triggered some soundless unseen vibration within her that spread like the quiver of a butterfly's wings from the furred chalice of her femininity to the tips of her breasts. 'No,' she whispered, though every nerve in her body now clamoured to shout Yes. 'No, no, you must not. Really!'

'Yes, I must,' Morand interrupted hoarsely. '*Really!*'

His exploring hand had found the creases of silk at the bend of her knee. His index burrowed into the warm, damp crevice behind.

And then abruptly he choked out something unintelligible as his fingertips sped above the black and crimson garter at Annette's stocking top and rested on the cool, satined swell of flesh beyond.

The arm around her waist was withdrawn and she tipped backwards off his knee to sprawl across the seat with her head resting against the fiacre's blinded window.

Morand was up as fast as a hare out of its trap at a dog race. She had fallen with her legs spread and he was between them, hunched down to knee apart her thighs, before she knew what was happening. Hot hands gripped her hips under the rucked up petticoats. He leaned over her as she opened her mouth to protest once more, but before she could utter a word his lips had closed over hers and his tongue, wet and lascivious, darted snakelike between her teeth to probe the warm cavern beyond.

Annette moaned softly under the onslaught, unaware through the fumes of his winey breath that she was permitting herself to respond, that her own tongue had leaped to couple with the invader, that her heart was thudding against the stays imprisoning her chest, that her pelvis had jerked involuntarily at the untoward violation of her flesh.

The Commissaire was shuddering with desire. Between their clasped bodies, his knuckled hands roved, snatched and poked with a life of their own.

One, sliding down from the hip, clenched flesh at the top of a thigh, surged forward and was repulsed by a circlet of lacy frills standing guard over the citadel he was urgent to storm. With the other an assault was made on his own garments. Hooked into the fly front of his tight trousers, his frenzied fingers ripped open the aperture with such force that a button flew off and clacked against a window.

Freed from the constriction and liberated further by the forceful displacement of a layer of underwear, the pulsating proof of his soldier spirit sprang smartly forwards and stood stiffly at attention awaiting orders.

But there were geographical hazards to overcome before the final command to attack could be given. Morand's free hand, making a reconnaissance in depth of the ruffles draped from Annette's shoulders, reported that the softly rounded orbs it wished to fondle were so incarcerated by camisole and corset that assistance would be needed if contact was to be made.

This was not immediately available, for its twin already had problems. So closely was the young woman's pleasuredrome protected by elasticated layers of linen and lace that no more than a couple of fingers could creep beneath the frilly stockade at a time.

Morand cursed under his breath as the probing tips smoothed across cool skin, touched a rougher, warmer surface, then encountered a scalding, hairy moistness that sent his pulses racing. But the imprisoned hand could reach no further; the drawers could not be dragged down because they were themselves captured at the waist by the tight-laced stays. There was nothing for it: the lacing would have to be loosened before a serious siege of that forbidden city could be staged. He snatched his hand away and attacked the buttons ranked down the front of the newly-repaired dress from neckline to waist.

Annette's hands meanwhile had fluttered like flame-blinded moths, at first ineffectually pushing at Morand's chest, then grappling weakly with his sinewy wrists, and finally inserting themselves between their two bodies in an attempt — not very strenuous, if the truth is told — to separate herself from his panting, thrusting maleness.

It was here that the slender fingers of her right hand, at first by chance and later by some deliberate if unconscious exercise of willpower, brushed against that sterling representative of his manly pride that bore such eloquent testimony to his hot-blooded desire for her.

Again it was through no conscious decision, considered and arrived at, that the fingers wrapped themselves around his strength; rather was it that her hand, curved like a horse-show magnet, was homing instinctively on an iron bar.

Morand gasped, pawing more hastily at the laces he was unthreading from their eyeholes beneath the drawn aside material of her bodice. The edges of the whaleboned corset gaped. And then suddenly his hands were full. Free like his own late prisoner from the restriction which had bound them so tightly, flattening their natural rotundity, her two breasts bounded joyfully into his clasp.

Squeezing and smoothing, the Commissaire's fingers traversed those swelling slopes while his palms, gyrating about their rosy summits, caressed each topmost peak to hardness against his hand.

Annette's hot breath played tantalizingly over his ear as her naked bosom heaved ever faster under his expert ministrations. Her free hand, seeking employment to match that of its sosie, knuckled two hirsute globes that underhung his rigid part. At once, instinctively, she twisted the wrist so that the tender glands fell into her cupped embrace. And then, with both hands pumping alternately, she began to stroke, to pull, to clench and to stretch.

Morand's breath hissed in. He was almost on the point of spending over that salacious grip. He lowered his head and sucked a nipple up into his mouth as his hands snaked once more beneath the supine dancer's petticoats to seize the waistband of her drawers, released now from the corset's restraint, and pull them down over her hips.

In a sudden silence — the hoofbeats had ceased and the fiacre was rocking on its cantilever springs — the cabbie's voice called from outside and above: 'Notre Dame de Lorette, sir. What number did you say?'

For the second time Commissaire Bruno Morand swore. He snapped up a blind, lowered the cab window, and shouted: 'Drive to the park at the Buttes de Chaumont and then bring us back!'

'And believe me, *mon vieux*,' Morand said to a friend

from the Police Judiciare that evening, 'if this little girl
doesn't turn out to be the hottest thing since chilis, I'll
resign my commission and sign on as a city garbage
collector!'

'You were that impressed?' said the PJ officer. They
were sitting over a beer at a lamplit pavement café in the
Place Dauphine.

'Impressed!' Morand echoed. 'I was damned near
violated once she got the hang of it and realized which
parts blended with what!' He stared upwards through the
leafy branches of a tree, chuckling. Fireworks spilled
streamers of red, green and gold across the sky over the
Grand Palais and the staccato crackle of their detonations
momentarily drowned the distant roar of the exhibition
crowd. 'With the slightest encouragement,' he said,
'Mademoiselle de Vervialle could become as randy – and
as successful if she so wished – as the *grandes
horizontales* at Maxim's and their counterparts around
the promenade bar at the Folies Bergère.'

'You actually took her while you were still in the
fiacre?'

Morand shook his head. 'She was panting for it, and
we had a good thirty minutes to spend, jogging to the
Buttes and back. But I fancied a half hour of mutual
frigging, and nothing more torrid than that, would bring
me a better tail when we finally arrived at Notre Dame
de Lorette than a rushed coupling in the cab. . .and the
possibility of second thoughts when it came to a second
time. Raising her up, I reckoned – the suspense, keeping
her on the cliff edge, so to speak –' would make the effect
all the more startling when at last she jumped.' He shook
his head again. 'And by God I was right!'

'Was she like that from the start? Randy and eager for
it, I mean?'

'Not on your life. Like any other little provincial, it

45

was all oh-don't and you-mustn't and let-me-go at first. But once she saw there was a coach and two horses ready to drive through the tunnel, curiosity, followed quickly by excitement, took over. The little bitch was in such a state when we got back from the Buttes that I could scarcely get her to adjust her dress decently enough to cross the sidewalk!'

'And in the hotel?' The PJ officer signalled a waiter to bring more beer.

'I had a bottle of champagne sent up to the room,' Morand said. 'And bless me, we had scarce consumed a quarter of it and she was tugging at the few remaining laces holding her stays together. "The whalebone sticking into my ribs is causing me great discomfort," said she. "Pray allow me to help you, then," said I. "For many hands, as they say, make light work, and it is a poor squire who leaves his lady languishing in the confines of an unsuitable attire".'

'You actually spoke to her like that? Like some Second Empire cavalier at a formal court ball?'

'In the seduction of provincials,' Morand said oracularly, 'the sophistication of the city-bred, genuine or feigned, is of great value.'

'And you stripped her — or she stripped herself — completely?'

'To the buff, *mon ami*. And in less time than it takes to tell.'

'And then?'

'Then it was off with the stays, the camisole, the bodice and the chemise; away with the skirts and petticoats and drawers. After which, since you ask, she lay on the bed cool as you please and watched — appreciatively, I like to think — while I removed my own garments. I never saw a quicker transition, nor one that was more complete, from prudery to naked lust!'

The Commissaire sighed, a faraway look in his eyes.
He placed a thin cheroot between his lips and lit it with
a wax vesta. 'My old man, of course, already summoned
on stage but not yet required to perform, was fairly
quivering with eagerness for the curtain to rise. I feasted
my eyes, a real banquet it was, while I disrobed. She lay
voluptuously still, only a slight quiver about the loins
betraying the emotion she experienced. Her breasts, I may
tell you, were superb, a little fuller perhaps than is
fashionable among the ladies of the Faubourg St Honoré
and the Chaussée d'Antin, but splendidly firm with the
rosy tips stiff as a baby's thumbs. The lower part of her
anatomy, sculpted as it were from alabaster, swept in
graceful curves from a small, trim waist to ample hips
whose fleshiness sheltered that last abrupt declivity
sloping down to the furry thicket where the Temple of
Love lay concealed.'

'Bruno,' said the PJ officer, 'you are a poet, the
troubador of the flesh.' He shifted in his seat. 'Also you
are making me envious.'

Morand drained his glass. Excitement in retrospect was
rendering him loquacious. 'As soon as she saw what I
had to offer,' he resumed, 'and related that to the task
for which it was designed, her breathing quickened, her
bosom rose and fell rapidly, and almost as a reflex her
shapely legs — still sheathed at my request in the black
stockings — spread themselves enough to show me the
smiling welcome that awaited me from the pale lips
between them. By this time I was maddened myself with
desire for the girl. I threw myself upon the bed. Her
motte was burning to the touch; the hairs on the
underside of the mound were wet. And the lips, pouting
now with expectation after so long a delay, glistened in
the discreet illumination welling from the pink-shaded
bedside lamp.'

47

'You went to work at once, without further ado or additional flirting?'

'Nothing could stop us. I was ready to make the proper introduction, but her hand, having once grasped and being eager to grip again, was there before me. In a trice the key was fast in the lock and the floodgates were opened! What a pump was primed then, Bruno my boy, said I a little later! What mingling of juices, what explosions of release as our hips ground together, the black stockings hooked over my back and her heels drumming on my spine!' The Commissaire smiled reminiscently. 'And that, my friend, was only the first of three!'

The inspector laughed. 'How fortunate,' he said, 'that we do not find ourselves on the far side of the Channel.'

'I do not understand you.'

'Why because among English officers, so it is said, it is not at all the thing − in fact it is frowned upon to the point of exclusion − for men among themselves to talk in this way of ladies while drinking in their mess hall.'

'To the devil with the English,' cried Commissaire Morand. 'What more *fitting* subject (if I may be permitted the term) is there for men to discuss together?'

CHAPTER FIVE

Annette lay awake most of the night after she returned to the Rue Halévy. Her mind reeled as she went over again and again the dizzying series of events which had overtaken her since she walked through the door of the police station charge room.

Could she really have behaved in such an abandoned, in such an unthinkably abandoned way with a man she had never met before?

The memories were too fresh — and far too exciting, if she was honest with herself — to leave any doubt about the answer to that particular question.

But the important question, really the only question when you stripped away the irrelevancies, was: why?

Why had she, who was such a fiery opponent of the idea that woman was no more than an object for the gratification of man, sunk as low as any notorious cocotte flaunting her charms at Maxim's?

What temporary insanity had swamped her sense of values?

Was she succumbing to her own baser instincts under the twin influences of alcohol and proximity? Did she — unconsciously perhaps and even more basely — feel that she was repaying a favour, and taking out insurance on favours to come? Or what?

Could it be that, whether she admitted it or not, she wanted a man of her own, and Bruno Morand fitted some pattern already formed in her subconscious mind? Could it really be as simple as that?

Towards dawn she fell into a fitful sleep and the warring images faded away. They were replaced in a waking dream in which she relived an outing the previous Sunday by stronger, more positive memories.

She was in a cab once more, driving around the outside of the exhibition to watch the army of workmen putting the final touches to pavilions and displays. The young man sitting beside her was twenty-two years old, tall and fair, with a drooping moustache and a grey derby with a black band on the back of his head. He was an earnest suitor, with lodgings in an attic across the street from her own room, and they had met several times for drinks at the café on the corner, and once spent Annette's free evening dancing at the Moulin de la Galette.

She was talking — dreams are no respecters of chronology — about Romero, the critic from *Figaro*. 'And what did he want this time?' asked the young man, whose name was Paul Duclos.

'What he always wants. He offers to write a flattering article about me, drawing attention to my. . .my talents as a dancer. Oh, he can do so much to help advance my career. . .at a price?'

'Meaning?'

'What do you think, Paul? There has to be an interview. At some nice quiet place, where we shall not be disturbed. A nice discreet little hotel, for instance.'

'What a swine!' the young man exclaimed angrily. 'Just let me get my hands on the fellow. I'll teach him to upset you with his vile — '

'Oh, it's not just that. He is one hazard among many.'

Paul put an arm around her shoulders. 'What is it that troubles you so?' he asked.

'Very nearly everything.' She sat forwards on the seat

50

as the cabbie whipped up the horses to cross an intersection. 'Life becomes dearer every day. It seems impossible for a girl without private means to make ends meet. And it appears equally hopeless to expect any kind of improvement in one's professional life – unless one is prepared to sell oneself to achieve it. Believe me, I am sick of the whole thing.'

'My poor dear,' he said sympathetically. 'I hate you having to put up with this kind of nonsense. I would do anything. . .but never mind: it will all change once we are married, I promise you.'

This time she disengaged herself completely, turning sideways to face him. 'I have not said I will marry you, Paul,' she replied.

'Oh, but you must. After all, we – '

'Paul, Paul,' she interrupted, laying a gloved hand on his arm. 'I am fond of you, truly I am. But you are a clerk in the office of an actuary.'

'There are chances of promotion. Monsieur Gilbert said – '

'In five years? In ten? I have no wish to hurt you, but I want something more than a shared apartment in Belleville, surrounded by babies and unpaid bills. Why should one not have the right, after all. . .?' She left the sentence unfinished, staring out of the window. The cab was halted halfway up the Champs Elysées. Behind iron railings, a large tree-shaded mansion stood back from the street. There were carriages drawn up around the semi-circular driveway, and through brightly lit casements men and women in evening dress could be seen beneath glittering chandeliers. 'Do you see that?' Annette cried passionately. 'That house once belonged to Napoleon III's mistress, Paiva. Do you know who lives there now? Louise Weber – La Goulue. An assistant washerwoman!'

'Annette – '

'Oh, certainly she was the so-called star of the Moulin Rouge, and the subject of paintings by that dwarf, Lautrec. But she didn't get there, and she didn't get that house, through her dancing. She got it the way Paiva did – lying on her back in a bed.'

'Annette!'

'Look at all the others! Look at La Belle Otéro! She cannot dance as well as I can, yet they are giving her a theatre all to herself down at the exhibition; she has bought herself one of the Marquis de Dion's horseless carriages; she has a diamond breastplate and a twelve-string choker of real pearls. Liane de Pougy has so many jewels that she cannot fit them all into her safe! Emilienne d'Alençon lives – '

'Annette,' the young man said for the third time, 'it does not become you to sound so envious.'

'I am not envious; I am angry. I do not grudge these women what they have. Everyone should have the chance to do as well. What infuriates me is that they are forced to earn it with their bodies and not with their talent.'

'My dear girl! What about Yvette Guilbert? What about that new soubrette with the big teeth. . .Mistinguett?'

'Exceptions. And you know what an exception does, Paul. But very well: take those who do have talent. Polaire, Gaby Deslys, Colette – '

'They are famous, as I say, *because* of their talent.'

'They may be now,' Annette said scornfully. 'But how do you think they got the opportunity to demonstrate that they did have talent? So far as their self-respect is concerned, they might just as well have been Liane de Lancy or Féfé or Tica la Rousse – any of those women who display themselves so shamelessly in the Bois or at the Neuilly Fair.'

Paul compressed his lips. 'I cannot understand why you keep on – '

'Because,' she burst out, ' the only way a girl can live an expensive life is to cheapen herself.'

'And you want to live an expensive life?'

'I want to live comfortably. Doesn't everyone? I want to have nice clothes and a nice home. Why shouldn't I? I want to be in a position where I do not have to worry myself sick each time a bill comes through the door. And I am determined to achieve that position. But I am damned – '

'Annette!'

'I am damned if I will prostitute myself to do it,' she finished defiantly.

'Prostitution is a relative term,' the man from *Figaro* said, sidling up to her on the other side of the bench. 'It depends very much on the point of view of the person using it. One man's tart is the tart's man's meal ticket! Brothers and sisters have I four, but my taste of honey is my wife's whore.'

'There are one million women in domestic service in France,' Annette shouted, thumping the café table. 'And every one of them has to face the fact, to accept the possibility, that she may be required to be *nice* to the master of the house. Or his son. Or even his wife sometimes. If she is not to lose her job, that is. It's disgusting.'

'Disgusting!' the Comte de la Férérière crowed. 'I wouldn't put up with it for an instant if I were you. How much do you want, chérie?' He removed his trousers and threw them out of the cab window.

Commissaire Morand leaned down from the coachman's seat. He was wearing a tall black hat with undertaker's black plumes on either side. Black plumes garlanded his naked waist.

'Black,' he said, 'is the colour of my true love's heart. But rosy red smiles her secret part.' He winked. 'First we shall have a drink at a little place I know.'

Annette tried to take her eyes away from that part of him below the garland, but the heat from his loins struck her like a blow.

She awoke with a start. A shaft of sunlight slanting through the skylight had moved across the bed to warm her face. It was a little after nine o'clock and the shouts of carters mingled with a rumble of wheels and the clip-clop of hooves rising from the street below.

Aware suddenly, guiltily, that her fingers were absently cupping and caressing her secret treasure, she snatched her hand away. But the middle finger was already wet.

She sat up and swung her feet to the floor. Her nude and nubile body, pinkly reflected in a cheval glass, still bore the marks of Bruno Morand's fingers and teeth.

She remembered in great detail the hotel in the Rue Notre Dame de Lorette. She recalled the sly, conspiratorial smirk of the chambermaid who had brought fresh towels and hot water to the room, the leer of the waiter bearing champagne, an air of complicity surprised on the face of the old woman behind the reception desk. She had noticed that Morand neither paid, nor was asked to pay, for the use of the room. It was clear, in fact, that he was an habitué of the place, had obviously taken other women there before, was doubtless allowed to use it as he wished in return for certain leniencies connected with his vice squad position.

The man was a philanderer, a lecher!

Why then did she hope so fervently, her heart beating fast and her breath quickening at the thought, that he would contact her again soon, as he had promised?

CHAPTER SIX

It was three days before Commissaire Morand 'made signs', as the French say. Annette was busy most evenings, making the rounds of the music-halls, cabarets and café-concerts, trying to replace her lost job at the Moulin Rouge. But although she went to them all — the Casino de Paris, Les Ambassadeurs, Ba-ta-clan, the Cigale, the Alcazar, even Mme Marchand's smokey and ill-ventilated Scala — the answer was always an abrupt negative. Clearly, from the Ollers' front office, the word had gone around: Mademoiselle de Vervialle was 'unreliable'; she had a dubious reputation with the police.

In the daytime, Annette explored with her friend Lucie Clément the attractions of the huge exhibition. Lucie was a midinette working part-time for the famous costumier Landolff, whose fabulous and exotic creations clothed half the socialites and most of the theatrical stars of Paris. At the moment she was laid off, and the two girls sampled the delights of specialities, sideshows, mime acts and marionette theatres in between visits to the comics at the House of Laughter and one of the exhibition's most successful displays — a tea room imitating the interior of a Trans-Siberian railway coach, where customers sipping infusions from onyx cups listened to the music of a balalaika orchestra as they watched panoramas of the Russian steppes unroll past the 'restaurant car' windows.

The only exhibit Annette firmly refused even to look at was the small theatre in the Queen's Walk, where a placard among the surrounding pleasure booths announced: *Three Splendid Performances A Day! Each One Consecrated to the World's Greatest Dancer: La Belle Otéro.*

It was on the corner of a wide alley leading to the reconstruction of a Swiss mountain village that the handsome Commissaire made his appearance.

A small caravan with the shafts canted upwards and the horse grazing nearby had been transformed into a mobile police station so that officers from different branches of the force could deal summarily with the pickpockets, confidence tricksters, prostitutes and touts attracted by the crowds in the exhibition grounds. Morand materialized, rather like an immortal in a Greek fable, through a mist of fine spray teased by a gust of wind from a group of stone dolphins spouting water into an ornamental pool.

'Mademoiselle de Vervialle!' he exclaimed, the wide mouth smiling to reveal strong white teeth. 'What a charming surprise!'

'Monsieur le Commissaire.' Annette was polite, if a little distant.

If he noticed that, Morand made no sign. 'You are enjoying the Spring sunshine amid the wonders of the world? With your delightful friend?' A small bow in the direction of the honey-haired Lucie.

Annette made the introduction. There was nothing else she could do.

My goodness, she was right! thought the midinette, who had been favoured with a strictly edited version of the meeting three days before. This one is one hundred percent man, all right! And good-looking with it! She took in the broad shoulders and erect carriage, the thick, straight eyebrows and determined chin. The grip of his hand was firm and masterful. Something very different from the vapid actuary's assistant she had met with her friend once at a Montmartre bal-musette − a youth whom privately she had found a little hangdog and lacking in the more positive virtues.

Perhaps this time Annette was on the way to a settled future with a man worthy of her, thought loyal Lucie. With a final approving glance at the Commissaire, she pleaded a conference with the female overseer at Landolff's workshop and discreetly left the two of them together.

'I saw you as soon as you entered the exhibition grounds,' Morand confessed once they were alone. 'I have been following you around, hoping to find an excuse − I am ashamed to say − to break up such a delightful twosome. Happily your friend is possessed of an extreme sensibility, saw at once the direction of my thoughts, and reacted in the most tactful fashion imaginable. I am most grateful for such delicacy. So. . .now that we are on our own, what would you like to do? I am off duty for the rest of the day.'

Annette thrust out of her mind the unbidden, forbidden thought of what her senses told her she would really like to do, hesitated. . .and as she paused, Morand spoke again. 'Perhaps a short trip on the river,' he suggested. 'We could observe the new pleasure grounds on either side that way from a different viewpoint. And then maybe . . .' He paused in his turn, then added: 'I know you live and have worked in the Montmartre *quartier*, but I wondered if it might interest you to go behind the scenes, as it were, of some of the more expensive − and, I have to say, raffish − establishments catering to the wealthy there?'

'I think that would be very nice,' Annette said primly

– consciously submerging the untoward thought, rising of its own lewd volition to the surface, that it might be even nicer to return to the hotel in the Rue Notre Dame de Lorette.

She need not have worried. Morand shepherded her through the crowds, past formal gardens brilliant with perfumed flowers, to a small landing stage projecting from the cobbled quay below the huge domed vault of the Gare d'Orsay. Here, instead of the stern-wheel pleasure boat crammed with sightseers she had half feared, he handed into a small grey steam launch with the words *River Police* in white letters on each side of the hull.

Two uniformed *agents* piloted the craft from a glassed-in cabin just aft of the fore-deck. A third, in overalls, tended the engine below the launch's tall, thin smokestack with its frilled iron collar at the top. Amidships, a short ladder led beneath a mahogany and glass hatchway to the diminutive saloon.

The Commissaire, after a word with the men at the wheel, cast off, and the boat chugged out into mid-stream.

Annette was standing beside the ensign floating from the stern halyard, watching the gaily coloured kiosks and booths float away beneath the plane trees lining the quay. Above the topmost branches, she could read, engraved in gold beneath the station's classical parapet, the names of the towns served by the railway: Orleans. . .Chartres . . .Tours. . .Angers . . .

Morand was standing beside her. 'We'll head downstream,' he said, 'past Boulogne and the Bois in the direction of Neuilly. It will not be of great interest until we are clear of the city, so I suggest we go below for the moment. It is pleasant in the warm sun, but after a time it provokes a thirst, don't you think?'

Without waiting for the girl's reply, he smiled, took her arm and led her to the companionway.

The saloon was very small, with gleaming mahogany and brass fittings: two cushioned seats, a folding table, a row of lockers each side of the door that led to the engine compartment.

The Commissaire opened one of the lockers and took out two wine glasses and a corkscrew. From another he removed a bottle of Chablis wrapped in a damp cloth. 'Not as cold, alas, as it might be,' he apologised, pulling the cork, 'but refreshing enough, I trust, to quench your thirst after that exhausting walk around the exhibition.' He filled the glasses, passed her one, and then raised his own. 'To your very good health, my dear. And may our friendship continue to be — dare I say it? — as *warm* as it was on the occasion of our first meeting!'

Annette was still standing. It was the first remark of a personal nature that he had made since their meeting. . .and it was *so* personal, with its echo of shared intimacies she scarcely dared admit even to herself, that she was taken by surprise and left without a reply. She raised her glass wordlessly, swallowed a large gulp of the wine, then sank onto one of the benches to avoid meeting Morand's eye.

He drank and refilled the two glasses.

'I don't think . . .' she began nervously. But the sentence remained unfinished because he set his drained glass on the table, strode forwards, seized her two arms above the elbow, and pulled her to her feet. Before she knew what was happening, he had crushed her to him and closed his mouth fiercely over hers.

For a moment Annette's breath was taken away. She felt her heart thudding against the hardness of his chest. Her breasts were squashed against the leather rim of her stays. Her knees began to tremble.

And then her lips were parting as the Commissaire's tongue forced its way between them, past the twin barriers of her teeth and into the hot clasp of her mouth.

Without any conscious volition on her part, her own tongue leaped forwards to meet the invader, twining around its moistly probing tip, flickering out in its turn to penetrate. Wet lips tremored and clung. Hips and bellies ground together. . .and she was aware suddenly of the rigid protuberance clamped against her pelvis just above the crotch.

Finally she freed her mouth, inserted her hands between their bodies and pushed herself away so that she was leaning back in his encircling embrace. 'Bruno,' she said tremulously, using his name for the first time, 'this, surely, is not the place . . .? I mean we cannot – '

'There is no better place – and no better time – than now,' he cut in roughly. 'I want you and I intend to have you. More importantly perhaps, I know very well that you want me!'

Annette was breathing hard. The man was positively shuddering with desire. And she herself was uncomfortably conscious of a wetness manifesting itself between her legs. But she had no time to analyse her own feelings or formulate her wishes, for Morand unclasped his hands, lifted her bodily and sat her upon the table. Before she could say anything, he whisked up the hem of her blue candy-striped dress and laid it, together with the petticoat and chemise beneath, across her thighs.

'*Bruno!*' she gasped again – he had gripped her knees and was spreading them apart – 'We *can't!* We mustn't! Not here. It's. . .why it's practically in public!' She gazed wildly out of the portholes on either side of the tiny saloon.

'Of course we can. And indeed we are, are we not?'

'But it's indecent, shameful.'

60

'A little shame adds spice to the variety of life,' Morand said. 'You will see.' He reached down and tore open the fastening of his trousers, grasped the stiff, upstanding proof of his desire for her, and manoeuvred it out into the open for her inspection.

She stared, fascinated in spite of herself, at its unyielding length, its throbbing tip. 'But the *crew*? We are not alone after all.'

'Boisset has to remain below with his engine.' He gestured at the mahogany door. 'The other two are far too busy in the wheelhouse to disturb us.' He nodded toward the starboard porthole.

Annette saw that traffic on the river was heavy. A tug hauling a string of coal barges loaded to the waterline was passing between two pleasure boats on its way upriver. Several skiffs and row-boats floated near the right bank and a paddle steamer was pulling away from a pier beyond the Trocadero gardens.

For a moment she was silent. Over the drumbeat of the launch's engine, the hiss and gurgle of water streaming past the hull was suddenly loud. Morand's fingers had crept up beneath the loose folds of skirt and underclothes and hooked themselves over the waistband of the girl's drawers. 'The sightseers in those pleasure boats could see us,' she complained.

'Then they'll see a more enticing sight,' he replied cheerfully, 'than the river could ever provide!'

Annette said no more. The knuckles of his two hands dug into the bare flesh of her belly. She shivered in anticipation, all thoughts of reproach and refusal swamped by the physical need that flamed abruptly through her loins.

Morand heard the sibilant intake of her breath as he snatched down the drawers — this pair free of the corset's imprisoning clasp — and dragged them over her thighs and down past the slender taper of her calves. She kicked off her shoes and shrugged her feet until the garment pooled on the deck between his feet.

His hands were back now on the cool skin above the garters that held up Annette's stockings. The fingers dug beneath her, clenched on the cheeks of her bottom; the thumbs gripped the top of her thighs. Very slowly, his blue eyes fixed on hers, he drew her forwards across the polished wood of the table top. When she was balanced on the very edge, he moved forwards until his staff of life, pricking out from his trousers like a flagstaff over the stern of a ship, quivered between her spread thighs.

Annette found it hard to breathe. She gazed with wonder at the engorged head. . .then, with an impulsive movement, she grabbed her skirt, petticoat and chemise and pulled them up around her waist.

Morand feasted his eyes on the lascivious spectacle — the pale thighs and dark stockings splayed on either side of that furred chalice that was cupped beneath a belly swelling indecently below a frou-frou of linen and lace. At the apex of this hairy triangle, a thin strip of pink glistened.

The grasp of his hands tightened again. . .but this time the young dancer, by now entranced with the lubricious tableau of which she formed a part, was ahead of him. Shuffling her bottom still further forwards, she allowed the tips of her toes to touch the floor and gently lowered herself until the damp hairs at the base of her belly brushed the tip of his baton.

Then, with a mischievous half-smile and a quizzical lift of the eyebrows, she parted the lips smiling so warm a welcome with the fingers of each hand.

Bruno Morand was quick to accept the unspoken invitation. He flexed his knees and then straightened his legs with a sudden thrust that forced the advance guard of his attack straight through the open gates of the citadel.

Annette groaned with ecstasy as she felt herself impaled on the spearhead of his desire. For a timeless moment she remained absolutely motionless, sensing with every nerve in her tautly strung body the remorseless advance of the man within her. Then with a wordless cry she jerked into action, pushing her hips forwards to meet his driving thrusts, recoiling only to urge herself forwards once more with even greater power.

She matched his accelerating rhythm with a rocking seesaw movement of her own, staring up at his flushed face wide-eyed, with her mouth hanging open and the breath thumped from her chest with each muscular surge of Morand's strong body.

Finally she hoisted her bottom back onto the table, raised her arms and locked her hands behind his head. Slowly, she leaned back until she was lying flat, drawing him down after her. She raised her legs and wrapped them over his back, pressing with her heels until he lay within her deeper than ever before.

The Commissaire's brow was dewed with perspiration. The backs of his legs shuddered. His hands clenched and unclenched on her naked waist; his breathing grew deep and hoarse as he felt the whole passionate force of his need concentrate in the fire that was stoked in his loins.

For a little while longer, assisted by the movement of the launch as it bobbed over successive waves of the wash from a passing steamer, they rocked in mutual exultation. But at last Annette moaned on a rising note, spasmodic contractions clasped and unclasped the scalding flesh that gripped his male pride, and her fingers dug into his shoulders as she trembled into her release with a long shuddering cry that rivalled the call of a siren floating from a boat on the river. At the same time Morand gasped aloud. Stimulated beyond belief by the girl's final surrender and total abandon, he sensed the floodgates damming the storm within him burst open to gush out the contents of his reservoir in frantic spurts.

The police launch rounded the southernmost bend in the river and headed north for Boulogne and the tree-shaded quiet of the Bois.

Although she had lived in the Montmartre district for more than a year, Annette was amazed to discover just how many cabarets, dives and unofficial brothels there were in the area. It was dusk when Morand began his rounds and the new electrical street lighting in the centre of the Boulevard de Clichy cast a pallid glow over the countenances of those denizens of the night already on the prowl in search of early – and easy – money. Whores settled themselves at the tables in the Moulin Rouge garden; further up the hill the lamplighters with their long poles cycled the steep, narrow streets to tip the triggers and flare the old gas lamps to life.

Morand took the girl to the Divan Japonais, Feyouac's, Parisiana, the Gaiété, Chez-Gaby and half a dozen less salubrious holes in the wall. They drank a bock at the scrubbed tables of Aristide Bruant's Mirliton – though the famous *chansonnier* was not due to appear and insult his customers until eleven o'clock – and made a short backstage visit to the Eden Palace music-hall.

Finally they took one of the interminable stone staircases that climbed towards the white dome of the Sacré Coeur, leaving it halfway up to traverse an alley which led them to the rear entrance of the Moulin de la Galette.

The square clapboard body of the windmill, which had been turned into a working-class dance hall in the 1870's, stood at the edge of an open heath on the western slope of the Montmartre *butte*. Market gardens, a tiny vineyard and a farm still flourished on that side of the hill, but these were already shuttered for the night as the narrow, crooked streets around them came to life. Strains of accordion music filtered already through the sound of many voices from the *Bal* below the mill.

The Commissaire shouldered his way through the crowd, glared at a group of apaches in striped jerseys and knotted kerchiefs until they moved away from a table, and installed Annette there. He ordered a carafe of dry white wine, then strode off to the bar.

He had done the same thing at each place they visited – a brief conversation with a barman, a cashier, the patron, while she was left sitting at the table, then a drink while he scanned the clientele and pointed out to her slumming socialites, members of the underworld, incognito politicians – and so on to the next place. So far as she could see over the press of drinkers and dancers, the conversations were hurried, almost furtive. Several times she fancied something changed hands. And at the Eden Palace there was no mistake about it: the stage manager definitely handed Morand a brown envelope. He nodded and stuffed it into an inside pocket before rejoining Annette.

At one of the nightclubs in Pigalle, the Commissaire excused himself and walked across to a table at which two elderly men sat with a magnum of champagne and a couple of over-painted women whose necklines were cut so low that almost all of their breasts were visible.

Morand addressed himself to one of the men – Annette was sure she knew the face from political cartoons in the newspapers – standing insolently with one foot up on a vacant chair as he wagged an admonitory finger. He talked for some time, and the man, red-faced at first with what she assumed was anger, soon changed his expression. His features registered discomfiture, sullenness and finally a sort of resignation as the policeman scribbled something on a card, dropped it on the table, then turned and walked away.

By the time they arrived at the Moulin de la Galette, a succession of beers, *coupes de champagne* and glasses of wine — none of which she noted, had been paid for — had flushed Annette's face, slurred her speech a little and provoked a certain confusion of mind that led her astray on matters of chronology.

Perhaps this was why she skipped the formal steps that decency required — and even more that convention decreed was never, but never the prerogative of the female sex — and made the suggestion herself.

When Morand finally sat down at the table and poured the wine, she laid gloved fingers on his arm and said shakily: 'Bruno — would a place like this — I mean, is there any chance — that is to say, would they have a private room here?' She stumbled over the last phrase and set her glass down rather hard, so that wine slopped over the rim onto the table.

'Why yes,' the Commissaire smiled, the heavy brows scaling his forehead in amusement, 'I do believe they would.'

He rose abruptly, left the table, and strode towards a small glassed-in office at one side of the bar.

Five minutes later, in a small wooden pavilion at the end of a garden surrounding the mill, he was stripping off his uniform.

Annette reclined on a wide coil-spring bed. For some reason she was feeling a little giddy.

Bruno, she though dreamily, really did have a splendid body. Broad shoulders tapered to a narrow waist and hips that were scarcely wider, the whole complex surface knitted together by layers of muscle as precisely outlined as the components of a medical illustration. The thatch

of springy hair from which his manhood arrowed forward
was unusually abundant, curling more than halfway to
his navel. But his deep chest, she was glad to see, was
smooth and hairless. Only his forearms, the backs of his
hands and the base of his spine were downed with a silky
fuzz. Below the twin hemispheres of his bottom, taut as
clenched fists, the same dusky growth feathered his sturdy
legs.

She was aware suddenly that she had unbuttoned the
front of the candy-striped dress and was now easing the
camisole top up over her corset. Her fingers plucked at
the laces joining the two sides of the basque.

Would it be like this, some distant part of her mind
wondered, if she and Bruno — well, anyway, someone
like Bruno — if they had a little house of their own?
Would there be this pent-up excitement, this almost
unbearable sense of anticipation each night when they
undressed and got ready for bed?

Could it go on for ever? she mused, gazing with
admiration at his upstanding figure, this thudding of the
heart, this fluttering of the nerve ends that quivered the
base of her belly and threatened to choke her breath in
her throat.

It would have to be someone *very* like him, someone
in fact *precisely* like him if she was to go on feeling the
same way. And even if there were babies in another room
— she had struggled out of her dress and pulled the
camisole over her head — the house or the apartment or
whatever would certainly not be in Belleville. And she
wouldn't blink an eye when the bills came through the
door. Not with the pay of a senior commissaire of police
in the capital . . .*Stop! She mustn't on any account think
this way. There was nothing, Lucie had told her, more
calculated to put a man off than —*

He was standing in front of her, his jutting part speared

67

in the direction of her face. 'You're not doing that very
well,' he said. 'Let me help you at least with the lacing
at the back.'

Annette giggled. 'My fingers feel too thick,' she
complained, turning to flop face down on the bed.

He bent over her and unfastened the corset with
experienced hands. Soon she was freed from its
imprisoning clasp, free to slide drawers, slip, petticoat
and the rest of her underclothes down over her hips and
thighs, to cast off the imprisoning whalebone and feel
at last the cool evening air fan the whole nude length of
her heated body.

Morand unpinned the burnished glory of her hair and
she rolled over onto her back. He leaned above her,
supporting himself with an arm planted each side of her
waist. His burning gaze swept over her shoulders and
breasts, her hips and belly and legs. Annette's breath
quickened as his eyes feasted a moment on the mound
of silky fur sheltering the entrance to that alcove of desire
where expectation was already signalling waves of
sensation throughout the lower half of her body.

The rest of his face seemed somehow blurred, but those
blue eyes were sharp and glittering in their concentration.
And sharp as a sword blade too was the image of that
weapon that now projected above her, quivering with the
evidence of the Commissaire's own desire and ready to
plunge into the sweet scabbard of his choice.

Instinctively, the dancer's hand reached out and
grasped it by the hilt.

She heard Morand's sharp intake of breath, and then
his hands too were occupied as he knelt up on the bed
between her slightly spread thighs.

His fingers teased through coppery fleece to home in
on the secret lips it concealed. With his other hand he
cupped the firm, fleshy globe of one breast, lowering his

head to pay tribute with lips and tongue to the beauty of its rosebud tip.

Annette shifted her position slightly, parting her legs again and drawing up her knees.

The Commissaire's exploring fingers had now discovered the tender warmth of her secret lips. Delicately, he caressed them until moisture welling over the tips told him that the liquid pearls of arousal already jewelled the depths beyond.

He allowed his index to sink deeper and she jerked, gasping aloud as he stroked with a skilful tenderness the hidden bud that activated the most passionate evidence of her female sexuality. Her arms crept towards him and her hands linked behind his neck, drawing him down onto her naked body.

Between his legs the part that bore such eloquent testimony to Morand's own sexuality was now at full stretch, quivering with eagerness. He lowered himself slowly, and as she drew up her knees still higher, the ready hand that had already made contact with his maleness gripped again and guided the throbbing head easily within the entrance to that temple of Venus where everything was made ready for him.

He pushed gently with his hips, and the entire stiff evidence of his need was swallowed in the hot wet embrace of her welcoming lips.

'Oh, Bruno!' she whispered deliriously. 'Oh, my dearest love!'

Morand made love to her with a fierce passion that was tempered nevertheless with affection. And he was too hardened a soldier on the battlefields of physical desire not to place a value on her pleasure that almost matched his own.

They fell at once into a coupling rhythm that raised them together on the crest of a wave that swept inexorably onward towards that point of no return where it would break with an unseen thunder that was felt rather than heard, engulfing them both in its fury.

The pace of their thrusting quickened, became urgent, critical. . .and in the instant that Bruno Morand expressed his devotion to her in a flooding spring tide of emotion, Annette's back arched up off the bed and she climaxed in a long shuddering cry that tailed off in a sobbed repetition of his name.

It was fifteen minutes later, and there was champagne in an ice bucket beside the bed, when she sprawled lazily across his prone body with her head resting on his flat belly. 'Bruno,' she murmured through the curtain of bronze hair draped over his loins, 'there is something I have always wanted to do.'

Her slender fingers wrapped around him, pulling him her way.

CHAPTER SEVEN

After their meeting at the Moulin de la Galette, a week passed before Annette saw the Commissaire again. She had still found no employment, and the little money she had was perilously diminished. Then one evening, returning to her lodgings after another fruitless trudge around the theatrical agencies, she found a folded slip of paper pushed beneath her door.

She smoothed it out and read the two lines of copperplate inscribed thereon:

I have places of interest to show you tonight. Be ready and I will call for you at half past nine o'clock.
                                                      B.M.

She was ready. She was nettled that seven whole days had passed without a single sign from her lover; she resented a little the impersonal, almost peremptory tone of the note; she was hungry, having lived on bread and cheese for the past forty-eight hours. But she was ready — laced tightly into a mustard-coloured damask dress, the most fashionable she had, with a high collar and a three-tiered skirt gathered up at the front to reveal the hem of a cream lace underskirt. Her hair was pinned up beneath a brown straw hat crowned with artificial flowers.

Morand was almost an hour late. He made no comment on her appearance, but he did offer an explanation − if not exactly an excuse − for the delay. And by implication the seven-day silence preceding it. 'My work, you see, requires me to be on call at any time and virtually any place,' said he. 'And with the extra crowds generated by this damned exhibition it becomes more and more difficult to plan ahead with any certainty.'

'You could perhaps keep me informed a little, nevertheless.' Annette was aware that the remark would not please him, but she made it just the same.

'Rather than make an arrangement which could subsequently be cancelled,' Morand said stiffly, 'I would prefer not to make it at all. Come now. . .tonight we will drink among the rich; we shall see, as the saying is, how the other half lives!'

'Bruno!' Her voice was apologetic but firm. 'It would be nice to drink − but you said nothing in your note. I have not eaten. In fact I have had nothing since early this morning.'

For an instant Morand's lips compressed in a grimace of impatience, then the ready smile was back in place and he said: 'Very well then. I dined earlier, but I . . .That is to say, we shall see what the Maître D at Wepler's sea-food brasserie on the Place Clichy can offer you. I will toy with a few mussels while you tuck in.'

What the Maître D offered was a Sole Véronique − the white fillets and their wine sauce surrounded by a ring of potato mousse topped by peeled grapes, washed down, of course, by a bottle of chilled Muscadet, the dry white elixir from the mouth of the Loire.

Annette was feeling very much better, very much more herself again and a little ashamed of her earlier tetchiness when they emerged into the crowded square and the Commissaire hailed a cab. It was almost midnight and the cobbled *place*, slanting downhill on the lower slopes of Montmartre, was crammed with nightlifers out on the

spree. 'Where are we going, so late in the day?' she asked
as he handed her into the fiacre.

'Somewhere,' said he, 'where vice, so-called, flourishes
in its purest — ha! ha! — and most licentious form. But
which the state, in its wisdom, permits to exist because
it provides a source of revenue.' He grinned. 'An
arrangement which brings pleasure to many and riches
to not a few.'

He paid off the cab at the corner of the Rue de
Monthyon, and they walked a hundred and fifty yards
to the steps and portico of No. 14. The two figures, set
in a fan-shaped, semicircular transom above a wide front
door of highly polished Acajou, were over-sized and
illuminated from behind. Morand climbed the steps and
tapped twice discreetly on a brass knocker fashioned like
a goat's head.

The door was opened at once by a fresh-faced young
girl wearing a long black dress with a starched white cap
and apron. 'Monsieur le Commissaire,' she greeted him.
'Madame is awaiting you in the Persian Room.'

Morand nodded and led Annette inside.

She received an impression of gilt chairs covered in
wine-red velvet, opulent hangings and a profusion of
oriental rugs beneath a painted ceiling. Framed portraits
on the walls lurked behind a dazzle of cut glass and
crystal. 'If you would come this way, please,' the
maidservant said.

The walls of the Persian Room were hidden by rich
and sumptuous tapestries between which, at equal
intervals, classical figures in black marble stood in niches
lit from below by electric light. The ceiling of the
octagonal room was divided into eight panels inlaid with
gold and a central dome painted with scenes from a
Dionysian banquet.

Rising to greet them from a Louis XV chaise-longue

half hidden by a carelessly flung white bearskin was a tall, upright woman of about fifty. She was dressed in a floor-length gown of black moiré taffeta that covered her from neck to wrist. There were no rings on her thin fingers, but a solitaire diamond the size of a pigeon's egg glittered from the centre of the black velvet band around her neck.

'Commissaire! How very nice!' The woman glided forward with an outstretched hand.

'Madame Renée. A pleasure as always.' Morand bent over the hand. He made no attempt to introduce Annette, who was favoured with a gracious nod and subsequently ignored.

Annette was content to stay in the background and observe. This was clearly one of the famous *maisons closes* or high-class brothels of which she had heard so much. It was a far cry from the women, often poorly dressed, she had seen at the VIIIth Arrondissement police station or even in the Moulin Rouge garden. She had never in her life been in a place that was so luxuriously furnished. Through a half-open door between two of the niches, she could see thin shafts of electric light focused on a huge bed framed by black curtains with golden tassels and fringes. And could the gleaming stickpins skewering the woman's auburn hair on top of her head really be genuine diamonds?

'The *Salon des Lords*, I am afraid, is occupied at the moment,' Madame Renée was saying. 'But if you would care to instal your friend in the Chinese Room, I will have refreshments sent in while you wait. The English are notoriously hurried about their special pleasures. I fear that it may indicate a sense of guilt added to the breeding we have come to expect.'

She picked a small silver bell from a *Directoire* table and tinkled it to summon the maidservant. The girl led

74

Morand and Annette through the entrance hall and up a gracefully curving marble staircase with a brass rail and crystal balusters.

A large open room occupied most of the first floor. Furnished with chesterfields upholstered in rich tapestry and a scatter of deep-button leather armchairs in front of a huge gilt mirror, it looked to Annette much as she would imagine an exclusive gentlemen's club. And there were indeed about a dozen men in evening dress, most of them elderly and prosperous looking, sprawled in the chairs or standing with glasses of champagne in their hands. A discreet murmur of conversation was punctuated here and there by the popping of a cork or the clink of bottle against glass.

What spoiled the club image was the fact that there were twice as many women in the room. All of them were expensively dressed, many were extremely beautiful. They were of all types: fair-haired and buxom, dark and intense, joking and jolly beneath a wild thatch of red. Most of the gowns were cut daringly low to expose as much flesh as possible. One Junoesque beauty with smouldering eyes and enormous firm breasts was bare to the waist; another, wearing a virginal night-gown, hid her body – yet contrived to reveal everything she had to offer – in a froth of Alençon lace.

'And all of these women,' Annette whispered, fascinated despite her convictions, 'sell themselves to the men who come here?'

'They are certainly all *disponsible*, that is to say available,' Morand replied in a low voice. 'At a price. But a man who comes here is not obliged to take a girl upstairs. He can just meet his friends and have a drink if he wishes. But if he should renounce the talent Madame Renée has to offer. . .well, the refreshments can prove expensive!'

She glanced around the big reception hall. Some of the men were in fact alone; others stood chatting to one or more women; some reclined on settees with foolish smiles, obviously being flattered by the half-dressed nymphs snuggled up beside them. One florid septuagenarian with a generous paunch dandled a giggling maiden who could not have been more than sixteen years old on his knee.

Laughter of a more intimate kind floated from a sophisticated group standing near a heavily carpeted staircase that rose from the far corner of the room. 'And if a man does take somebody upstairs?' Annette queried as the maid preceded them to the floor above. 'How much would he have to pay then?'

'Ten to fifteen Louis,' the Commissaire said. 'Minimum. More of course for those with. . .specialized . . .tastes. Sometimes much more.'

'Ten to fifteen Louis!' Annette breathed. 'Why that's twice as much as I earn in a whole – '

She broke off as a couple rounded a bend in the staircase and stepped down towards them. The man, a young exquisite sporting a wispy moustache, was dressed in a lemon yellow suit with a violet silk waistcoat and a floppy bow tie. His companion, a busty, heavy-featured blond of about forty, wore a black riding habit with a tall silk hat. As they passed on the stairway, she raised the hem of her skirt to tuck a short leather whip into the top of one riding boot. 'And next time, *mon petit*,' she said in a deep, husky voice, 'you do not present yourself late and keep your mistress waiting, or it will be the worse for you, I promise.'

'Yes, Madame,' the young man said. 'I am very sorry, Madame. My most humble apologies.'

'You see what I mean,' Morand whispered as they were led along a dimly lit landing floored with deep-pile Axminster. 'That was the young Marquis de Passalboni.

Twenty-five Louis, or I miss my guess. But he's probably been chained up here for several hours.'

The maid unlocked a door and ushered them through into the room beyond. 'Madame Renée instructs me to say, Commissaire, that you will find a. . .message. . . awaiting you if you would pass by the office on your way out.'

Morand nodded. 'Thank you, Marie. You may knock upon the door when the *Salon des Lords* is free.'

'Everything seems to be free for you, Bruno,' Annette ventured when the girl had withdrawn. 'Tell me, why have you brought me to this place?'

'My position brings me certain advantages,' Morand said. 'The proprietors of such places would be foolish not to offer them, would they not? And I would be even more foolish to refuse what is freely offered.'

'You have clearly been here before. And I mean here upstairs. The formula trips easily from your lips. So I ask you again' — there was a hint of acid sharpening Annette's voice — 'why do you bring me?'

Morand laughed. 'I have never pretended to be a saint. As to the last question, I bring you for your instruction and, I hope, edification! I bring you because I have to come here anyway. Most importantly, I bring you, rather than another, because it is *you* whom I have chosen.'

And with that, the nearest he had ever come to an affectionate remark or a display of emotion, the girl had to be content.

The Chinese Room was a complete contrast to the richly furnished apartments below. Islanded in a sea of *chinoiserie*, hard cushions on the bare floor surrounded a low table set with fragile teacups in silver filigree cradles. Huge pottery vases decorated with enamelled flowers stood between a series of bamboo screens that framed shadowy landscapes and bright birds painted on silk. A set of Mah-Jongg tiles was laid out on a brass tray-table supported on intricately carved wooden legs.

Annette studied a collection of ivory figurines, a group of bronze horses on a lacquered commode inlaid with mother-of-pearl. 'What an extraordinary room!' she exclaimed. 'This looks exactly. . .I mean surely all this stuff is genuine? Some of it looks antique.'

'Well, it wasn't imported from Birmingham,' Morand smiled. 'Nor was it knocked together by amateur carpenters in the Zone. But you have yet to see the room's most enticing secret. Come over here.'

He placed her in front of an oval mirror set in a heavily scrolled, painted wood surround that was hung on one wall. With a finger and thumb, he slid aside a small circular boss in the centre of a scroll. 'Have a look through that,' he said.

She stooped slightly, put her eye to the hole that was revealed. . .and gasped.

She was staring through a spy-hole equipped with a magnifying lens into an adjoining chamber. There were four people in the room, three women and a man, and all of them were naked.

'The Negro Room,' Morand said behind her. 'Although the term, as you see, is used in its broadest sense.'

The room was high-ceilinged, with a glass dome. A palm tree growing in a tub spread its fronds beneath the dome, and there was a reconstruction of a thatched native hut projecting from one wall. The man, who could have been a schoolmaster or a lawyer, wore gold-rimmed spectacles. He stood with his feet apart beside a spiky, broad-leaved bush in front of which pineapples and a hand of bananas were piled. A black African girl, whose hands and feet appeared to be manacled, knelt on the straw-covered floor in front of him. Behind her, a tall, full-bosomed mulatto woman who played the part of a slave driver drew a plaited leather quirt between her fingers. The African's head was moving to and fro in an accelerating rhythm, and Annette's breath hissed in for the second time when she saw what the 'slave' was doing. It was only then that she noticed the fourth member of the quartet — a slender Kashmiri girl who sat cross-legged on a mat beneath the thatch, watching the debauch with expressionless eyes. She wore an elaborate headdress from which a single teardrop pearl hung over the middle of her forehead.

'Oh, but this is ridiculous, this is absurd,' Annette cried, turning her head away from the spy-hole. 'I really cannot take this seriously. Do these people know they are being watched?'

'The girls certainly do.' Morand shrugged. 'The man may or may not. Possibly that's what he pays for: it's not absurd to him.'

'Well, I think it's silly.'

'It may be,' Morand said. 'But it's pretty tame compared to some of the stuff Léo Taxil is peddling in his article this week.'

'Léo who? Did you say Taxil? I'm afraid I never heard of him.'

'A journalist, the muck-raking type who deals in sensation. But he does occasionally stumble on the truth. For the past three weeks he has been regaling his avid public with an exaggerated account of depravity and vice in the city. It's the old story: you "expose" something, fulminate against it, and say this should be stopped — and of course the public appetite is whetted for more scandal the next week.'

'What is the particular revelation this week?'

'I shall read it to you, if you wish.' The Commissaire drew a thrice-folded sheet of newspaper from his pocket and opened it out. He cleared his throat and read aloud:

"'I have it on the best authority that one of the more disreputable *maisons de tolérance* — not that in the Rue de Monthyon and not Madame Kelly's Chabanais — boasts for the pleasure of its dubious clients what is described as a 'funerary' chamber'. This is no less than a lupanar for would-be necrophiliacs!

"'The walls are lined with black satin and strewn with tears of silver. In the centre is a very luxurious catafalque with a lady lying inert in an open coffin, her head resting on a velvet cushion. Around her are long candles in silver holders, incense-burners and livid-hued illuminations. The lustful madman who has parted with ten Louis for the séance is then introduced. He is shown a *prie-dieu* on which he may kneel. A harmonium, placed in a neighbouring closet, will play *De Profundis*. Then, to the strains of this funeral music, the vampire will precipitate himself upon the girl simulating the deceased.'''

'There follows another quarter column calling on the authorities to close the place down, which of course they will ignore.' Morand folded the paper and put it away.

Annette shuddered. 'Vampires! That certainly sounds like something Bram Stoker might have written. Why, do you suppose, does he include a disclaimer concerning this place and — what is it called? — the Chabanais?'

'Because Taxil receives a retainer from them, and it would never do even to suggest that *they* were closed down. They are happy, on the other hand, to see such revelations in general because it may well steer more customers their way.'

'Dear God' — Annette closed her eyes and sank down onto one of the cushions — 'is there nobody in any of these places disposed to behave normally, the way nature intended?'

'Indeed there is.' Morand stood above her and placed

a hand on each of her shoulders. He drew her to her feet. 'As you shall see the moment the famous *Salon des Lords* is vacated.'

She smiled up at him, touching his cheek with two fingers. 'Why, Bruno, do you choose this particular English room when there are so many?'

'Because it is comfortable,' Morand said promptly. 'Soft rugs on the floor, a fire burning in the grate, a splendid four-poster bed with a feather mattress. And also because there are no spy-holes!'

CHAPTER EIGHT

Whether or not she had been unconsciously stimulated by the scenes of depravity at No. 14 Rue de Monthyon, Annette de Vervialle was at her most tempestuous once installed beneath the mirrored canopy of the four-poster in the *Salon des Lords*. Even Morand was astonished — if delighted — at the lewdness of her demands and the total abandon with which she reacted to his own.

And it was she who insisted, late though it was, that they did in fact subsequently visit No. 6 Rue des Moulins as the Commissaire had at first intended.

Here, in a house as sumptuously decorated as the first, they were shown into a fantastically ornate room, panelled in mock-Gothic style, whose centre-piece was an enormous bed of carved mahogany that was shaped like a shell. 'It belonged once,' the servant girl who brought the hot water said reverently, 'to the courtesan Paiva.' The head-board was also shell-shaped, and from it — in imitation of the world-famed *Venus Rising* masterpiece — a life-size naked goddess gazed benignly down on Annette as she sobbed out her ecstasies.

Before they left, Morand vanished into an office at the rear of the building — to add, the girl guessed, one more envelope to those already stored in his bulky inner pocket.

He sent her home in a fiacre — the cabbie, somewhat sourly, declined to accept payment when they reached the Rue Halévy — but refused her invitation to spend what remained of the night in her own bed. There were, he said, certain duties he must attend to before dawn which it would be 'inappropriate' for her to share.

Annette slept for most of the next day. She left her lodgings late in the afternoon with mixed emotions. That she was in love with Bruno Morand there was no doubt: just to be near him aroused her physically to the point where it became literally uncomfortable not to be able to touch; he was a handsome and entertaining escort; the thought of a permanent relationship — yes, of marriage and children — was almost unbearably enticing; she was wined and dined well when she was with him, even if he never actually had to pay. On the other hand, although he was sympathetic about her lack of a job, he never suggested helping out, he never offered her money — and, worse still, she had no means of contacting him and she never knew when she would see him next.

She had exactly thirty-five francs and a few sous in her purse. That was all the money she had in the world. The rent was overdue. She had applied, without success, for work at every music-hall, *Bal*, café-concert, cabaret, nightclub and variety theatre in Paris. Posts at the exhibition had all been filled long ago. She could think of nowhere else to try. And the only relative she had was a spinster aunt who was a schoolteacher in Toulouse. Even if she would have been welcome there, she doubted if she had enough money to pay the train fare. Thoughts of Bruno apart, the future looked bleak.

The sky clouded over. Now a light rain began to fall. All at once exhausted, she allowed depression to overtake her and sank into a chair beneath the awning of a pavement café in the Rue St Lazare. She ordered a coffee and a croissant. What did it matter? She was hungry, she was tired; whether she had thirty five francs in her purse or thirty four made no difference.

She was licking the last crumbs of the croissant from her fingers when the shower moved on and the sun came out again. A shadow fell across the small round marble table at which she was sitting. She looked up. A man was standing in front of her — a short, bulky man with a red face and bristling side-whiskers. He wore a hard hat with a curly brim, a pale check suit and highly polished black boots.

For a moment Annette wondered why he looked familiar. Then she remembered: it was Rochard, the vice-squad inspector who had been so objectionable when she was taken to the police station, the boor who had refused so angrily even to listen to her explanations. She drained her coffee cup, left a coin on the table and rose hastily to her feet.

'Don't leave,' Rochard said, stepping forward to bar the way with his squat body. 'I want to talk to you.'

'I do not think there is anything you could say, Inspector, that could possibly interest me,' Annette said icily.

'I understand how you feel — about the other night, I mean. But you don't want to take it so hard. You must be a beginner or a part-timer or *you'd* understand: it's all part of the game, after all.' He pushed her back into her chair, drew another forwards from a nearby table, and sat down beside her. He leaned forwards, lowering his voice confidentially to speak in a manner that was almost avuncular. 'Besides, I have a suggestion to make to you.'

'A. . .suggestion?' She recoiled slightly. His breath, playing hotly on her face, was tainted with garlic.

'Yes. If you still feel the same, that is. If it's so important to you *not* to be thought of as a whore; if it pains you so much to be down in the books — and you *are* down, you know — then there are ways . . .' He glanced over his shoulder. The neighbouring tables were unoccupied. 'Cards from the index can get mislaid. . .records can even be altered.' His small dark eyes were glistening. There were blackheads, she saw, in the flushed skin on either side of his nose.

'What are you saying?'

Suddenly one of his hands was on her knee. She could feel the warmth of the palm through the stuff of her dress. 'A nice girl like you,' Rochard said thickly. 'A nice, big, beautiful, healthy, well-formed girl like you . . .' The hand rose so that the knuckles brushed against the swell of her breast. There were black hairs lining the back of each finger. 'There's a little hotel just around the corner in the Rue Clauzel. You be nice to me, *ma poule*, and I'll see what I can do.'

At the beginning of her training as a dancer at the age of thirteen, Annette had taken an extra course in acrobatics. Her muscular coordination was still superb. In a whirl of two-handed activity, she struck away the fingers that were now squeezing her breast and hit him across the face, open-handed, with all her strength. 'You disgusting little pig!' she cried.

The force of the blow jerked the policeman's head back. His hat fell off and rolled into a puddle at the edge of the sidewalk. By the time he lumbered to his feet to retrieve it, the domed crown was sodden with muddy water.

He stood glaring at the girl. His face was crimson. Several customers sitting just outside the door had witnessed the scene and were laughing openly. 'You'll be sorry for that, you cheap little slut!' Rochard hissed. 'If you're so high and mighty and la-di-da, what the devil are you doing, trolling outside a *brasserie des filles*?'

He strutted away, carrying his damaged hat in one hand. After ten paces, he turned and shook his fist. 'You'll be sorry!' he said again.

Annette was puzzling over his last taunt. She looked around her more carefully and saw that the man was right.

All the customers were men. Instead of waiters wearing long aprons, the food and drink were served by buxom girls with low-cut white blouses and skirts short enough to reveal ankles — sometimes even a hint of calf. It was indeed, as Rochard had said, a so-called *brasserie des filles* — one of 200 such places in the city whose rivalry had reduced the number of licensed brothels from 150 to less than a hundred. Disguised as ordinary cafés, these establishments and the girls who worked them were exempt from the severe regulations governing the *maisons closes* and their inmates. The head of the Paris Sûreté had recently written a report pointing out that there were 1,100 serving girls dispensing beer who were prepared to go upstairs with a customer for a consideration at brasseries 'where the large street numbers have been replaced by shop windows to give sufficient indication of the kind of commerce being practised therein.'

Annette rose hastily and started to cross the street. Once again somebody stood in her way, just as she was stepping off the pavement. This time it was a slightly built young woman of about thirty, wearing a cheap gingham dress in red and white checks. Above her thin, peaky features, dark, straggling hair was skewered up beneath a straw hat with a black band. 'Well, fancy seeing you!' she exclaimed. 'Just the kind of person I was looking for.' She coughed, holding dark-veined hands to her chest. 'What a piece of luck!'

As soon as she spoke, even more so with the cough, Annette recognized her. It was the prostitute she had confided in when she was held in the charge room of the VIIIth Arrondissement police station.

'Trying to work the brassies, are you?' the girl

continued. 'Not worth it, if you ask me. The types who want to play stick to their francs like glue. It can be dangerous too: the girls inside don't welcome the competition.'

'I was just leaving,' Annette said. 'I had not realized that the place – '

'No luck, eh? Well, the street's even tougher with this damned clean-up. But look. . .if you want to make a bit extra, I can put something your way. Nothing to do with the game either. But it does need someone with a little class. That's why I was glad to see you.'

Annette knew from experience that it was hopeless trying to convince the girl that she herself was not 'on the game'. And if what she proposed had nothing to do with it either. . .well, there was no harm listening. 'Well,' she said doubtfully, 'if you think . . .'

'Come on up the Red Rooster,' the girl persuaded. 'We'll drink a bock and I'll tell you all about it.'

The Red Rooster was a steamy café in a poor quarter off the Place Blanche. Rough-looking men in working clothes crowded the zinc-topped bar or played *belote* at tables in the rear part of the room. The few women there were looked as if they were waiting for dusk so they could promenade the streets. The place was loud with conversation and bawdy laughter.

The girl's name was Lily Leblanc. 'You looked very down,' she said sympathetically when they were sitting in the window with their small glasses of dark beer. 'Things not going too well?'

'At the moment you saw me, it was fury,' Annette replied. 'That poisonous little toad Rochard had just propositioned me.'

'Don't even speak to me of the damned *flics*,' Lily cried. '*Ils ne sont que des ordures*. They're just a load of rubbish.'

'But apart from that. . .well, no, things are not too good.' Relieved to find a confidante − her friend Lucie had gone to stay with her family in Brittany − Annette poured out the whole story, omitting only the fact that the man she was so unsure of was also a policeman.

'Men!' Lily said angrily when she had finished. 'They're all the bloody same. Once they've got their hole they don't want to know.' She swallowed a mouthful of beer and looked up at Annette with a remarkably shrewd pair of eyes. 'You know,' she mused, 'I reckon that maybe you're straight after all. But. . .I don't know why. . .I've taken a fancy to you, dear, and I'd like to help. I can too, because, like I said before, you've got class, and that's what I need right now.'

Annette smiled. 'Very well. Talk me into whatever it is.'

Lily plucked at her lower lip. 'It's not *entirely* legal,' she admitted. 'But anyone who loses out can well afford to do so.'

'Tell me about it.'

'It comes down to this: me and my mates, we've had enough. Running away from the *flics* so that we can lift our skirts for any bastard that has the cash to pay for it no longer makes any sense.' She smiled crookedly. 'The game, you could say, is no longer worth the candle! So we're going to try something else.'

'Good for you.'

'You have to know, first, that what they call the crime scene, here in Montmartre and down in Montparnasse, is well and truly sewn up. Big René and Jo the Terror have a stranglehold on the villains. Nobody lifts a bent finger without those two collecting their rakeoff. Even a straight kid must know that, I guess?'

Annette knew. René Lambert and Jo Hainnault were virtual bosses of the Paris underworld. By threats, blackmail and the use of physical force, over ten years they had imposed an iron grip, a pioneer version of the protection racket that brought them a percentage of the take from all organized crime in the capital.

'René and Jo,' Lily said, 'would never tolerate a woman muscling in, as the Americans call it. But that only applies to the bigtime scams. The whole point of my plan is that it would be smalltime.'

Annette was fascinated. Moral considerations that might have swayed her before her own brush with the law were now forgotten. 'Go on,' she said.

'René and Jo can't be bothered with petty crooks — bag-snatchers and walk-in burglars and people who sell forged lottery tickets and that kind of thing. They're after the big hauls pulled in by the organized gangs. What me and my mates aim to do is recruit those very small-timers, the types who work on their own, that the Big Two ignore.'

'But if you are going to recruit a number of people,' Annette objected, 'surely, once you organize them. . .I mean, I see your point, but once these small-timers become a gang – '

'Of course. They would be no different from the others. But if, despite a discreet organization, we were to restrict ourselves to the kind of jobs that were too small to interest them. . .and if we did enough of those jobs in a short time – ' Lily shrugged, smiled and shook her head. 'Maybe, if we were clever, we could make more than we do now – enough in any case to keep a roof over our heads – and still stay out of their clutches. It might be risky, but it would be a sight better than making it on our backs, no?'

'I do so agree,' Annette enthused. 'And I appreciate your thinking of me, but I don't know that I am really qualified – '

'I'm not suggesting you joining the gang,' Lily said. 'That wouldn't work, I agree. But before we start operating, we need capital. Not much but enough to keep us going while we organize. And for that I plan a one-off operation that takes places at several different places at the same time. Which is where you come in.' She held up a thin hand as Annette was about to interrupt. 'I will explain. You have heard, of course, of Boni de Castellane?'

'Who has not?' Annette replied. The Comte Boniface de Castellane was a rich dandy who had set himself up, along with a coterie of intimates, as the arbiter of fashion among the socialites of Paris. If Boni and his aristocratic dilettante friend, Comte Robert de Montesquiou-Fézenac, approved, then a style of dress, a leisure activity, a form of speech was 'in'; if they didn't, it was out.

'De Castellane is giving a party.' Lily said, 'to celebrate the opening of the exhibition. You know the kind of thing: a thousand bottles of champagne, five hundred lobsters, dozens of skewered lambs cooked in a garden tricked out to look like an oriental palace court-yard, with Negro slaves serving at seventy-foot tables and a hundred flamingoes imported from Africa in the shrubbery. The only thing different about this one is that it's a costume ball, with fancy dress representing the different nations exhibiting.'

Annette looked puzzled, and Lily explained:

'There are between two and three hundred guests. Their costumes have been chosen – and paid for – by Castellane himself. And they are all being made by Landolff. My plan hinges on the fact that all these guests have to go to the costumier's workshop for fittings at fixed times – otherwise there would be chaos, and they'd never be finished in time.'

'So?'

'So we select a few of the richest, find out when they will be occupied at Landolff's, and nick a few trinkets — Fabergé eggs, miniatures, bibelots, silver snuff boxes, etcetera — while they are away.'

'Yes, but —' Annette frowned. 'Surely the fittings will be during the daytime? You can't very well burgle their homes in daylight: there'll be concierges and servants and —'

'No burglaries,' Lily cut in. 'We send in ladies. Who will say they have an appointment with the lady of the house. The servants will ask them to wait. . .and while they are there they will pocket whatever is handy and small, getting out before the boss returns.' Lily grinned. 'That's why I need classy folks like Milady and you — you remember Milady, the tart with her nose in the air? — folks who can carry off a socialite rôle.'

Annette was still dubious. 'Even so, I don't quite see. . .I mean, how will you know the exact times each of these women have their appointments at Landolff's? And even if we could carry if off, there's the question of clothes. This rag's the best thing I've got, and look at it!' She held up disdainfully a fistful of the mustard-coloured damask.

'All taken care of — by the same set of facts. Landolff doesn't pay very well, and some of the seamstresses earn a little money on the side. . .well, our way. We happen to know about it, so we can lean on them a little, because Landolff would sack them if he found out.'

'You blackmail them?'

'Not in a serious way. But in return for our keeping quiet, they will let us have a list detailing the appointment times. As for the clothes, well we have. . .shall we say persuaded?. . .them to lend us for the couple of hours necessary a few of the fabulous gowns that are almost finished or awaiting delivery to the noblewomen who ordered them.'

'You seem to have thought of everything. Well, almost everything. How, for example, do we talk our way into these houses?'

'Pierre the Penman will see to that. He's a forger — lottery tickets, identity papers and that kind of thing. He'll supply you with perfect visiting cards saying you're Lady Muck from the provinces, complete with letter of introduction from the Marquise Whoever.'

'He sounds a good contact,' smiled Annette. 'Who else do you plan to recruit?'

'Not a bad lot. There's the fence of course, who'll take the stuff we nick off our hands. Then, for this first fund-raising hit, there's just us girls — me and Milady, Fat Berthe, Suzy Half-Pint and Jacqui the Jerker. Plus you, of course, if you'll do it.'

'Jacqui the Jerker!' Annette echoed. 'What kind of name — ?'

'Poor Jacqui! She's so ugly she has to turn her tricks in an unlit alley, otherwise marks would take fright and run! But it don't matter in this case: Pierre will fix her up as a German baroness.'

'No men among your "small-timers"?'

'Oh, sure. But, like I say, not for this first operation. Later, apart from Pierre, there'll be a queer called Le Géroflé, the wallflower. He's a second-storey man. And Young Benoit. And someone I haven't fixed yet, for muscle, for protection. And of course Turkey Phiz. He's a pickpocket, a dip.'

'What does Young Benoit do?' Annette was intrigued by this bizarre collection of underworld nicknames.

'Benoit? Looks about seventeen, but he's forty if he's a day. He plays the country cousin, the rube up for the first time in the big city. He's the guv'nor at the ring job, among other cons.'

'The ring job?'

'You *are* green, aren't you!' Lily said. 'The operator has his pocket filled with rings. They come at one franc a dozen. Brass and glass, but they could be gold and diamonds in bright sunlight, see. He threads a little price tag on each one: fifty francs, a hundred, maybe even two-fifty if the district he's working is swank enough.'

'What does he do with them?'

'Well, he waits outside a jeweller's shop until a likely mark comes along, doesn't he? Two ladies out shopping together is ideal. Then he drops one of the rings just behind them, pretends to find it on the pavement, and stops them, saying didn't *they* just drop this? When they tell him no, he acts the hick for all he's worth, thick Normandy accent and all. He says, oh dear, he doesn't know what to do with it, and all that. Then, seeing the tag, they figure some rich fool has dropped it on the way out of the shop. And ten to one their greed will get the better of them, and the bitches will exchange glances and decide to cheat him out of his find. They'll offer to take it off his hands, to help him out, and give him ten or twenty francs as a favour.'

Lily's laugh turned into a fit of coughing. When she had caught her breath she added: 'Some favour — when he paid a franc for it, along with eleven others, and they think it's worth a hundred!'

'And of course they cannot complain,' Annette said, 'because that would mean admitting that *they* tried to cheat!'

'You got it. Now, since we're talking money . . .' Lily leaned forwards with her thin elbows on the table. 'Will you come in with us — just on this first trick? I have to know at once, but say you'll do it, please. I can guarantee you ten Louis, maybe twelve if everything goes well.'

Annette bit her lip. It was a difficult decision to take on the spur of the moment. Stealing of course was wrong — even from rich people who would not really suffer from the loss! In view of her desperate financial position, the offer was on the other hand tempting, there was no doubt about that. Staring absently over Lily's shoulder, her eyes focused suddenly on the windmill above the entrance to the Moulin Rouge garden, visible at the end of the alley, on the far side of the Place Blanche.

The sight crystallized her predicament and the young prostitute's in a single image, concentrating all her fury and frustration at the unfairness of life in a single surge of defiance. Very well. The world of men had decided to cast her in a villain's rôle, had they? They were determined to treat her as a bad girl? All right, in that case she would damned well *be* a bad girl. Just this once anyway.

She nodded across the table at Lily. 'I'll do it,' she said.

CHAPTER NINE

It was three days later, and Annette had already been summoned twice for exploratory talks with Lily and Milady, when next she saw her policeman beau.

She had been inside the exhibition grounds. A friend had told her that one of the waitresses at the chic and luxurious new restaurant overlooking Paris from the second level of the Eiffel Tower had been taken ill and a replacement was needed. Alas, by the time she had hurried across from the St Lazare neighbourhood and climbed more than 750 stairs the post had already been filled.

She was walking disconsolately away from the vast, splayed, cast-iron pillar containing the staircase when she saw Morand — striding her way from one of his mobile police stations between the tower and the domed facade of the eighteenth-century École Militaire. His handsome face creased instantly into a welcoming smile. 'Annette! But what a splendid surprise!' He approached her with outstretched hands.

'Maybe one day *you* will give *me* a surprise,' she replied — just a trifle acidly — as she permitted herself to be kissed on each cheek.

Morand laughed off the rebuke. 'A policeman's lot!' he quoted. 'You know the difficulties, my dear. Now. . .I have a few minutes. What would you like to do?'

A mischievous smile illuminated her face. 'I would like

to go to the top of the Tower,' she said. 'Right to the very top. In an elevator!'

For a moment the Commissaire frowned, then the narrowed eyes widened at a sudden thought. 'An excellent idea,' said he. 'There is a lift in each leg of the structure. We will take the one reserved for officials and personnel.'

There was a uniformed attendant outside the double grille closing in the cage, and a small notice warning: *Pass Holders Only*. But as soon as he saw Morand, the man touched his cap with a forefinger and at once slid back the outer and inner gates.

The cage was richly panelled in mahogany, with mirror glass covering the back wall. There were four buttons on the control panel, three black and one red, with a manual lever beneath. Morand thumbed the top button and the gates clanged shut.

As soon as the cage rose out of sight of the attendant, the Commissaire swung towards Annette — as she knew he would — and wrapped his arms around her pliant body. One hand cupped the swell of her bottom, the middle finger pressing the thin stuff of her dress into the crack between the two rounded cheeks. The other hand moved around from between her shoulderblades until the palm cradled the weight of a breast as he crushed her against him. Below the basque of her corset she could feel the hard pressure of his maleness jammed against her belly.

Whether it was because of a naturally rebellious nature, because she wished in a subtle way to get her own back, or simply because her talks with Lily had renewed her confidence, Annette never knew. But a minor devil certainly got into her that day, and she determined that this time, for a change, the game would be played her way: instead of merely acting, she would direct! And if the gallant officer was — perhaps just a little? — discomfited, well that was too bad.

Nobody was paying the piper? she thought to herself as the now familiar tremors coursed through her loins. Very well, then it was she who would call the tune!

Freeing herself from his embrace, she hooked the fingers of her own hand into the fly of his tight trousers and ripped them open. The hand plunged inside, yanked aside underclothes and grabbed the hot and rigid proof of his masculinity, jerking it forward into the open air.

Morand's jaw dropped and his breath hissed inwards. In the instant that he stood there, bemused, the hard stem of flesh projecting from his trousered thighs, she dragged her drawers down to her knees. Then, whirling about, she whisked skirt, underskirt and petticoat up around her waist and turned to face the mirror.

The Commissaire was thunderstruck. 'Annette!' he gasped. 'You cannot. . .you must not . . .'

'Oh, but I have, haven't I?' she taunted. She stepped out of the drawers. 'You have something I want, Bruno. Something I want very badly. Give it to me now.'

The lift rose slowly past the Tower's first stage.

Several visitors stood on the platform, waiting for one of the public elevators to arrive. One or two of them glanced across as the service cage passed on its way up.

'*Annette!*' This time Morand's voice was almost a yelp. 'Those people! Some of them could see!' He stared aghast at the obscene tableau in the cage — the girl's naked pink rump below the bunched clothes, the bare columns of thighs with a tuft of chestnut hair visible between, the calves and knees covered by horizontally striped blue and white hose secured by pink satin garters. And his own upright figure with its stiff and reddened stalk protruding through the gap in his savaged trousers.

'How lucky for them!' Annette quipped. 'But Bruno, dearest, we can see too, can we not?' She tapped the mirror glass.

'But. . .you must be mad! I am in uniform. If I was recognized . . .'

'They won't recognize that fellow who looks so eager to perform. At least I hope not. But if you are not quite sure — why then either you must remove the uniform or find some place to hide your cavalier. I wonder now what secret place of concealment we could think of?'

Morand choked. The cage must be half way to the second stage. He could feel the blood pulsing through the veins in his temple. But at the same time, and despite his fury at being upstaged in what he considered to be a man's prerogative, the blood was also hammering through more sensitive parts of his anatomy. The very lewdness of the situation, even the fact that the initiative had been taken, quite literally, out of his hands, the astonishing sight of the half-nude young woman — all these things excited him to a pitch where he could scarcely contain himself. The sensations coursing through every fibre of his nervous system concentrated in the spearhead of his desire.

She was still facing the mirror. 'Kneel down, Bruno,' she commanded. 'We must be approaching the next stage.'

For a tenth of a second he hesitated. . .and then, as lust overcame his fear of ridicule and he saw at the same time what she meant, he sank down behind her until he was sitting on his heels, with his two knees touching the glass.

'Why, you little . . .' he began, with his lips touching the satin skin above the divide in her bottom. But Annette was now lowering herself too.

Straddling her legs, she sank slowly down until she was squatting over Morand's lap, and the rigid part of him that had been designed expressly for the purpose was lodged between the moist lips of her lovers' tryst. He gasped with pleasure as she rotated her hips, easing the way until the whole of his manhood was swallowed in the soft clasp of flesh and he was entirely within her body.

'There,' she said dreamily. 'Your cavalier is safely sheltered. I knew that somehow, between us, we would find a place for him to hide.' Ruffling out her skirt and underclothes, she spread them around her so that the lower half of the Commissaire's body was completely covered.

The floor of the second stage sank into sight beyond the steel grille gates of the cage. There were a dozen tourists waiting to descend. Those of them who looked saw the back view of a man in a dark uniform, apparently sitting on the floor with a young woman perched on his lap. Aha! Morand imagined them saying over the fierce beating of his heart. There's the French for you! The moment they're alone, the fellow cuddles his girl and steals a kiss!

If only they knew! If only his Superintendent knew!

The lift continued upwards. There was still more than 500 feet to go before the third and last stage. But now his desire was consuming him. He reached over Annette's shoulder and stabbed the red button. The cage shuddered to a halt between floors.

Both of them were panting now with anticipation and excitement — at the daring of what they were doing and the shame that they should find it so stimulating.

Annette bundled her skirts together and tucked them into the belt she wore around her waist, freeing her two hands. Gently, she withdrew herself from Morand's throbbing maleness until she was half standing, feet astride, in front of the mirror. She leaned forwards and supported herself with her palms flattened against the glass.

The Commissaire was on his feet, dragging his

unbuttoned trousers down over his thighs and knees. He was breathing hard. His blue eyes glittered. 'My God, Annette,' he said hoarsely, 'I knew I was right, but you really are the most adorable . . .'

He broke off with a gasp of ecstasy. She had reached one hand back between her straddled legs and grasped his stiff part, guiding it between the warm globes of her backside until the swollen head touched the damp fur between her thighs.

Bracing his hips so that the upper part of him did not move, Morand stepped out of his trousers and underslip.

Both of the girl's hands were flat against the glass again. He stole one hand around her, swept it down her belly and parted the hot lips nestled at the apex of her pubic triangle. She shivered, feeling the engorged head nudge the entrance to her secret cave.

Morand's other hand, resting firmly on one of her hips, pressed Annette's pelvis down, so that as she arched her back and he flexed his knees, he slid his whole length easily within her again.

She stared fascinated at the double image in the mirror, the two bodies fused, the faces open-mouthed with the intoxication of love, the four eyes blank with need.

Mindlessly, her body supported now by her brow resting against the mirror, her hands unfastened buttons and laces on bodice and camisole so that her breasts hung free between the open edges of her dress.

Morand had started a slow and rhythmic movement of his own hips, alternately advancing and receding his stiffness to tease groans of pleasure from his willing mistress. Steadying her with one hand, he sought and found the tiny bud of her innermost delight with the fingers of the other, caressing it to an awareness that startled shudders over her whole frame.

'Down!' she gasped a moment later. 'Get down again, Bruno, and squat on your heels.'

He obeyed at once, and she lowered herself after him, retaining the tip of his rigid part within her grasp by muscular contraction.

Once more she was poised over his lap, rising and falling in invisible stirrups as she gently — oh, very gently — massaged his upright stalk with the amorous clasp of her body.

Balancing himself on his heels, Morand stared over her shoulder in a trance of delight. Below the belly and between the splayed legs of the nymph gazing at him lasciviously from the mirror, the open pink lips of Annette's treasure closed seductively over the stem that impaled her. Around the soft mounds of the image's breasts, fingers that he knew were his kneaded and stroked. And from behind her shoulder, the face of Commissaire Bruno Morand, the head of the city's vice squad, glared accusingly at his own.

The hell with the damned Commissaire! He was off duty was he not?

Morand allowed her a few seconds more to admire the plastic masterpiece provided by the junction of their parts, then he released the breasts, grasped her naked hips, and levered her to her feet above him.

He drew her slightly away from the mirror, so that she was bent almost at right angles, her outstretched hands still pressed to the glass, the twin globes of her bottom and the furred cleft between them exposed to his salacious gaze.

Then, thumbing apart those fleshy hemispheres, he plunged in again the intrepid diver who had only seconds before broken surface.

This time his thrusts were longer, harder, deeper, the invasion of Annette's secret flesh more ferocious, the coupling of their two bodies more urgent. A tremor, a shudder, a shivering spasm shook the girl's torso. Her quaking loins contracted. Delirious sensations stormed outwards from the hidden temple of her delight and she climaxed with a long sobbing outcry of joy.

The strength of her release and the hot pulsing clasp of those contractions provoked in Bruno Morand an irresistible and relentless surge of excitement that nothing could arrest, and his quivering part leaped within her to pay tribute in a spurting flood that left them both exhausted on the floor of the stationary elevator.

It was only after they had dressed themselves with trembling fingers, reactivated the hydraulic lift mechanism and stepped out onto the Eiffel Tower's top platform, one thousand feet above the roar of the exhibition, that Annette spoke. Hugging Morand's arm to her bosom, she murmured: 'Even when I was little, I never dreamed that I would end up raping a policeman!'

CHAPTER TEN

For reasons of security, the first meeting of Lily Leblanc's
gang, or at least the nucleus of it, took place at some
distance from Montmartre. An unusual grouping of petty
crooks, which would certainly be remarked locally, stood
a much better chance of passing unobserved by the
underworld bosses, it was felt, if it occurred in the wastes
of La Villette, on the north-eastern boundary of the city.

They met at a guingette, or open-air bar, on the banks
of the St Denis canal. Annette decided to walk there,
although it was a long way, almost four miles, from where
she lived. This was partly to save money, partly to clarify
her own feelings in the light of what she had agreed to
do, and partly because it was a balmy sunny morning.
In the end she was glad she had done so because her route
lay across the zone – a desolate no-man's-land between
the city centre, the outer boulevards and the fortifications
which had once encircled Paris, where the poor, the
forgotten and those without hope lived out their wretched
lives. It was the sight among the shantytowns of the rag-
pickers and gypsies and scrap-metal scavengers, of their
ill-fed, barefoot children in the mud, that steeled her
resolve to continue a course of action that was beginning
to scare her with its implications.

La Villette had been the subject of one of Aristide
Bruant's bitterest and most caustic 'social accusation'
songs, but Annette doubted if any of the socialites who

flocked every night to the Mirliton to hear the *chansonnier* attack their kind had been within a mile of the guingette. It called itself the Auberge des Poissonniers, although there could have been no fish to catch in the weed-scummed canal for many years. It was approached by a dirt road that wound through a deserted area waist-high with weeds, pockmarked with dumps of refuse. In the distance, beyond a wilderness of railway yards, she could see the severe geometry of gas-holders in the Quarter of the Evangelists. The roofs and chimneys of workers' cottages bounded a patch of neglected allotments on the far side of the water.

Annette shivered. There were certainly patches of open country that remained among the slums of Montmartre, but they were pastoral idylls compared to the bleakness of this urban desert. A cool wind rustled the dry grasses and stirred dust from the surface of the road. She shivered again and hurried toward the auberge.

She appeared to be the last to arrive. Lily and her friends were already sitting at cast-iron tables on a cracked cement terrace overlooking the canal. Milady was there, splendid in damson brocade edged with white lace. Beside her, the coarse-featured, thick-lipped woman they called Jacqui the Jerker was wearing a worn brown velvet dress with a feathered hat that looked as though it had been washed up on a beach after a storm. Suzy Half-Pint and Fat Berthe had once worked the halls as a comedy act. Their disparity in build was accentuated by the fact that they dressed alike — in horizontal stripes of blue and white — and by the fact that the enormous Berthe had a high, piping voice while Suzy spoke in deep, hoarse tones that would not have discredited a fairground barker. Lily wore lavender-coloured silk.

Although they were not directly concerned with the costume ball operation, three of the men she had recruited were there. It was not difficult for Annette to decide which was which.

The pickpocket known as Turkey Phiz was a bulky, middle-aged man with a red face and loose folds of flesh quivering beneath his jaw that bore a laughable resemblance to the wattles of a Christmas bird. Young Benoit, too, merited his name. He was slender, athletic-looking in a coltish way, with a frank pink face that was unmarked except for a scatter of freckles under each candid eye. The forger was a tall, thin, saturnine fellow with a heavy moustache and black, black hair growing low on his forehead. It was he who stepped forwards and drew out a chair for Annette to sit on.

A waiter in a long white apron was leaning against the auberge doorway beneath a rusty iron pergola half covered with vines. Lily beckoned him over and ordered jugs of wine for everyone. 'This first round is mine,' she announced, 'since I asked you to trudge all the way out here. After that, the expenses, like the profits, will have to be shared equally between all of us.' She looked around the group, grinned, and then continued: 'Now. . .you have all been briefed individually, but this is the first time we have all been together, so I will detail today's operation again, from top to bottom.'

The plan was simple enough. Turkey Phiz had brought the 'borrowed' robes from Landolff's workshop in a two-horse carriage, which was waiting behind the auberge. Once the six women were dressed, he would drive them into the city, dropping each one off at the correct address, at a time when the owner would herself be at Landolff's for a fitting. The 'ladies', each equipped by Pierre the Penman with a believable identity, would allow themselves thirty minutes to pocket whatever they could lay hands on that was small enough to conceal in a muff or a handbag, and then, as though tired of waiting, let themselves out — preferably without encountering the servants. Finally they would make their way to a pick-up point near the Arc de Triomphe, where Turkey Phiz would be waiting to return them to the auberge. Before dark, the dresses would be back where they belonged.

There would, Lily said, be no difficulty getting to the pick-up, because all six of the houses chosen were nearby in the snob XVIth Arrondissement, between the Arc de Triomphe and the river. She added: 'There is just one more thing. Some of you may be worried, frightened you won't be able to carry off the toff's rôle you've been given. But remember this: you won't actually have to face the noble bitches you're supposed to have an appointment with. All you have to do is convince the servants!'

Yes, Annette thought to herself, that's all very well. But servants in upper-class houses were often better judges of breeding than their owners. And as for being worried. . .well, she was already trembling inside.

The house chosen for Annette was the Paris home of the Comtesse van den Bergh. It was in the Avenue Kléber, a huge mansion with an arched entrance and a central courtyard. Turkey Phiz, in coachman's livery, drove smartly through the arch and reined in the horses by the steps that led to the entrance doors. Jumping down, he ran around and opened the door of the carriage with a flourish, handing her to the steps with a deep bow. Inside, the other girls ducked back out of sight, giggling, for Annette was the first to be 'delivered'.

She ran up the steps, twirling a small parasol, and withdrew the heavy, polished brass knob of the bell. Somewhere within the mansion, at basement level she thought, the summons jangled. Turkey Phiz climbed to his seat, whipped up the horses, and drove away.

Suddenly Annette felt very much alone, very

vulnerable. She was wearing a lilac taffeta dress with a square-cut neck and huge leg-of-mutton sleeves that narrowed to a tight wrist. The bodice was heavily encrusted with amethysts, pearls and rhinestones, and there were silk flowers appliquéd to a violet organza overskirt that was draped around the lower half of the bell-shaped garment. A wide hat swathed in mauve velvet hid her hair.

The finery rationed out to the other girls was equally impressive, especially a hip-hugging, peacock blue sheath with a hobble skirt that Lily herself wore. The dress, with its large, loosely folded standaway collar, had been designed by Paquin and then sent to Landolff for the addition of semi-precious stones around the bust. Once laced into it, Lily, with her thin-featured, perky face, carried off splendidly the rôle of niece to an Alsatian industrialist that Pierre had written for her. Annette's visiting card identified her as Madame Geneviève Lalande d'Estournel. Her letter of introduction was from her supposed father-in-law, a provincial Marquis with a château near Lyon.

The doors were opened by a footman wearing a striped, sleeved waistcoat, his eyebrows superciliously raised. 'The Comtesse van den Bergh is expecting me,' Annette said as haughtily as she could, hoping that the knocking together of her knees was not audible.

'Madame la Comtesse is not at home,' the servant said.

'What? But I was distinctly told. . .the afternoon after my arrival in Paris . . . Surely she cannot have forgotten even a *distant* relative?'

'Madame is at the couturier's. She is not expected back for some time.'

'The couturier? Oh, I see. It is not as though it was a *social* occasion. Perhaps I am a trifle in advance: after all no precise time was agreed. Never mind.' She stared over the man's shoulder, a trick she had learned from Milady ('Never look them in the eye. Treat them like shit. They expect it.'). 'I shall await her return. You may show me into the salon.'

For a moment the footman hesitated, his lips pursed.

'Well, what are you waiting for? Am I to stand here all afternoon?' Annette allowed her voice to sharpen angrily. She tossed her card, along with the envelope containing the letter of introduction, onto a silver salver that lay on a Louis XIV marquetry table just inside the front doors.

The servant conceded defeat. He bowed. 'If Madame would be so good as to follow me . . .'

On the far side of the black-and-white marble squares that checkered the big hallway, a staircase with a brass rail curved gracefully to the first floor. Opposite the stairhead, the footman flung back ivory-coloured double doors picked out in gold and ushered Annette into a huge room overlooking a garden.

He bowed again and withdrew.

Military ancestors in dress uniform and ladies in ball gowns stared disapprovingly down at her from gold frames as she looked hastily around her. She saw tapestry-covered shieldback chairs and settees, glass cases filled with Dresden and Sèvres, more marquetry, an antique Burgundian commode piled high with illustrated books. Gilt cupids supported a barrel clock under a glass dome crowning the carved wood chimney-piece.

More importantly, the room was strewn with a variety of small tables, almost all of them crowded with pocketable items. Her sweeping glance registered snuff-boxes, vinaigrettes, Lalique figurines, animals in ivory and jade, a silver basket filled with china eggs.

She swung around. The doors were open and the footman was in the room again. This time his manner was markedly more obsequious. It was clear that he must have read the eulogistic letter in the unsealed envelope she had left below. 'If Madame would care for some refreshment while she waits?' he suggested. 'An infusion perhaps, or a tisane?'

'Thank you, no. You may leave me.' She turned her back on him and walked to the windows.

'Very good, Madame.' The man retired and closed the doors.

A stone balustrade stretched across the three floor-length windows. Beyond it, a walled garden was shaded by chestnut trees already in leaf. Picked out by a ray of sunlight filtering through, stone urns planted with geraniums flanked two classical figures on plinths. Annette wished she was down there, lying peacefully on the lawn.

She turned back into the salon. The miniatures she had been particularly briefed on by Pierre the Penman were hung in a close group at one side of the fireplace. The prize example — so she had been told — was a tiny Nicholas Hilliard portrait of the Earl of Essex, a favourite bedfellow of Elizabeth I of England. The white ruff, the feathered hat and slashed doublet sleeves, no less than the sardonic expression on the subject's face, identified the painting easily enough. She unhooked the frame from the wall and dropped it into the brocade reticule that she carried.

A vinaigrette next, cut crystal with a gold stopper. Into the pouch. A tub-shaped pillbox in chased silver, a diminutive elephant, exquisitely carved from ivory, part of a collection spread over the marble top of a Breton buffet. Not more than five, they had said. A snuff-box, then? There were thirteen, on a glass-topped octagonal table. She selected one with an inlaid mother-of-pearl lid, was about to stow it away when she noticed, in the bright light streaming through the windows, that there was now a small rectangle on the glass that was shinier than the rest of the surface. Evidently the table had not been dusted for some time! So much, she thought, for the prissy footman!

Hastily, she moved around the boxes to cover the table top a different way. If the servants neglected the dusting, they were not likely to notice a different arrangement. She added the snuff-box to the rest of her booty and took a last look around.

Horrors! Unmistakable in that light, a darker patch on the wall shrieked out that a miniature had gone from the middle of the group. There was no way to hide that. Regretfully, she withdrew the Hilliard from her reticule and hung it back.

She was looking around for a replacement when the doors were flung open yet again and the footman announced: 'Monsieur Lionel Giotto.'

A tall, soberly dressed young man with fair hair walked into the room.

'My dear lady,' he said, striding forward with an outstretched hand, 'I beseech you to forgive me for this unannounced intrusion. But since I was calling on our Commercial Counsellor, who lives in the same street . . .' He left the sentence unfinished. From his heavy accent, Annette assumed he was American.

Hurriedly, she put down a majolica trinket box that she had been considering. But before she could reply, Giotto had seized her hand, bent low over it, and touched it with his lips. 'I trust the fact that our mothers were distant cousins will excuse me,' he said.

Then, straightening, he plunged a hand into an inner pocket and produced an embossed envelope. 'However, I have here, *ma chère Comtesse*, a letter of introduction from our mutual acquaintance, the Ambassador.' He held out the envelope.

Annette, at first bemused, realized what had happened.

The footman, having forgotten the name she had given, had failed to make the introduction and withdrawn before he could be rebuked. And the young man, seeing before him a woman dressed in the height of fashion, had naturally assumed this must be his intended hostess. He had mistaken her for the Comtesse van den Bergh!

Smiling, she was about to correct the misunderstanding . . .when suddenly she had second thoughts.

Lionel Giotto was *very* good-looking. The eyes beneath that straw-coloured thatch were as bright and as blue as Bruno's. He was tall and extremely well built: the lightweight suit he wore, with its long, waisted jacket, did nothing to hide the muscularity of his frame. A firm, decisive jaw completed the picture. Might it not be amusing — just for a minute; she was about to leave anyway — to accept the rôle in which fate had cast her? To play along with the suggestion that she was a great lady, with this huge house and all its servants at her disposal?

Giotto was smiling at her appreciatively. Teeth gleamed white in his lean brown face. She knew at once that their attraction was mutual. The devil riding her during that shameless scene in the Eiffel tower swung his cloven hoof across the saddle again.

'But of course, Monsieur, I am delighted to see you,' she drawled. 'Any friend of the dear Ambassador is welcome in this house. Do you — ah — do you plan to remain long in Paris?'

'A few weeks, certainly. Mainly I am here on account of the exhibition. But a newspaper in my home town, *The Boston Evening Transcript*, has asked me to write a series of articles on the Paris underworld. . .which may indeed be a more rewarding assignment.'

'Really? How amusing.'

'I am not, of course, an expert on low life . . .'

'Quite.'

' . . .but one or two of your compatriots, a journalist who writes for *Figaro*, a police officer, have kindly offered to assist me.' Giotto hesitated, aware that the subject was not interesting the beautiful young woman in front of him. 'Er. . .have you yourself visited the exhibition?' he finished lamely.

Annette raised her eyebrows. 'Certainly not, Monsieur. One does not mingle with the riffraff in such places.'

'No. Of course not. Forgive me.' The young man was confused. 'I thought perhaps. . .with the Ambassador or the President. . .a private view . . .?'

Annette grinned, taking pity on him. The game was beginning to bore her anyway, especially since her real self was rapidly warming to his open and frank personality. 'Tell me about yourself,' she said confidingly, putting the envelope down among the snuff-boxes.

The next ten minutes passed very quickly. She was toying with an intriguing thought as she listened to him: what if he was as bogus as she was? What if he had accepted her so easily as the Comtesse because he was as unfamiliar as she with the world of socialites? Suppose the letter in the envelope was as spurious as the one she had left downstairs, the work of some other Pierre who specialized in forgeries?

That would be the supreme irony, she reflected — the two of them, each speaking from a false position, each attempting to bridge a gap that did not in fact exist! She wished it was true. She wished he really was some kind of walk-in robber like herself. . .because there would be a chance then of further meetings.

Where? How? Giotto's eyes were sparkling. She tried to banish the scene from her imagination, but in her mind's eye she saw herself naked and spreadeagled on the bed in the hotel room in the Rue Notre Dame de Lorette; she saw him poised above her, felt her breasts squashed by his manly weight as he lowered —

Unfamiliar noises from the far side of the doors jerked her back to reality. Quick feet tapping across the marble floor, footsteps on the stairway, rustle of paper and a faint thump. Then a female voice: 'The costume didn't require a second fitting after all. Take the box into my boudoir, Gaston, and give it to Françoise . . . Visitors, did you say?' The footsteps approached the salon doors.

An icy hand clutched at Annette's heart. The real Comtesse had returned unexpectedly! She would know at once. Annette would be exposed as an impostor: she could never explain why she had allowed Giotto to believe she was the châtelaine. He would turn from her in disgust. Worse, Madame van den Bergh would notice the missing objects the moment she entered the room. The mind's eye reopened: it revealed Annette standing once again beneath the high desk in the police station charge room. 'The accused already has a record . . .' the desk sergeant began.

The doors of the salon opened.

A tall young woman stood there, dressed in an elegantly cut, floor-length black riding habit. She was big-bosomed and small-waisted, with chestnut hair a little darker than Annette's own, and wide green eyes.

For perhaps two seconds she remained, staring at the couple in the salon. The she rushed toward Annette with outstretched hands. 'I am Geneviève Lalande d'Estournel,' she announced in a deep, mellifluous voice. 'My dear Comtesse van den Bergh, how gracious of you to receive me!'

CHAPTER ELEVEN

My dearest Lucie [Annette wrote to her friend in Brittany].

Things have been happening here in Paris that you have to know about!

As a change from the forces of law and order — and, it must be admitted, in defiance of any positive declarations therefrom — your (dis)obedient servant has been trying the forces of evil! Or at any rate the forces of those opposed to our so-called Guardians of the Peace.

I joke not, dear friend. A chance encounter with one of those 'fallen women' with whom I was for a short and unhappy time incarcerated has led me to plunge, oh very discreetly, into the water 'on the other side of the fence'. The more so since my fortunes are very seriously depleted. But do not worry on my account: I am by no means submerged!

I judge it prudent not to go into detail here (you shall be regaled with the details immediately you return). Suffice it to say that, on a recent afternoon, I was masquerading as a certain high-born lady when a personable young foreigner — an American with a doctorate in philosophy, believe it or not — appeared and took me for the genuine article. Perhaps foolishly, I did not disabuse him. . .and then, horror of horrors, just as we were getting along famously, the genuine article did materialize!

You can imagine my feelings: all, I thought, was lost.

But Fate gave to the proceedings a most unexpected twist. Instead of being vexed (as well she might have been), the lady entered as it were into the spirit of the thing. Lucie, she accepted me as 'herself' — and claimed that she was the person I had pretended to be when I talked my way into her house!

Yes, yes, the situation was confused, to say the least. Not least because the young American had come with letters of introduction and the real lady had therefore to prompt me to say in her place those things she would have said had the situation been normal. To thank him for his visit, to ask him to call again, and that sort of thing. What he must have thought of these two women and their highly artificial, sometimes hesitant dialogue I shall never know.

In any case, beneath the surface glitter, I was continually asking myself: why? Why had she not immediately denounced me? Why had she not only accepted my deception but immediately compounded it with one of her own?

The answer was not vouchsafed until the American gentleman had stayed the polite amount of time required by convention and then taken his leave.

Dagmar van den Bergh — for that was the name of the Comtesse I was impersonating — holds, you must know, a very particular position in Paris society. Along with Gabrielle Dorziat and Marie-Ange Foucault de la Roquette, she is a leading light among the Amazones *— those followers of the Sapphic cult who can be seen daily exercising their Russian Wolfhounds in the gardens of the Luxembourg Palace or riding, black-habited and tall-hatted, in the Bois. Why such (not to mince words)* Lesbian *activity should suddenly have become so 'fashionable' among the rich and famous we are not told.*

But its prevalence is such that scandal-mongers like the journalist Jean Lorrain permit themselves openly to discuss it in their articles. Only last week I saw a libellous drawing in l'Aurore, where the satirist Caran d'Ache illustrated in caricature the wives of two noble senators skating in far too intimate a posture at the Palais de Glace!

Ordinary folks such as you and me, of course, imagine that the Amazones are simply playing tit-for-tat with husbands who leave them to fret at home while they (the husbands) dally with expensive mistresses at Maxim's and the Café de la Paix.

But I digress. It is enough to say here that the Comtesse is − very much! − of that persuasion.

And that the reason she saved my reputation in the way she did was − that she wanted to ruin it!

Well, let us say compromise it. My beauty (!), she assured me, was such that she had to find out more about me, what I was doing in her house, and so on.

This of course emerged only after the American had gone. For I admitted at once my sin, begged her forgiveness, and indeed asked why she had not denounced me at once.

'My dear young woman,' said she, 'I know the Lalande d'Estournel family − shall we say intimately? − and I know you are not one of them. What I do not know is who you really are, and I thought the best way to find out more about so ravishing a creature was to play your game and see where it led me.'

Well of course it led her to another deception, though she did not know it. For she was so compassionate, so warm and understanding that I had not the heart to say that my aim had been to rob her. I made up some barely plausible tale about a scurrilous journalist (whom I did not name) who had persuaded me to infiltrate the home

of a well-known Amazone *so that I could provide him
with 'background material' on what he called the life-
style of such people. She was unaware, naturally, that
the whole point of my expedition had been to leave before
she returned, so that we should never have met at all.*

*She said: 'now that you are here, you shall see that life-
style for yourself. But also, perhaps, you will be able to
tell me something of yours. For I have seldom seen so
perfect an alabaster neck rising from such a superb pair
of shoulders. Nor indeed such a seductive body boasting
a skin texture like your own. You must tell me, my dear,'
(said she), 'just how you contrive to keep that
complexion.'*

*This left me, you will realize at once, in the most
awkward of predicaments. I was, you see, most
expensively dressed and turned out, and she would have
assumed — even if my behaviour itself was highly
questionable — that I came at least from some level of
society comparable with her own. I was therefore
forbidden yet again from telling the truth. . .and certainly
from the revelation that I was a penniless ex-dancer with
a police record who had been dismissed from the chorus
of a music-hall.*

*What, I wonder, would you have done, Lucie? You
would never, of course, have placed yourself in such a
position in the first place. For me at that point the only
thought was flight. Flight and sheer fright. More
especially because my hostess (as she now seemed to be)
had already laid a hand on my arm as she bade me relax
on a chaise longue, and shortly afterwards moved cool
fingers up my neck while tucking back an errant curl
escaping from under my hat. This last accompanied of
course with fulsome compliments concerning the hair
itself — its colour, its texture, its style and I know not
what else.*

My dear friend, I fled! Not solely because of these attentions and what they could imply, but because — dare I admit it? — I was myself at the mercy of sensations that troubled me greatly. Sensations I refuse to admit, even to you.

I mumbled an excuse and ran, literally ran, from the salon.

But the worst was to come. I was halfway across the marble tiles of the entrance hall, reaching for the handles of the entrance doors, when the Comtesse appeared on the landing above. Leaning over the stair rail, she smiled at me and called out: 'I hope you get a good price for the snuff-boxes and things!'

Oh, Lucie, I was scarlet with mortification. She had known all the time, but been too well-bred to mention the subject!

Now, however, I must be sufficiently ill-bred to leave you — with the promise that you shall be the very first to learn of any further development concerning any of the above; and the assurance that I remain ever your friend and confidante — Annette.

Part Two

Lionel

CHAPTER TWELVE

The *Exposition Universelle* stretched from the Place de la Concorde to the Trocadéro on the right bank of the Seine; across the river, the Quai des Nations followed the waterfront and pavilions housing the scientific marvels of the age filled the whole huge rectangle of the Champ de Mars, between the Eiffel Tower and the École Militaire.

On the morning after Lionel Giotto's brief visit to the mansion in the Avenue Kléber, the American and Felix Romero met for coffee at Fouquet's and then strolled down the Champs Elysées to the main entrance.

'On the Left Bank,' the drama critic said, 'in among all that mechanical display, there is a mobile police station where I can introduce you to the officer most likely to assist you in your researches concerning the – ah – darker side of our city life.'

'That is kind of you,' Giotto said. 'I shall be most – '

He stopped in his tracks, staring up at the gigantic arched gateway with its exaggerated curves and florid decorations. 'Good God,' he exclaimed, 'I have only been here after dark before: this is the first time I noticed her!'

He gestured towards the cupola crowning the entrance arch. On top of the dome there was a golden ball. And perched on top of the ball was the garishly coloured statue of a young woman dressed and coiffed in the latest Place Vendôme style.

The man from *Figaro* coughed. 'Yes. . .well. . .we are a trifle ashamed of the lady, if the truth be told,' he admitted. 'Binet, the architect responsible, was commissioned to create something. . .modern. It seems to me that all he produced was something vulgar. She is supposed to be a symbol of the city of Paris.' He shook his head sadly.

Lionel laughed. 'But so she is!' he said. 'To visitors like me at any rate. Gay Paree and all those naughty girls! Though I can see why the City Fathers might disapprove. Didn't I read some tirade against her in the *Revue Blanche*?'

'You did indeed,' said Romero. 'In the same issue they roasted the organizers for showing too many Impressionists in the Palace of Painting. According to them, Renoir and Cézanne are out of date: the real avant-garde should be on display.'

'The real avant-garde?'

'You know. That little Spanish fellow. Pizzicato? Piccato? They want him and his coterie.'

'Well, there's not a great deal of the avant-garde about *that*!' the American said, pointing at the florid bulk of the Grande Palais — which, like its smaller companion across the street, had been built specially for the exhibition.

Romero stopped and shaded his eyes against the glare of the Spring sunshine. 'Do you know what those groups are called?' he asked, indicating the rearing horses and chariots on each corner of the roof mansarding the vast neo-baroque building. '"Harmony Routing Discord" and "Immortality Vanquishing Time". Can you imagine!'

Lionel chuckled again. 'I prefer the kind of harmony one can arrive at with ladies like the one on the golden ball!' he said.

'Ah! Well, of course . . .' Romero caressed his lower

lip with the tip of his tongue. He straightened his necktie. 'If real ladies interest you, there is always the *promenoir* of the Folies Bergère. A real treasure trove, my dear sir, on some nights. Or the Café de la Paix in the afternoons. The Bals-Musettes of Montmartre if you like the rougher stuff. And then of course there is the Palais de Glace — after four o'clock, of course. Before that time it is the preserve of the chic and the *mondaine*.'

'To say nothing of the houses with oversize street numbers,' Giotto smiled.

'Yes, of course. But I was rather confining myself to amateur talent. Once you get into the professional field, money becomes involved in a big way.'

'Talking of women,' Lionel said casually, 'do you by chance happen to know the Comtesse van den Bergh? She has a house in the Avenue Kléber.'

'I never met the lady. I know *of* her, of course. *She* can be seen at the Palais de Glace *before* four o'clock. But her tastes, I fear, drive her toward her own sex rather than ours. Like Colette and the Marquise de Belbeuf, she is a notorious *Amazone*.'

Lionel frowned. 'Really? You surprise me, Monsieur. When I met her yesterday, I distinctively had the impression. . .I mean I fancied that I detected between us the possibility of. . .but no matter. Doubtless I was mistaken.'

'That, Monsieur, is easy enough. Pretty as a picture they are, some of these *gouines*. They are not all heavy-rumped, jackbooted farm labourers with the wrong organs down here.' The critic twirled his hand in an indecent gesture.

'Her friend now — Geneviève someone; I forget the name — she could have been that way. For my money anyway. And now I come to think of it, there was a most curious, almost evasive, atmosphere between them while

I was there.' He shrugged. 'Oh, well: I guess there are as good fish in the sea as ever came out of it.'

Romero was no longer listening. They had arrived at a gravelled plot between two exhibition pavilions where one of the caravans used as a mobile commissariat was installed. A small crowd had gathered: provincials with their families, who had been gazing open-mouthed at the exhibition set pieces, a young German governess doing her best to control three unruly schoolgirls, two Italians in silk hats. A couple of *agents* were manhandling a thin-faced man in ragged clothes up the steps and into the caravan. 'A pickpocket, I suppose,' Romero said. He turned to an officer standing nearby. 'Good morning, Commissaire. I bring you a colleague anxious to share your knowledge of the higher echelons of crime in this city: Doctor Lionel Giotto, from Boston, in the United States of America.'

'A pleasure indeed, after dealing with the likes of this wretched fellow,' said Bruno Morand, turning around with an outstretched hand.

The girl was plump and jolly. She was about thirty, Lionel Giotto thought. Unpinned, her long black hair fell almost to her waist. A dark blue, tightly swathed velvet dress that flared out below the hips hugged the upper part of her fleshy body.

She flashed him a conspiratorial smile as she started slowly to unfasten the double row of buttons regimenting the blue bodice.

He had found her, following Romero's advice, at the Folies-Bergère. The place was a surprise to him. Behind a normal auditorium surrounded by boxes, a forest of slender pillars supported the gallery. And behind them, at the level of the stalls, the whole theatre was cradled by the notorious *promenoir* – a huge semicircle curving away each side of a bar presided over by the busty blonde in black and white stripes immortalised by the painter Manet.

There were tables and chairs at strategic intervals around the *promenoir*, but most of the people crowding it stood or strolled, in pairs, in groups or singly — and those on their own were there for a purpose unconnected with the attractions on stage.

Competing with the jugglers and acrobats and singers and dancers and daringly undressed showgirls, several hundred young women every night peddled their own attractions in the city's largest shop window for sex. And unlike the artists on stage these girls could be talked to, offered drinks and bargained with openly. They were high-class material too, Giotto was intrigued to see.

The police Commissaire, Morand, had told him that prostitutes who were permitted to use the *promenoir* as a kind of prolongation of the Rue Richter sidewalk paid a subscription of twenty francs a month for the privilege. Marchand, the Folies' manager, insisted that every girl should wear gloves and a hat with feathers. 'Quite a tyrant, is old Marchand,' Morand said. 'Stands by the fountain in the lobby to make sure they don't sell back the candies and flowers bought for them in kiosks there. But he's got a heart. If one of the birds isn't sufficiently well dressed to please him, he'll advance her money to buy a new outfit. No interest when she refunds it either.'

The American dancer Loie Fuller was on stage when Giotto arrived. He had seen her act in Boston and New York, but paused at the back of the stalls to admire her barefoot arabesques, marvelling once more at her original approach — a human flame among special effects of luminous gases, wreathed in incandescent veils.

'She's wonderful, don't you think?' a soft voice said at his elbow. 'She uses photography and electrical lights as well, in a little theatre she has all to herself at the exhibition.'

Lionel turned around. The girl in the blue dress.

She had smiling eyes and a snub nose. The expression on her face was half-amused and half-challenging. At first he was unwilling to believe she was a 'business girl' — if only because, unlike the other promenading girls, she displayed no bare flesh above the bust, which was in any case covered by a feather boa. But then she took his arm in a familiar way and said: 'A nice gentleman like you all on his own! Aren't you going to buy a girl a drink?'

And of course he was hooked, gaffed and landed.

At the beginning of the evening, Lionel had had no intention of propositioning a woman, and certainly not of paying for her favours. At least that is what he told himself on the way to the Rue Richter. Why else, on the other hand, would he have gone to the Folies? When there were more comfortable theatres, with better shows, far nearer the Hotel Meurice, where he was staying?

Just to look, perhaps? To observe and make mental notes? He was, after all, in Paris to write a series of articles on the underworld — was he not? And whores, high class and low class, formed part of the underworld — did they not? It was part of his assignment, surely, to regard the activities of each. At close quarters. And to determine wherein they differed. Was that not why he had come to the Folies?

If you believe that, he could hear the cynical Commissaire say, you will, my dear sir, believe anything!

They were sitting on high stools at the bar, with their heels hooked over a brass footrail, drinking glasses of pink champagne. Inconsequentially, Lionel was reminded of an old music-hall song taught to him by his father, who had learned it in London, during The Great Exhibition of 1852.

It was called *A Dark Girl Dressed In Blue*.

If he remembered correctly, the subject of the song had been a confidence trickster, who had parted a country cousin from his money.

Was this blue girl too, at the time of this other great exhibition, equally 'on the make'?

Well. . .he was investigating the underworld, wasn't he?

Her name, rather to his surprise, was Nellie. She came from Brittany, from a small town called Vannes, near the fishing port of Lorient. Her father was a trawlerman, but the catch had been bad for three years running, there were no jobs to be had for young girls in the provinces, and she had come to Paris to seek her fortune rather than slave away in service in some draughty country house. The rest of the story was straight out of the sociology text book.

But the girl had a sense of humour. By the third glass of champagne Lionel was finding her increasingly attractive.

The way she moved each time she turned towards him; the soft, loose way the flesh moved within her bodice, which showed that her breasts were free above the stays; the very way her haunches spread on the wide, flat stool, stirring inside him the imagination of the warm, secret furrow between. . .all these things heightened his awareness — heightened it uncomfortably after the fourth glass — of his enforced celibacy ever since his ship left New York.

She had made no overt proposition: the girls licensed by Marchand were supposed to be sufficiently desirable to stimulate a first approach from the men who wanted them. Which left a girl free, if by chance she disliked a prospective client, to make a polite refusal on the pretence that she was not 'like that'. This way, Morand had said, the mark's pride remained uninjured — and Marchand retained his client at the Folies.

Nellie replaced her empty glass on the bar counter. Over the mingled aromas of patchouli, coffee, sweat and cigar smoke, Lionel sensed the musky female scent of her as she leaned forwards.

The tightness at the top of his thighs was definitely uncomfortable now. 'Do you. . .do you live far from here, Nellie?' he asked huskily.

'Oh, bless you, yes!' she laughed. 'North of the Porte de la Chapelle, in St Denis.'

'Oh.' Lionel looked momentarily crestfallen. 'I had thought perhaps. . .I mean —'

'On the other hand,' the girl continued smoothly, 'if a gentleman wished to further an interesting discussion in less rowdy surroundings, I know a comfortable and discreet place, not expensive, in the Rue Saulnier, not a hundred yards from here.'

'Splendid! There will be refreshments, I trust?'

'Naturally. And I fancy we had best make haste, because' — her eyes slid towards his loins — 'I see there is a fellow down there even more anxious to make the journey than you are!'

'We shall go at once,' said Lionel, slapping coins on the counter.

The hotel offered neither the luxury nor the variety of high-class brothels like the Chabanais, but it was, as Nellie had promised, comfortable. The room was large, with a fire burning in the grate, a wide brass bedstead, and a curtained-off cubicle housing bidet and lavabo. A side table in the centre of the amber broadloom carpet carried an ice-bucket of champagne and two glasses.

When Nellie had finished unbuttoning the blue dress and opened the front of the bodice, he saw that her breasts were, as he had thought, large and a little soft.

But the skin was satin-smooth and the sight of those pear-shaped mounds swelling above the confines of a tightly laced blue corset did nothing to diminish the ache constricting his upstanding part. He unfastened his trouser fly.

'My goodness, what a whopper!' she exclaimed, stepping out of her skirt and petticoats as he exposed his manhood.

'Look,' Lionel said, 'you do not have to pretend or attempt to flatter. I am not of the kind that sets a great store by size. I know from locker-room experience at college that I am no bigger — although certainly no smaller — than anyone else.' He stripped off trousers and underwear to stand with the organ under discussion speared out from beneath his flat belly like an Embassy flagstaff.

'Very well, Monsieur Average,' said Nellie, seizing it as if it was a handle and drawing him to the bed. 'Bare the rest of yourself while I retire behind this curtain for two minutes.'

'It seems nevertheless well designed for the task for which it was constructed,' she resumed when she reappeared, wearing nothing but the corset and black silk stockings. She lay on the bed with the long dark hair spread out like a fan around her head and shoulders.

Lionel stood looking at her. The tiresome formalities of commerce had been disposed of when he paid for the room: he could regard her as a woman and not an object he had hired for a certain space of time. 'In any case,' she had told him, 'we shall be in no hurry. You may take as much time as you wish. I am not like those girls in the Place Pigalle who turn a dozen tricks of an evening. One gentleman, one night, is my motto. Especially when he is a fine upstanding fellow I fancy, like yourself.'

'Do you. . .that is to say. . .is that sufficient. . .

income. . .to keep you,' he said awkwardly, 'the way you wish?'

'Lord, no,' Nellie laughed. 'This, you might say, is like an extra, for the small luxuries of life. In the daytime I work as a seamstress for a man called Landolff, a costumier. But this is the part I prefer — tho' it's more pleasure than work, to tell the truth.'

That at least *was* probably true, the young American reflected, gazing with increasing approval at the lush curves of the body spreadeagled on the bed. Nellie's eyes were luminous and misty. The rosy tips of her breasts, cradled now in her own two hands, were erect and quivering. The blue panels of the corset rose and fell rapidly with the rhythm of her breathing. Her parted lips glistened.

And beneath the lower edge of the wasp-waisted foundation garment, nestled in the triangle of black hair between her thighs, that second pair of lips, dewed already with moisture, seemed to him to smile invitingly.

Willingly, his pulses now racing and the evidence of his lust throbbing more rigidly than ever, he accepted the invitation. Full length upon the bed, he paid tribute with his own lips to the pink buds so temptingly held towards him. His hands, sculpting the slender taper of the young woman's shapely legs, rose to the cool swell of thighs still damp from the water in the bidet. His fingers dabbled lasciviously within the hot, wet entrance to her secret shrine.

Nellie's whole body was trembling with desire. 'Your soldier,' she breathed huskily, 'will catch cold, standing there at attention for so long without a warm welcome somewhere within.' She gripped him again with practised fingers. 'Can we not, between us, find a place where he can exercise his military talents in comfort?'

With an inarticulate cry, Lionel lowered himself

between her legs and allowed her hand to make the introduction he craved. With a thrust of her hips she rose to meet him, and they settled at once into a languorous rhythm. . .which soon accelerated to a crescendo which left Nellie gasping out her release while he fountained his own ecstasy into her receptive body.

Unstabled again, his cavalier relaxed off duty after the long-awaited call to arms. The level in the champagne bottle gradually sank.

'My goodness,' Nellie said dreamily, 'that was so good it could easily become a habit! Now that we know each other a little, perhaps we could venture together on a longer. . .exploration? With some persuasion, I could even be tempted to stay the night here.'

'Nothing,' Lionel said truthfully, 'could please me better.' He refilled her glass and held it towards her.

She leaned his way, her mouth half open, one heavy breast drooped against his naked arm. 'My gentleman,' she crooned throatily. 'With you I could make it a night of *love*!' She swallowed the champagne, let the empty glass fall to the carpet, and lay back on the bed. One hand crept down to fondle his maleness, the other to cup the twin dependencies below.

Lolling between Lionel's thighs, the soldier rose stiffly to attention once more under her expert manipulation.

This time their coupling was more venturesome, more inventive. . .and much longer drawn out. Lionel was raised time and again to the very pinnacle of delight.

Why was it then, as he lay speared deep within the hot clasp of her flesh, that his mind constantly superimposed on her excited face the image of the woman he knew as the Comtesse van den Bergh?

CHAPTER THIRTEEN

Like any wealthy young man of his generation, Lionel Giotto found that a great part of his time and energy was spent in the contemplation — and if possible the company — of women.

Practical research into the mysteries and inconsistencies underlying the behaviour — at times infuriating, at times exhilarating — of this enigmatic race occupied much of his waking, and a good deal of what should have been his sleeping, hours.

He had of course, like any good college man, been on intimate terms with prostitutes before.

But he had not, as the saying is, 'had recourse' to them, in the sense that he was unsuccessful in finding sexual partners elsewhere.

A number of young ladies of good family with whom he was acquainted could bear witness to that.

But he had never before established a genuinely satisfactory physical relationship with a 'business girl'. And Nellie was certainly the first to arouse in him feelings that were, if not of love, at least those of complicity, a camaraderie of shared joys.

He found the experience rewarding, and filed it away mentally as part of that wider education he hoped to acquire through his visit to Europe.

It was in the same spirit of empiric, almost scientific, research that he decided to investigate an annexe to the

Japanese pavilion in the exhibition grounds. Commissaire Morand had indicated the place with a casual wave of the hand on the way to show the young American one of the more unsavoury taverns in Montparnasse. It was described as The Tea-House of Ultimate Bliss.

'Geishas, they call them,' Morand said. 'Their morals, you understand, are not like ours. The Japanese, I mean. These girls are trained, almost from birth, to please men in a number or artful ways, some of them even beneficial to the health. But there is no social stigma attached to the profession. They are in no sense looked down upon in the way we regard whores. Like doctors or barbers or the experts of pedicure, the young ladies simply supply a service.'

'A health service indeed,' Lionel concurred. And he determined — for purely academic reasons, naturally — to find out for himself exactly the quality of the services supplied by these socially accepted oriental ladies.

Tinkling music from behind the bamboo screen greeted him as he was ushered from a somewhat bare reception hall into an inner courtyard where two fountains played between flowerbeds bright with hibiscus and poinsettia and blood-red peonies.

A woman wrapped in an equally vivid kimono glided forward to take him by the hand. She was short, no more than five feet tall, with glossy black hair coiled high above her head around an ornate tortoise-shell comb. She could have been any age from thirteen to thirty.

Bead curtains hid perhaps a dozen open doorways around the patio. Led through one of them, Lionel found himself in a small two-room suite separated by an arched opening. A low table surrounded by cushions occupied the middle of the outer chamber, which was walled with panels of silk, hand-painted to show, in an economic, almost perfunctory style, scenes of rural life in Japan.

The furnishings of the inner chamber were hidden behind veils of steam.

The Japanese woman clapped her hands together. At once a young girl, equally short, appeared in the archway. Swathed in a black kimono printed with designs of the rising sun, she carried a tray loaded with fragile bowls encrusted in gold leaf and a tall, slender pot with a long spout and a handle sheathed in wickerwork. A close-fitting helmet of raven hair encased her head.

She sat down cross-legged on one of the cushions and poured pale amber tea into the bowls.

The woman with the comb seated herself and signalled Lionel to do the same. Two other girls, who could have been twins of the one with the tray, appeared through the steam and joined the party.

Lionel supposed they had been chosen because they spoke French. But the French they spoke was incomprehensible to him, and their English reduced to a handful of pidgin phrases. The intellectual content of the conversation was thus somewhat limited.

Beside these slender exquisites with their ivory hands and flat, expressionless, almond eyes, he felt gauche and awkward, a heavy-limbed rustic whose feet were too big and his fingers too thick. He sipped the aromatic, almost tasteless tea, and wished he hadn't come.

Then the older woman clapped her hands again and the three girls rose and led the way to the inner chamber. Stumbling after them, he was astonished – and at last gratified – to see that as soon as she had skipped up the two steps beneath the arch, each of them unwrapped and discarded her kimono, so that she stood nude amidst the wreathing layers of steam.

Inconsequentially, he thought of Loie Fuller and her diaphanous dancer's costume at the Folies Bergère. But the skeins of vapour eddying around these three naked nymphs were subtler and far more provocative than anything that could be produced on a music-hall stage.

Wisps of transparent white curled around their tiny, pointed breasts, hugged their waists and wrapped insolent fingers between their thighs and the upper part of their almost hairless bodies.

Lionel could see now that the steam came from a bank of heated stones doused with water in the manner of a Scandinavian sauna. A high, narrow table covered by a white sheet stood at one side of a sunken bath filled with a liquid topped by green foam. A wide divan shielded by screens of bamboo and printed silk completed the furnishings.

'Please. . .gen'leman to remove clothing?' one of the girls said in a high singsong voice. Lionel hesitated. . .and then complied. Nobody was offering to assist him, and it was clearly a matter of the utmost urgency that he should be on equal terms with this ravishing trio. He stripped off jacket, trousers, necktie, shirt and underwear and dropped them on the tiled floor. While he clambered hastily out of socks and shoes, one of the girls picked up his clothes, folded them, and draped the outer garments across one end of the divan. He stood naked before them, that part of him most sensitive to female allure already stirring from its nest between his thighs.

'Western gen'leman prepare for eastern massage,' the girl who had spoken before announced.

Lionel had no need to reply. A second Geisha produced a stoneware pot and the third dipped in three fingers, scooped out a thick wad of sweet-smelling grease and slapped it on his belly. 'On table, plees,' the first girl said.

He climbed up and lay on his back. The table was covered with thick white hospital rubber which was momentarily cool to his heated shoulders and bottom. But he had no more than registered the fact when six hands attacked the ball of grease, smoothing it away from his navel, up over his chest, his arms, his thighs, kneading and stroking and massaging until the whole frontal surface of his frame gleamed silkily with its oily sheen.

His fleshy pride, his only untouched part – although soft fingers had certainly burrowed into the creases of his groin – was now at full stretch and standing away from his abdomen, fairly quivering from the attention it had so far been denied. But the girl who spoke English ordered him suddenly to turn onto his face, and the three of them spun him over and at once began the same treatment to his back and buttocks and calves.

Lionel was in transports of sensual delight. And now the sliding, palping hands were replaced by thighs and bellies and delicate breasts rubbing the oleaginous grease across and into his skin as the three girls draped themselves over him in an orchestrated smother of scented flesh. And not only was his back the target of this slithering assault: jerked to and fro by the Geishas' expert manoeuvring, he found the oiled facade of his body itself caressed by the friction of skin against slippery rubber.

He groaned aloud in ecstasy, fearful that this combined attack on all his senses would provoke the climactic eruption whose commencement was already signalled by a bursting sensation in his loins.

Reaching behind him with one arm, he tried to grasp a moving limb, a breast, a handful of flesh. But his hand was slapped away. 'Bath now,' the English speaker said – and he was left abruptly alone, quivering with readiness, on a knife-edge between retreat and the final plunge.

The three girls lifted him from the table as easily as if he had been a manikin in a shop window and lowered him into the bath.

The water was hot, so hot that its clasp on the tingling surface of his body made him gasp.

Six hands swooped in once again to the attack, lathering him from head to foot with perfumed froth, exploring the convexities and concavities of his muscular form like small soft animals, kneading the oil into his pores as the gorged head of his fleshy stem just broke the surface of the water.

He gave himself up wholly to their ministrations, noting dazedly as they bent over the bath how the delightful curves of their little love mounds were accentuated by the lack of hair, how the clefts that concealed the entrance to each temple of delight allowed nevertheless the tiniest glimpse of those forbidden portals he was so eager to force.

Too soon the ritual ablution was over. When they raised him from the bath the water ran off him at once to leave his skin as pink and soft as a baby's.

He was on the divan now. Such lighting as there had been in the chamber had been discreetly lowered by an unseen hand. In the scented gloom, Lionel was enveloped — there is no other word for it — by a swarm of limbs still humid from the last frail scarves of steam wafted out through the archway by some errant current of air.

He was aware of hands and mouths and thighs: probing, stroking hands; thighs that gripped and slid; a trio of wet mouths that sucked and licked and tongued. And this time his own hands were permitted to roam. His fingers clenched on delicate rounded buttocks, felt themselves swallowed up in the hot clasp of liquid flesh. Small breasts brushed their contours across his belly and down his thighs. The erect buds, almost purple in the case of the girl who spoke, teased his eyelids, paid fleeting visits to his parted lips and in one case wandered lasciviously the length of his trembling stem.

Hands followed them. One hand, two hands, three, the fingers pulling, stretching, squeezing. Every nerve in his frame was on fire. The pressure in his loins threatened to explode in a climax as violent as any he had ever known. His gasping breaths were shrill with need.

And then suddenly, instead of three bodies skilfully handling a fourth, the tangle of limbs on the divan was transformed into a single unit − a four-backed, eight-legged beast with what seemed like a hundred hands, all of them excruciatingly active.

The beast writhed and bucked and panted and gasped. Unintelligible endearments escaped its four slavering mouths.

The whole, thought Lionel, abandoning his entire being to the onslaught on his senses, was most definitely more in this case than the sum of the parts. . .delicious individually though the parts might be!

The tempo changed. The tremoring components of this breathy sandwich of flesh reoriented themselves in a specific direction. Remorselessly, lips and fingers homed in on the shuddering centre of his desire. A downy curve brushed his lips, escaping his probing tongue, to be replaced at once by the taut swell of a breast. That part of him clamoring to be freed of its intolerable load was suddenly the focus of the Geishas' attentions. Once again he was stretched and pulled and kneaded and jerked.

The pace of these insistent caresses quickened, hardened, quickened again and finally accelerated with the force of a wave creaming in to some foreign shore. His shuddering hips spasmed; his buttocks clenched as an intruding finger impaled him; he opened his mouth and roared.

The wave broke.

The older woman with the comb and the built-up hair

stood beside him with his clothes folded over one arm. Limp and exhausted, Lionel rolled off the divan. There was no sign of the three girls. The chamber was brightly lit once more and the bath, still steaming, beckoned. He felt quite wonderful.

Music from behind the screens fluted and twanged as he plunged into the water. When he emerged, refreshed and content, the woman towelled him dry then helped him to dress.

He had left the Japanese pavilion and walked halfway to the Eiffel Tower this time before he experienced a pang of regret at the absence of the Comtesse van den Bergh.

CHAPTER FOURTEEN

'There's one to watch,' said Commissaire Bruno Morand. 'There! On the far side of the fountain: the red-faced fellow in the striped suit!'

Giotto glanced across a triangle of grass already trampled almost bare by the daily influx of visitors to the exhibition. The man looked innocent enough. He wore a straw hat with a black band. A country farmer perhaps, up to see the sights.

'Which of the crooked categories you mentioned?' the American asked with a smile. 'A bag-snatcher? A tout selling forged lottery coupons or spurious entrance tickets to the shows?'

'A pickpocket,' Morand said. 'Come. . .we'll keep an eye on him from a distance.'

The man in the striped suit seemed to have tripped over the curved rim of a circular basin surrounding the fountain. He staggered a few steps, almost fell, and saved himself only by clutching the arm of a stout gentleman admiring the display of Spring flowers in a bed bordering the pathway. For a moment the two of them teetered over multicoloured ranks of primula and polyanthus, and then, with a muttered apology and a perfunctory raising of his hat, the man in the striped suit hurried away.

'There you are!' Morand enthused. 'The classic pass!'

Lionel was frowning. 'I am afraid I don't quite . . .?'

'The classic dip formula, man! Knock into the mark,

145

then lift his watch and wallet as you beg his pardon. That's Turkey Phiz, one of the most notorious – and, incidentally, one of the clumsiest lifters in Paris. Even so, I'm surprised to see a man of his experience use such an old trick.'

'Turkey Phiz?'

'That's what they call him in the underworld. Make haste now. . .we shall see what the Phiz is up to. And when we get closer you will see why they call him that.'

Shouldering aside two blue-overalled workmen blocking their way, Morand led his guest after the pickpocket. As they drew nearer, Lionel saw at once why the man had been given his nickname. In addition to the red jowls, a hooked nose, mutton-chop whiskers and the fact that he strutted rather than walked combined to give the fellow a ludicrously birdlike appearance.

Turkey Phiz turned right along the northern bank of the river and spring-heeled down the Queen's Walk. The Commissaire and Lionel were fifty yards behind, passing the sideshows that flanked the Belle Otéro theatre, when a dandyfied young man walked out of the artists' entrance and headed for the Grand Palais. He wore yellow, elastic-sided boots, a lavender suit, and an embroidered waistcoat in the palest lemon-coloured silk. Morand swept off his képi and bowed. 'Good morning, Monsieur le Comte,' he said in a peculiarly deferential tone.

The young man stared haughtily, lifted his straw hat high above his head, favoured the policeman with a brief nod, and passed on.

'Who was that?' Lionel asked curiously.

'Boni de Castellane.'

'*Bony?* Bonnie?'

'The Comte Boniface de Castellane.' Morand made the name sound like a boast. 'He is very rich. He is married

146

to a countrywoman of yours, the heiress Barbara Jay Gould.'

'Of course! That is where I have heard the name before.'

'He is also a little. . .how shall I say?. . .raffish. They say he won his wife from a friend in a game of cards.' Morand looked over his shoulder. 'In certain of the more exclusive salons, he is no longer accepted.'

'If he wears suits like that, I am not surprised,' said Lionel.

'In Paris society nevertheless, it is still he who sets *la mode*, especially among the younger set. You saw the way he raised his hat? That is the latest fad. To remove the hat with a flourish and hold it low in the old way is, according to Monsieur le Comte, both vulgar and an invitation to receive a crown full of coins!'

Outside a pleasure-booth selling hot sausages and sweetmeats, a youth was unloading flat trays of cakes and pastries from a horse-drawn delivery van. Beside the van, two policemen in uniform surveyed the passing crowds. Morand stepped into a space between two groups of tourists and signalled to them, moving one hand with a circular motion and then pointing at Turkey Phiz. At once they moved forwards and seized the petty crook by the arms before he had time to realize what was happening or turn to run.

'I thought you were head of the vice squad,' Lionel began, 'and yet here you are, occupying yourself with the riffraff who – '

'That is true,' Morand interrupted. 'It is true that my business here really has to do with the whores and their touts who infest the place. But because we are so short of competent men, the Minister has asked me to broaden my field of reference, as it were, and help in the drive to clean some of the other filth from our streets during the run of the exhibition. In any case I would naturally assist my colleagues in the Sûrêté Nationale if I came across — as I have today — something in their own line.'

Turkey Phiz was expostulating violently when they came up to him. 'Who the devil do you think you are? Let me go at once,' he blustered. 'I've done nothing. You have no right to hold me, no right at all — Oh, good day, Monsieur le Commissaire. What a surprise! Would you mind telling your roughnecks that a man has a right to walk through an exhibition if he pleases?'

'Come on, Phiz,' Morand said gruffly. 'Hand them over.'

'Hand what over? What do you mean?'

'The stuff you took off that fat mug by the fountain.'

'By the *fountain*? What fat mug? I don't know what you're talking about.' The pickpocket's red-veined face was a mask of injured innocence.

One of the uniformed men looked at Morand and raised an inquiring eyebrow. The Commissaire nodded. 'Take him behind that kiosk and frisk him,' he said.

Giotto followed as the three representatives of the law escorted their struggling and protesting victim around to the rear of a booth selling newspapers and cigars and guides to the exhibition. One of the *agents* dispersed the small crowd which had collected at the sound of raised voices, and then under Morand's direction the search began. But although Turkey Phiz was forced to strip off his outer garments and submit to a body search, although the pockets and linings of his suit were turned inside out, there was no sign of any property that did not belong to him, and certainly no evidence of a stolen watch or wallet. The small amount of money he carried was stuffed into a shabby imitation leather purse, he wore no watch, and the only other things on his person were a bunch of keys, a pipe and tobacco pouch, identification papers, and an entry ticket to the exhibition.

'You see?' he said angrily as they handed him back his clothes. 'I told you, didn't I? How many times does a law-abiding citizen have to be arrested, wrongfully arrested, before you bastards accept the fact of his innocence? How often do I have to complain – ?'

'All right, Phiz, give it a miss,' Morand said curtly. 'So you passed the stuff on to a confederate before we nabbed you. Just watch it in future, that's all. And as for a man with your record calling himself a law-abiding citizen . . .!' He shook his head, then added: 'We shall be looking for you again when the fat mug makes his complaint to the exhibition police.'

Turkey Phiz shrugged himself furiously into his jacket and stalked away without another word.

But when Morand and Lionel chanced to see him near the Palace of Laughter twenty minutes later, the stout gentleman assured them after a hasty slapping of his pockets that neither his watch nor his wallet was missing. And it was not until they were sitting down to an early lunch near the Trocadero some time after that, that the American, preparing to pay the bill, felt in his own fob pocket and exclaimed in dismay: 'My God! My gold watch has gone!'

The gold watch together with Giotto's well-filled wallet and a gold pencil, was handed over to Turkey Phiz at five o'clock that evening in the back room of a brasserie near the Place de la Bastille, by the two men in working overalls who had obstructed Morand and the American when they set off in pursuit of the pickpocket.

'It's a new technique I worked out,' Phiz said proudly to Lily Leblanc some time after midnight. 'With my face, I was getting too well-known as a dip. So I thought I'd *capitalize* on that. As soon as there's someone watching me, I do the old trip-up routine on some type — *but I don't take a thing*. Then, when the birds who reckon they've sussed me out give chase, Armand and Maurice pull the same trick and dip *them*. Only they're too keen to nab me to notice. . .and then when they do catch up with me, of course I'm clean!'

Lily giggled. 'Smart,' she approved. 'But why only dip the foreigner? Wouldn't it have been better sport to take something off that shit, Morand?'

Turkey Phiz shook his head until the red wattles shivered. 'Not that one,' he said decidedly. 'He's too *much* of a shit, and bent as a hairpin as well. He'd have you framed on some fake charge and sent up for five as soon as look at you.'

'Well,' Lily said, 'it's all part of our capital gains. Thanks for the loot, Phiz: I'll see you get your cut as soon as the stuff is fenced.' She rummaged in a flat leather shopping-bag, coming up with a small sealed brown envelope. 'And here's your share from the dodge we pulled while the rich ladies were prettying themselves at Landolff's.'

The pickpocket nodded and stuffed the envelope into an inner pocket. 'Buy you a drink?' he offered. 'On me, personally?'

Lily shook her head. 'Good of you, Phiz,' she said. 'But I have to go up the hill to the Rooster. Annette hasn't had her cut yet.'

'She's got possibilities, that kid,' Turkey Phiz acknowledged. 'But keep an open eye: I thought I saw her with Morand, down by the Eiffel Tower, a couple of days ago.'

In turn, Lily nodded. 'You never know,' she said.

It was Morand who had told Lionel about the Red

Rooster. 'Spend an evening there if you really want to imbibe some local colour,' the Commissaire advised. 'No good my coming with you. The place would be empty in thirty seconds. But it should be good copy: it's a non-tourist joint catering for the poorer folks in an alley off the Rue Lepic. Midinettes, delivery boys and shop assistants from Notre Dame de Lorette rubbing shoulders with tarts, ponces and small-time crooks, that kind of thing. Between midnight and two if you want to see some action.'

The American stared through steamed-up windows into the noisy, crowded café-bar at ten minutes to twelve. Inside, someone was playing an accordion. The light from a gas lamp at the end of the alley showed an amorous couple hunched in a doorway. Beyond it, horse-drawn traffic clip-clopped around the Place Blanche as the late-night crowd streamed from the Moulin Rouge.

Lionel pushed open the door of the bar and went in.

As he had expected, the noisy hubbub of shouts and laughter subsided at once. A sea of faces turned his way. But he looked inoffensive, he was clearly not a *flic*, and he didn't gawp openly, the way so many foreigners did. By the time he reached a vacant table at the far end of the smoke-filled room from the bar, conversation had resumed. Once, not wishing to seem too American, he had ordered an absinthe it was in full swing again.

A great deal of it centered on an enormous fat woman behind the bar. Known all over Montmartre simply as Mamma, she was — Morand had said — the shoulder on which the entire neighbourhood wept. At the moment she was dividing her attention between a group of loud-voiced costers recounting some complex anecdote concerning the fruit market and a pile of thick white plates on which she was ladling out her *plat du jour* — rabbit stew with onions, according to a notice chalked on a blackboard behind the bar. It smelled, Lionel thought, delicious.

Mamma slapped five plates down on a narrow wooden trestle around which three men and two girls who were obviously prostitutes were squeezed. On the way back to the bar she stopped at an empty table where a young, freckle-faced man sat with a thin dark girl in a brown dress. 'Hey, Lily,' she complained, 'that's not a park bench you're sitting on, you know! We expect customers to order something when they come in here.'

'It's no gold mine I'm sitting on either,' the dark girl snapped, 'whatever the gossips say. I'm not hungry, I don't want a drink, but I have to wait for Annette . . .Oh, very well: I'll have a bock, and Young Benoit here can pay for his own.'

A shout of laughter greeted this exchange and the big woman bustled back to her bar. Lionel's attention was diverted by a quarrel between four card-players at the table next to his own. The next time he looked toward the door, the man called Benoit had gone and Lily, her peaky face still flushed, was sitting alone in a darkened booth at the back of the room, the beer untasted in front of her.

The accordionist was playing again, a nostalgic waltz hinting at lost love and the joys of yesterday. Lionel saw that the musician was a youth with a club foot, sitting on a wooden stairway visible through an open door behind the bar.

Discreetly, he took out a notebook and gazed around the boisterous crowd — the card-players, the costers, the tarts and their Jules, Mamma overflowing her counter and Lily in her booth . . .

Lionel started. He half rose from his chair. Lily was no longer alone. She was handing a small sealed envelope to a bronze-haired beauty wearing a mustard-coloured dress. The American's heart thudded in his chest. There could be no mistake.

The newcomer was the Comtesse van den Bergh.

As he watched, she put the envelope into a purse, smiled at Lily, then turned and hurried to the door.

Before Lionel could gather his wits together or call out, the door had swung open and shut, and she was in the alley.

Fumbling awkwardly, he produced some coins, threw them down beside his empty glass, and shoved his way between the crowded tables to follow her.

He ran out into the alley. A light rain had begun to fall and the cobbles were wet. The lovers were still wrapped together beneath the street lamp.

He stared up towards the Place Blanche. The lights of the Moulin Rouge had been extinguished. A horse with its head drooping stood between the shafts of a stationary cab on the far side of the deserted square. There was no sign of the woman in the mustard-coloured dress.

The other way then? He swung hastily around.

Fifty yards away, the alley turned a corner. A dim shape, faintly illuminated by reflected light, vanished around the bend. He heard the echo of receding footsteps.

Lionel ran for the corner.

Beyond it, the alley led to a wide street. He halted and looked each way. Street lamps, mirrored in the shining asphalt, illuminated the empty sidewalks in each direction. Two hundred yards away, a fiacre turned and headed uphill towards the Boulevard de Clichy.

But of the Comtesse ven den Bergh there was no sign.

CHAPTER FIFTEEN

Heavy rain fell throughout the next day, and the day after that. Lionel went to the Palais de Glace in the afternoons, drank innumerable apéritifs at the Café de la Paix, dined twice at Le Grand Véfour. But he saw no sign of the Comtesse.

On the third morning, when the sun shone again and the wet streets of the capital steamed, he hired a carriage and went to the Bois de Boulogne.

For two hours he had the coachman drive up and down the most popular rides, but although there were perhaps two dozen black-habited *Amazones* on horseback among the promenading gentry and their cavaliers none resembled the copper-haired beauty he was eager to contact. Once he saw the woman he had met at Dagmar van den Bergh's house — Geneviève something-or-other, was it not? — but she had cantered past on a magnificent bay and was lost to sight before he could catch her eye.

In the afternoon he went to the gardens of the Luxembourg Palace. Of the ladies pacing the gravelled walks between the beds of zinnias and lobelia, many held dogs on a leash. Some, certainly, were exercising Russian Wolfhounds. Of these a small number could well have been followers of the Sapphic cult. But none resembled the Comtesse with the tawny hair.

Absence, they say, makes the heart grow fonder. In Lionel's case the total absence of success — and thus of the person he wished to see — steeled his heart to the extent that he determined to find his quarry if it was the last thing he did. Even if it was someone with whom he had exchanged no more than a few words, even if the lady in question was a lesbian, even if the idea that there could conceivably be something between them was pure fantasy. The quest had become an obsession with him.

At last, in desperation, he decided on unconstitutional means. To the devil, he thought, with protocol. He would call again, in person, at the house in the Avenue Kléber.

Social convention demanded that, after an initial call, a gentleman wishing to pursue a relationship with a lady must await an invitation from her before venturing a second meeting.

He would throw that absurd custom to the winds. Choosing his time carefully — late enough not to disturb a siesta, too early to compromise the arrival of invited guests or a planned sortie — he had the hired carriage drive him into the courtyard at four thirty in the afternoon. Telling the coachman to wait, he ran up the steps and rang the bell.

When the supercilious footman answered, he handed him a card and said peremptorily, 'See that Madame la Comtesse receives this immediately', before the servant had a chance to tell him that the lady was 'not at home'. On the back of the card he had scrawled: *Forgive, I pray you, the breach of protocol, but it is most urgent, imperative in fact, that I see you at once — even for two minutes.*

Waiting on the black and white checkerboard marble of the hallway while the man retired upstairs, Lionel felt like a knight in a game of chess. Would it be one square forwards and two to the side? Or one aside and then two forwards to place him in direct line with the Queen?

Two minutes later the footman reappeared. 'Madame la Comtesse will receive you,' he said disapprovingly. 'But

I am to inform you, sir, that she is obliged to leave shortly. The carriage will be calling for her at five.'

Lionel nodded. He followed the man upstairs once again. The footman threw open the double doors of the salon and announced: 'Monsieur Lionel Giotto.'

The American hurried in to the big room with an outstretched hand. 'Madame, you must pardon this intrusion,' he began, 'but I could find no other way . . .'

He broke off, frowning. The tall, big-bosomed woman standing by the buffet wore an elegant afternoon dress striped in crimson and rose satin. Her upswept chestnut hair was fashionably coiffed.

But she was not the woman he expected to see.

She was the horsewoman he had seen riding in the Bois, the friend he still thought of as Geneviève something-or-other.

Lionel was confused as well as disappointed. 'I am sorry,' he stammered, 'I had hoped that Madame la Comtesse. . .I mean, that is to say I thought I might see . . .'

'I am Dagmar van den Bergh,' the woman said calmly.

He stared at her open-mouthed. 'But I thought . . .?'

'I am afraid, Monsieur, that you were the victim of a rather unfeeling conceit, a silly game, on your first visit,' said the Comtesse. 'I apologize for this. But, for reasons I cannot at the moment divulge, I was at the time unable to admit the deception. I trust that it has not caused you too much trouble?'

'Er. . .no, Madame. Not at all,' Lionel said politely but untruthfully.

'You wished to see me on some urgent matter?' She was looking at the card in her hand.

'The fact is,' said Lionel, floundering. 'Well, the fact is . . .' He swallowed. 'Madame la Comtesse, you are the most beautiful, one of the most beautiful women I have

157

ever. . .I mean, I think any man would agree you're an absolute stunner . . .'

'But?' Dagmar van den Bergh was smiling now.

' . . .but to be honest, if you will not think me unforgivably ungallant, the urgent matter I wished to discuss was with the other lady, the one I *thought* was the Comtesse van den Bergh.'

'I see.'

'If you could . . .' Lionel said wretchedly, flushing to the roots of his hair. 'If it would not be considered too forward, I would consider it a great favour to be told the lady's name. And if possible where she may be found.'

'I would be happy to comply with your request, Monsieur,' Dagmar said. 'But unfortunately I do not know the answer to either question.'

His jaw dropped. 'You don't *know*?'

She shook her head. 'She said she was a Lalande d'Estournel, but that is not so. I had only. . .well, recently. . .met her, you understand. And, alas, I know neither her address nor her real name.'

'But that's damned awful!' Lionel cried despite himself. 'Forgive me, Madame. What I meant to say was that this is indeed a setback.'

'For me, too, as it happens,' the Comtesse agreed. 'There are reasons, personal reasons with which I will not bore you, why I myself am anxious to see the lady again. Come, let us make a bargain: I shall try my hardest to locate her; you will doubtless be doing the same. If I should succeed, I undertake to let you know at once, provided you promise to do the same for me in the case of your own success. Can you agree to that?'

'Willingly,' Lionel said. 'I should tell you that I have already tried a great number of places.' He enumerated them, leaving out only the fruitless sighting at the Red Rooster.

Dagmar nodded. 'There are many other possibilities. It is a big city, at the moment a very busy one. And of course she may have arrived at one of the places you looked, ten minutes after you left. Or left just before you got there. Lacking a name, it is difficult.'

He sighed, thinking again of the Red Rooster. 'We must just keep on looking,' he said.

'I will make a suggestion,' said Dagmar. 'I suspect, though I have no proof, that you will be far more likely to run her to earth in Montmartre than in the Faubourg St Honoré or the Chaussée d'Antin.'

'I shall go there tonight,' Lionel promised.

He went to the Mirliton, on the Boulevard Rochechouart, to hear Aristide Bruant. He sat on a hard bench with no back, at a scrubbed wooden table nursing a *Formidable*, a huge glass tankard holding half a gallon of beer.

The place served nothing but beer. By ten o'clock it was crowded. Socialites from the right bank, bohemians from the left and working-class customers from the neighbourhood jammed themselves in beneath a ceiling decorated with antique weapons and wooden carvings to applaud the master of 'sung poetry' as he immortalized the 'thieves, whores and pavement romeos' who were the heroes of his new urban folklore.

Bruant had made his name on the same premises, when the cabaret was owned by Rudolph Salis and named *Le Chat Noir* – the Black Cat. He was world-famous now, and co-director of the fashionable *Concert de l'Époque* near the Bastille, but he still returned each night to his original home to provoke the bourgeois with his revelations of life among the poor and the hopeless of the city's outer slums.

He made his appearance at eleven o'clock as advertised – a burly man with fierce eyes and a bitter smile beneath

a shock of black hair. He was dressed in a black corduroy
suit, a scarlet flannel shirt and black boots. 'All right,'
he roared, glancing disdainfully around the packed room.
'I suppose I shall have to sing for you. I shall sing *A La
Villette* – though I don't expect you're intelligent enough
to understand it.'

Applause, whistles, the stamping of feet.

'And if you've got to join in, herd of camels that you
are,' Bruant shouted, 'keep to the choruses and at least
try to bray in tune!'

A pianist in a corner beside the bar struck a chord and
the *chansonnier* launched himself into the number. Lionel
thought he had never heard a voice so cutting, so metallic,
so vindictive. But he was in fact less concerned with the
song – whose vernacular *argot* was incomprehensible to
him – than with something he had seen on the far side
of the room.

As Bruant stalked up and down, declaiming his vitriolic
phrases, the American noticed beyond him, sitting with
her back to a Chéret poster advertising Les
Ambassadeurs, a thin girl with a peaky face. It was the
young woman called Lily, the one he had seen at the Red
Rooster with the beauty he was looking for.

She was sitting among a crowd of locals, but as far
as he could see appeared to have no particular escort.
That was a good beginning: he had no desire to get into
a bar-room fight with a jealous apache! When at last
Bruant took a break, he shouldered his way through the
noisy, applauding audience and sat down beside her.
'Mademoiselle,' he said, 'could I have a word with you?'

She glanced at him. 'You're too late,' she said. 'A
month too late. I'm not on the game any more.'

'It's not that. I just hoped that you might – '

'I told you no! Now why don't you just piss off?' Her
voice rose angrily. Lionel saw hostile faces turn his way.

'I'm not trying to proposition you, for God's sake,' he said urgently. 'But there's money in it just for a piece of information.'

Lily turned to face him. 'What kind of money? What piece?'

'A name, that's all. An address if possible. Fifty francs?'

Her eyes narrowed. 'Maybe you'd better tell me about it?'

'That's all I'm trying to do,' Lionel said. 'I saw you in the Red Rooster three, four days ago. You told the fat woman behind the bar that you were waiting for someone called Annette.'

'What if I was?'

'I'm not interested in that. But later I saw you hand an envelope to another girl, a very pretty girl with auburn hair. She was wearing a mustard-coloured dress. I'm not interested in the envelope either; I'm not interested in your business at all. But this girl –'

'But that *was* Annette, for goodness' sake! What do you want with her?'

'I want to meet her again, that's all. But I don't know her name, and I thought –'

'Why do you want to meet her? You're not some kind of cop, are you?'

'Good heavens, no. I want to meet her because, well, I did meet her once before but it seems the name I was given –'

'Wait a minute!' Lily's glance was suddenly knowing. 'You're American, aren't you?'

'What if I am?' – mimicking her own defensive tone.

'And you met her in some posh house on the Avenue Kléber?'

'That is so. But – ?'

'Now I understand. She *thought* maybe she had made

161

a hit with you. You're telling me it was reciproc, right?'

'You could say that. I mean, all I want is to ask her out to dinner, but I was already given *two* wrong names. If you could tell me her real name, maybe we might be able to get together.'

'I forget her real name,' Lily said. 'But the name she uses in Paris is Annette de Vervialle. She's a dancer. Or she was – at the Moulin Rouge. I don't know her address, but she lives someplace over St Lazare. If you were to try the cafés around there . . .'

'I'll certainly try,' Lionel said. 'You can't tell me any more, like where she works or anything?'

'I don't *know* any more. As for work . . .' Lily shrugged, appeared suddenly to remember something, then shook her head. Whatever it was, Lionel sensed, it was going to stay private. Perhaps it was in some way connected to the mysterious envelope. But he knew better than to press for more details now. It was clear that Lily was not exactly in favour of the police; if she suspected in any way that he was engaged on any kind of investigation, she could pass the word along and he would lose Annette de Vervialle forever.

'You are very kind,' he said, passing her money under the table. 'I sure appreciate your help.'

For the first time she smiled. 'My pleasure,' she said. 'A friend of a friend, you know. Come to think of it, you're a good-looking fellow. If you have another fifty to spare, I could change my mind – just this once.'

'I appreciate that too,' Lionel said. 'But right now I have to hurry back to the Avenue Kléber: Dagmar. . .that is to say, the Comtesse. . .is as anxious to contact your friend Annette as I am.'

'I'll bet,' said Lily with a chuckle. 'My, my, what a popular girl we are!'

CHAPTER SIXTEEN

Madame Renée passed a beringed hand over the black marble skull of a statue standing in a niche at one side of the Persian Room at No. 14, Rue de Monthyon. She examined her fingertips for traces of dust and nodded her head in satisfaction. The new girl from Strasbourg was going to work out all right. They were too stolid, too lacking in flair and fantasy to make good cocottes, the Alsatians, but they did know how to work. It was the German blood that made them such good servants.

She switched on the central chandelier. Light flashing back from the mosaics surrounding the painted ceiling showed up a certain dullness, a lack of glitter and brilliance in several of the pendant crystals. Madame Renée tutted. The woman responsible for cleaning the glass must be rebuked. She was Provençale of course. What could you expect from the lazy South?

She lowered herself into a carved Louis XIII chair with a high back and rang a small handbell to summon the waitress who would bring her a glass of champagne. It was going to be a busy night. The busty, nubile dancer, Cléo de Mérode, whose nude statue by the sculptor Falguière had caused such a scandal in academic circles, was due in at midnight. Ten minutes later her 'protector' would arrive in a closed carriage with drawn blinds and be ushered in through a side entrance that led to a private staircase. As the protector was no less than Leopold II, the King of the Belgians, the utmost discretion was necessary. A police presence had been arranged to move on possible sightseers, the illumination behind the oversize street numbers above the entrance doors had been extinguished, a certain number of unobtrusive but muscular gentlemen were disposed about the premises. But one needed eyes everywhere these days.

One hour before midnight, two senators and their wives, who favoured an exchange of partners every half hour, must be smuggled up to share the Baghdad Suite. And before that there was the policeman, Morand, again with his own woman. And some American he had recommended.

Madame Renée sighed. That was four rooms taken. Of course they paid well (except for the policeman, who not only expected the service free but also received a substantial sum each week), but that was not the point. Such a large 'outside' use of the house was unfair on her own girls, for it cut down the number of tricks that could be turned with the regulars and casuals who would drift in later.

As for Cléo de Mérode, apart from being kept by royalty, she was highly paid as a stage performer, so why did she not move her own establishment to an address where the comings and goings of her guests were less likely to be overlooked? Another sigh. A shrug. These *Horizontales* were a law unto themselves. They had their own hierarchy. To live the opulent lives they led, such 'public' mistresses required the 'protection' of one king, bishop or president, two arch-dukes, three or four barons – or, in the case of mere vicomtes, one for each day of the week! And as for the furs and jewels. . .the very least among them could expect a fashionable apartment, a sable coat, several rows of pearls, a hired carriage and seventy-five Louis a month spending money. Some of them — Otéro, Emilienne d'Alençon, Manon Loti, the flame-haired temptress Tica la Rousse — a great deal more.

Madame Renée finished her champagne and rose to her feet. The Commissaire and his little cocotte had arrived. She arranged a welcoming smile on her face and moved toward the entrance lobby with an outstretched hand.

There could be no possible doubt about it, Lionel Giotto thought. The fact admitted no contradiction. Whether or not it was evident to other people was of little importance: the fact was that *he* knew.

He was drunk. There was no other word for it. He had drink taken. He was intoxicated, inebriated, tiddly. It was champagne mostly, with some exceedingly strong herbal *digestif* after dinner at the Comtesse's house.

And now here he was at this high-class cat-house recommended by the police captain, with these two extraordinary women. He didn't quite remember how they had gotten there; he supposed Dagmar van den Bergh had a carriage. He remembered his surprise when she had expressed a wish to come here, for the three of them to come. He guessed he must have mentioned the place in his more loquacious mood. Before that liqueur had blanked off past and future and left only a present that was still a little blurred. Blurred but intriguing. Exciting, too.

For here he was, naked, in a room that looked like a stage set for a South Sea Islands' melodrama, while the two women . . .

Naked?

Yes, he remembered the dinner party now. To discuss tactics after he had reported his discovery of the girl's real name. Annette de Vervialle, wasn't it? They didn't discuss much because this other woman was there.

Baroness Gisela von Zwickenheim: a strapping thirty-year-old with hair paler than his own. An old friend, Dagmar had said. From Lower Saxony, where the wine came in *boxbeutels* shaped like a goatherd's water-carrier. A little more champagne, *cher ami*?

But why, he remembered asking, did they suddenly want to go to this *maison de passe*, of dubious reputation he had no doubt? And he saw again Dagmar's small, secret smile, and heard her reply: 'Experience, my friend. As the philosophers say, all experience is rewarding.' she looked at the Baroness. 'In one way or another.'

Naked now, he wondered once more: why here? Why not in that huge house where there is every comfort? And then, more urgently: why me? What have I to do with these devotees of the Sapphic cult?

The answers to all those questions was before his eyes. He had no recollection of undressing – or being undressed – and he certainly remembered nothing of their arrival at No. 14 Rue de Monthyon. Yet here – emerging from the *cabinet de toilette* hidden beneath the thatched roof of the native hut – were Dagmar and Gisela, each as nude as he himself, each calm and unruffled as if they were still at dinner. Truly, he thought, there has to be something *perverse* about the Comtesse.

But perversity in his own make-up? Certainly not! So why should that part of him destined for private coupling with a normal woman be provoked to a state of excitation by the sight of two women who, by the standards of correct society – and especially Boston society – were abnormal?

Because, he told himself fiercely, individually each of them was about fifty times more alluring than all of the scantily dressed showgirls on the Paris stage put together. He didn't want to put these two together either. But separately . . .!

There were some resemblances of course. But what linked them in some way more closely were the differences rather than the characteristics they shared. Each was generously fleshed in the region of the bust, unusually so in the case of the German. Both had small, trim waists and billowing hips. But the Comtesse's hands were long, thin and elegant with birdlike wrists, while Baroness von Zwickenheim, broad across the palm and strong in the arm, flexed square-tipped fingers that were workmanlike and muscular. Dagmar's legs tapered exquisitely to slender ankles; Gisela's athletic limbs were shaped like those of a horsewoman or dancer. More distinctive than any of these things was the difference of regard. Gisela von Zwickenheim's expression was challenging, open, practically aggressive, while her friend's was secretive, almost sly, hinting at subtleties yet to be revealed.

Lionel, if asked, would have been hard put to it to express a preference. The part of him most immediate in its reaction to the opposite sex was categoric: *all* naked women were exciting.

That excitement registered itself in a stiffness, a rigidity, a sense of eagerness almost bursting, that became more uncomfortable every second.

'A good, fine stud here,' Gisela said, wrapping competent fingers around his thickened and pulsing stem. 'Almost in the stallion class, wouldn't you say?'

Lionel was lying on his side, supporting himself on one elbow. Dagmar was beside him, on her back with her legs spread. Gisela sat on the edge of the bed. He could not remember climbing up onto it.

'Stroke her,' the German woman commanded, gripping hard and starting a slow pumping movement. She lifted Lionel's free hand. 'No, not there . . .There! That's right: a liddle tongue, *ja*, between the lips.'

'Oh, yes!' Dagmar murmured, lifting her hips to meet

his inquiring finger. '*There!*. . .No, not there, not quite. . .Show him where, *Liebchen* – show him how to do it.'

Dazedly, Lionel felt his middle finger lifted, the tip pressed down, rotated. His finger slid in a warm clasp of flesh, penetrating where that other throbbing part of him was eager to be.

Dagmar was becoming excited, too. She threshed from side to side on the bed, her big breasts rising and falling fast, lips drawn back from her teeth. One hand clenched and unclenched on the bedcovers; with the other she kneaded the flesh on the inside of Gisela's thigh.

'A big fellow here, eh?' the Baroness said, bestowing an extra squeeze and pull. 'I think maybe you better can find a good warm place to put him, no?' With her free hand, she grasped Dagmar's knee, prising her splayed legs farther apart. Reinforcing her grip on his upstanding part so that he was forced to lever himself up and follow, she pulled Lionel toward her until he was kneeling between the Comtesse's thighs. Then she released her hold and pushed with both hands on the base of his spine, lowering him face down towards the spreadeagled brunette.

'Put him in,' she said huskily, inserting a guiding hand between their two hot bodies. 'There! Now! Make love to her; do it; give it to her! I want to see.'

Supporting himself on his two hands, the young American felt himself drawn upwards and inwards, swallowed by the silky heat of that perfumed flesh whose secret shrine he had never thought to penetrate.

Bemusedly, he raised his head. The Baroness had moved. She was cradling Dagmar's face between tender fingers and kissing her passionately on the mouth.

'Good Lord,' exclaimed Bruno Morand, his eye to the

secret spyhole in the Chinese room. 'Look at my foreigner! Now what do you think of that?'

'What foreigner? What are you talking about?' Annette had emerged from the washroom and was folding her clothes over the back of a chair. The ritual abandon of their lovemaking had now reached such a pitch that they preferred to renounce the preliminaries and the undressing and, as the Commissaire put it, 'jump right in at the deep end of the pool'.

'What foreigner?' he repeated now. 'An American. A journalist I was asked to show around the hot spots. I told him to come here. But the young devil has got himself *two* women! Real beauties, too! Here, come and see for yourself.'

Annette shook her head. 'I prefer my lovemaking at first hand. Come here, Bruno: we get little enough time together – although I can never quite understand why – without wasting what there is watching other people!' She stole up behind him, sank to her knees and wrapped her arms around his waist, brushing her lips caressingly across the base of his spine. Her hands trailed downwards, cupped, gripped; Morand's distended member, already stirring thickly in anticipation, hardened at once and stretched to full length. He swung around and dropped his hands to her shoulders, allowing those sensitive lips to continue the ministrations they had started behind him on a more suitable subject in front.

Two minutes later his calves were tremoring and the muscles of his bottom contracting and relaxing in turn with each thrusting osculation of her warm wet mouth. Catching his breath, he freed himself gently, leaned down, and with a swift movement picked her up and carried her to a low divan on the far side of the room.

She lay naked on her back with her heels spread and her knees raised. She held out her arms towards him. 'Oh,

Bruno,' she breathed, 'I want you so! Come to me, beloved; do it to me now!'

Morand knelt between her parted thighs, bent himself double, and began feverishly kissing the satin slope of her belly, tracking his own lips downwards and through the tawny curls sheltering her most private entrance until he could probe with an exploring tongue the tender bud throbbing within.

Annette gasped. Her hips arched up off the bed until his tongue was buried inside her. With an eager finger and thumb she reached for the head of his upstanding part and coaxed it towards her heated loins.

He straightened suddenly, sat back on his heels, and grabbed her by her fleshy hips, pulling her towards him until his excited stem nudged the downy covering of her love mound.

Annette shivered. Raising her hips again, she lifted her legs to seize his waist in a scissors grip, crossing her ankles behind his back. In a slow belly-dance rhythm, she rotated those hips, pressing him closer with her heels. A lascivious smile animated her face. Both hands intruded now between their bodies, holding, guiding.

Morand's rigid pride, succumbing to the forces cajoling on every side, slid between soft lips of flesh, penetrated farther, and was swallowed up by moisture and heat. His breath hissed between his teeth as the dark, wiry hair sheathing the focal point of his loins ground fiercely against the silken mat furring her most private place.

He fell into a dreamlike rocking motion, swaying back and forth in ecstatic rhythm so that their two frames interconnected with the reciprocal precision of a well-oiled machine.

Annette licked her lips. Her fingers were wrapped around those two parts of him that hung below his moving shaft. She gazed at him through slitted eyes, the breasts bobbing on her labouring chest. 'Who needs to watch other people?' she murmured lazily.

On the far side of the wall, in the Negro Room, Lionel Giotto was the centre of a tangle of limbs sprawled over most of the high bed.

The alcoholic fog blanketing his mind had begun to dissipate, but it had by no means disappeared. His memories of the past two hours were hazy in the extreme. He remembered crying out aloud as the writhing of Dagmar's pliant body and the slamming of her hips against his pelvic bone produced a series of shuddering spasms that exploded his long-held-in-check passion into the receptacle destined for it.

He remembered – was it that time or the next? – Gisela von Zwickenheim exclaiming aloud: '*Ja, ja!* Is good, very good!' And then the deep contralto laugh, and: 'You ask me why? Because I wish it, my friend. You do it good, you see, and she like it. But afterwards she realize I do it even better!'

Was this afterwards? Lionel wondered. Who cared? He was adrift on a sea of delicious sensation. The flesh, the whole flesh, and nothing but the flesh! he mused drunkenly.

He was lying face down across a soft body, with unseen hands fondling his willing member into yet another state of alert and his own fingers rolling the erect bud tipping an invisible breast. On his other side, wet fingers slid over his free hand as it plunged in and out of some anonymous but palpitating female shrine. In front of his face, pouting between two slender banks of blonde hair, pink lips invited his attention. Cool thighs clamped each side of his head as he lowered it and accepted the invitation.

Seconds later – as it seemed – when the sighs and gasps on either side had momentarily lapsed, he raised a head no longer held fast and gazed into the Baroness's challenging green eyes. She was lying along the bed, and the face above the breast he was manipulating was now buried between the same thighs that had gripped him. Beneath his weight — it had to be Dagmar, of course — flesh jerked and heels drummed on the bed covers. 'Kiss me again,' Gisela commanded, 'only this time on the mouth.'

It was later — a long time? a short time? — that, for the third member of the trio, the night fused into a single delirious continuum — an endless series of sensual components, one passing into another with no awareness of time or space or even identity. For him there was softness and hardness, coolness and heat, breasts and bellies and lips and thighs in an ever-changing pattern of limbs — his? hers? whose? — that left the mind dazed and the heart hammering while a host of hands smoothed and squeezed.

In one moment of crystal clarity, Lionel imagined he was back with the Geishas in The Tea-House of Ultimate Bliss. . . but no: this was less formal, much less of a ritual, more *personal*, the pulse beating wildly among this banquet of flesh as he erupted once more into climax and the encroaching darkness . . .

Lionel slept.

'He will not waken until morning,' Dagmar said quietly. 'Madame Renée will arrange a carriage. But we. . .I think we should leave now.'

'But yes, but yes!' The Baroness put an arm around her waist. 'For us, dear one, the night is young!'

It was one of the few times — Annette de Vervialle thought, choking out her third (fourth? fifth?) release as she lay spreadeagled with the Commissaire speared deep within her — that they had made love naked, on a bed,

172

in what she still considered to be the normal position. Just like a married couple. At home in their own house. She sighed..

'Oh, Bruno,' she groaned. 'I do so adore you. You are such a wonderful lover; you make me so happy. I do so wish – '

'You are the most remarkable, the most surprising, the most *extra*-ordinary partner yourself!' Morand said swiftly as she twined her legs around his back. 'You excite me as nobody ever has.' He stifled her reply with kisses.

Ten minutes later he levered himself off the divan and went into the washing cubicle. Soon afterwards Annette opened her eyes sleepily and saw that he was dressing. 'But. . .what are you doing? Where are you going?' she demanded, knuckling the tiredness from her eyes.

'I have to leave,' Morand said. 'I didn't want to spoil our evening by mentioning it before.' And then, smoothly: 'My job. . .a last-minute call. There's an informer I have to see in Montparnasse.'

'I will come with you,' she began, starting up from the bed covers.

'Impossible.' He took her by the shoulders and pressed her firmly back. 'It is a real den of thieves, an insalubrious place to say the least. There will be no women there at all.'

'But, dearest, I thought . . .' She was almost in tears.

'Hush, *ma poule*. I have arranged with Madame Renée to have a cab waiting to take you home. It will be here' – he looked at his watch – 'in twenty minutes. You must forgive me for not escorting you. It is a disappointment for me too. But duty is duty.'

He kissed her and left.

There was still a murmur of conversation spiced with female laughter from the big first-floor reception hall when Annette stole down the stairway into an atmosphere of brandy and cigar smoke. In the street outside, she saw that the numerals above the door were illuminated again.

Her cab was waiting at the kerbside. In front of it was a highly-polished victoria with a liveried coachman and a coat of arms emblazoned on the door.

The cabbie had climbed down and opened the door of the fiacre for her when the entrance to No. 14 was flung wide again and two expensively dressed women swept down the steps. To her astonishment, Annette recognized Dagmar van den Bergh, her arm linked with that of a tall blonde woman.

The recognition was mutual. For an instant the Comtesse hesitated. . .and then, with a murmured aside to her friend, she disengaged herself and approached Annette with an outstretched hand. 'My dear, what a surprise!' she enthused. 'I never thought. . .but never mind. This coincidence could not have occurred at a better time!'

Annette, covered with embarrassment at the recollection of their last meeting, found herself tongue-tied.

'I have a friend, you see, the gentleman you. . .met. . .at my house. You remember? The American.' For the briefest instant the Comtesse's eyes flicked towards the house behind them. 'And he is anxious, most anxious to renew your acquaintance. So now, you see, after this fortuitous meeting, I shall be able to oblige him. You must call on me tomorrow afternoon and I will arrange the introduction.'

'Madame, you are very kind,' Annette stammered, confused, 'but I do not know that −'

'I will not take no for an answer,' Dagmar van den Bergh said.

CHAPTER SEVENTEEN

My dearest Lucie,

So many things have happened since last I wrote to you that I do not know where to begin.

Or indeed how to find words to continue once begun I have!

You will remember of course the story of my policeman beau. Well, since I wrote, the affaire has progressed not one whit. Oh, yes — we still meet from time to time, as often, or as infrequently, as Monsieur sees fit to decree. But of any kind of permanent relationship there is no sign, whereas I had hoped — perhaps foolishly — that maybe one day . . .but I must not dwell on what will doubtless turn out to be a fantasy, even tho', as I understand, the pay of an established Commissaire is largely sufficient for two. Suffice it to say that when we do meet those turbulent emotions he so unexpectedly aroused in me still hold me in their thrall. I remain a slave to my animal instincts, you see, when dear Bruno is (you will pardon the expression) at hand.

Meanwhile another complication, perhaps even an escape, has manifested itself.

I believe I mentioned once that I encountered, in somewhat equivocal circumstances, a fashionable lady known as the Comtesse van den Bergh. On the same occasion a wealthy young American was temporarily present. I forget his name, but I remember that he was a most personable individual. Anyway, it appears that he has expressed a wish to see me again. The Comtesse, whom I met by chance yesterday (again in rather unusual circumstances), has apparently undertaken to effect this re-introduction. And I was bidden later in the day to her private mansion in the Avenue Kléber, to learn the details of this assignation. . .if that truly is what it is.

The Comtesse, you must know, is one of those modern females who can be seen horse-riding in the Bois or, still wearing her tall hat and black habit, exercising two Russian Wolfhounds in the gardens of the Luxembourg Palace.

She is a tall, big-bosomed lady, small of waist and generous of hip, customarily wearing handmade boots of the finest kid, which button not at the front but the side, the better to display her shapely calves. I would put her age at around thirty-five years.

I think I may have described the house to you before. The Comtesse (I have seen no sign of any Comte) received me in the first-floor salon that overlooks the tree-shaded garden at the corner of the Rue Galilée. She was wearing a most becoming gown of jade green taffeta, much ruched around the lower part and gathered behind the waist into a small peplum or bustle which echoed in some way the few curls allowed to depend from her chignon.

A servant, a pretty young girl in a starched cap and apron, served us minted tea and madeleines while the Comtesse explained the mechanics of the introduction, which is to be formal (in the Ritz hotel, no less!). The girl then withdrew, carrying away the silver tray, and I fancied that I intercepted a glance exchanged between her and my hostess that I can only describe as one of complicity. I was not mistaken, as you shall see.

I had risen to take my leave when the Comtesse said:

'Must you hurry away, my dear? There are so many things we could discuss.'

A trifle reluctantly, though the expression in her wide green eyes was so persuasive that it would have been ill-bred to refuse, I reseated myself and drew off my gloves once more. She laid a hand on my arm. *'In addition,'* said she, *'there is a favour I have to ask you.'*

I looked at her inquiringly, my own expression as noncommittal as I could make it. What could she mean? What could she possibly want from me? Certainly not a loan!! An introduction then, in return for her kindness to me? But to whom? Who could I possibly know—?

'I have to go this evening, you see, to a grand ball given by Anna de Noailles.' Her deep mellifluous voice broke into my thoughts. *'And my personal maid has been sent to Paquin to collect my new gown. Meanwhile, I am dying to get out of these wretched stays, bathe, and rest awhile before I am required to dress for the evening. And I was wondering'* — the green eyes were pleading — *'it is an impertinence on my part, I know, but I was wondering if you would be kind enough to help me. The stays lace up the back, you see, and I am quite unable to unfasten them myself.'*

Seeing me hesitate, and perhaps divining my thoughts, she added: *'It would not be proper for me to order a mere parlourmaid to assist in so personal a service.'*

How, Lucie, could I politely refuse? A small intimacy between women. . .no more than might be required in the powder room of a restaurant or hotel. . .and, I have to confess, a slight case of flattery! I was proud to be the confidante, as it were, of so great a lady.

There was, too, that extra complication: I had once abused her hospitality, even pocketed a few trifles, but she had never once referred to this on either of our two

177

subsequent meetings. How then could I deny her what
she was asking of me now?

I agreed and we went upstairs to her boudoir.

It was, as you would expect, an extremely feminine
room, with hangings of rich material, velvet swags and
many small, delicate objects, doubtless the gifts of
admirers, that could have come from Cartier or Fabergé,
but I will not tire you now with its description: that must
await our next meeting. For the moment, it is what
happens within the boudoir that concerns us!

At first all was very seemly. The Comtesse unhooked
the back of her dress and I helped her slide it forwards
over her arms until the lace-edged sleeves pulled free. I
went to hang it up for her. . .and, oh, Lucie, the clothes
she has! But never mind that now. She stepped out of
all her fine linen underclothes (except of course for the
drawers with their black tapes and silken frills) and
offered me her back. The corset was clearly from one of
the most expensive couturiers, with inserts of salmon-
coloured leather separating the pockets of whalebone and
the pink satin panels on the outsides of waist and basque.

I worked fast, familiar with the task from my days at
the Moulin Rouge. but it was nearly fifteen minutes
before the foundation was loose enough, with the laces
properly looped, for her to emerge. Above the red weals
left by the constriction, the skin of her shoulders was
creamy smooth and the colour of old ivory. And at once,
as she massaged her waist — which I swear had been
tightened to no more than nineteen inches! — I was aware
of the warm body scent rising from the perfumed flesh
of a woman too long a slave to the dictates of fashion.

Without turning to face me, she walked away and
through a white-painted door whose panels were picked
out in gold. A moment later, I heard her voice call: 'Come
in, come in. . .see how you like my beignoir!'

I went into the bathroom. Lucie, the tub was enormous! Almost level with the white sheepskin rugs on the floor, it was made of grey and white marble veined with gold, and the taps too were plated in gold! I must have exclaimed aloud, for she laughed, tying the waist belt of a white silk peignoir trimmed with grey fur at the neck, wrists and hem. The surface of the steaming water in the bath was covered in foam, and the vapour rising from it carried some cloying and heady fragrance I could not identify. 'It is still a trifle hot,' the Comtesse said. 'Come back into the boudoir: there is a new perfume from Worth on which I would value your opinion.' And she picked up a small flask in heavy crystal with an ornate cut-glass stopper, and led the way.

Back in front of her mirror, she unpinned her hair and shook it free. I was astonished. A great mass of auburn ringlets tumbled about her shoulders, gleaming with tawny highlights in the late afternoon sun shining through the tall windows. She smiled and unstoppered the bottle. 'Come here, my dear,' said she, 'and let me dab a little on your wrist.'

As I approached, she upended the crystal flask over a morsel of cotton wool, and was about to lean forwards as I extended my hand, when she caught her elbow on a heavy japanned jewel box that lay on the dressing table and seemed almost to overbalance on her stool. The flask flew from her grasp, spilling a gout of livid green liquid down the front of my dress — the mustard damask with the three layers of ruffles at the neck, the only half-way decent dress I have.

'Oh!' cried the Comtesse, starting to her feet. 'Oh, my goodness! How insufferably clumsy of me! You will never forgive me: I am afraid your pretty dress is quite spoiled.'

What could I say? The dress was indeed ruined, and the smell of the concentrated essence was overpowering.

I was in fact quite immoderately angry at her carelessness. Rich people! I thought furiously. What is one dress more or less to them? All they have to do is send out for another. . .but the Comtesse, most contrite, was speaking again.

'I will have my laundrywoman attend to it at once, and if it cannot properly be cleaned and the odour removed, Landolff shall make you another exactly the same. In the meantime you must borrow one of mine . . .I have an afternoon tea robe in blue silk moiré that is a little small for me: it should fit you exactly. Come, you shall try it on – and if it does fit you must keep it. Really, I am so very sorry.'

And then, before I could reply, 'You must take that off at once,' said she, 'and soak it before the stain takes hold. No, no, I insist. Let me unhook the back for you.'

Again, before I had time to protest – and indeed what else could I do, it being out of the question to leave with my dress in the state it was? – the garment was unfastened and around my feet, the Comtesse had tugged a tasselled bell-pull, and a motherly woman in a starched pinafore had materialized to take the dress away.

So there I was in my stays and knickers, marooned until she chose to find me the blue silk substitute, in my lady's boudoir! And it was then I realized, thru' some unconscious movement she made, that my hostess was nude beneath her peignoir.

What do I mean – unconscious?

'Let me loosen your own laces a little,' she said. 'You must be fatigued, coming all this way to see me, and then this fuss about the dress. I fear it is entirely my fault. The least I can do is make you comfortable while we wait to hear the report on that stain from below stairs. Perhaps then, before we try the blue dress, you would care to relax your muscles in a warm bath?'

I cannot explain, dear Lucie, in no way can I explain in any logical fashion that which followed. I found myself in a curiously languorous state, face down upon a luxurious four-poster bed covered in fur rugs, with the Comtesse kneeling up behind me, her cool fingers busy about the laces and the knuckles occasionally kneading my heated skin. Perhaps I had become a trifle drowsy – indeed at one time I wondered if mint had been the sole additive flavouring the tea – but at any rate I was suddenly aware that the stays had loosened so much that the hooks linking the two busks in front could become – indeed had already become – unfastened!

I rolled onto my back, about to remonstrate. She was leaning over me, and I saw then that the belt of the peignoir was unknotted and the edges yawning apart to reveal her breasts. She was, as I have said, full-bosomed, but these fleshy, perfumed hemispheres, even if slightly pearshaped, were clearly as firm and taut as those of a girl not yet out of her teens.

As if mesmerized, I stared down the valley between those swelling mounds to that triangle below the graceful sweep of her belly where the golden tints of her hair were reproduced in silky profusion. I cannot understand why, but at that moment I experienced a sensation close to that overwhelming me when my policeman removed my stays in the hotel in the Rue Notre Dame de Lorette. The situation was by no means equivalent, *yet in some obscure way my reactions were! And so I did not demur when I felt her soft fingertip laid on my arm, and the voice above me intoned: 'You must know of course that your skin is of the most ravishing texture, and your* poitrine, *your bust, in its perfection the envy of any sculptor!'*

I murmured something unintelligible. I seemed temporarily bereft of speech. The forefinger of her other hand was now tracing arabesques on the flesh of my thigh between the leg of my drawers and my stocking top. She lay down, extending herself beside me in such a way that my left hand, resting passively by my hip, was trapped between the fur cover and the warm skin of her abdomen.

What was I to do? I knew that this woman was a leader of the notorious Amazones. *It came to me suddenly, too – if her lady's maid was really at the couturier's, who could have drawn the bath that was still too hot to get into when we came upstairs? Surely the woman who had taken my dress? And if that, why not the Comtesse's stays?*

I remembered the glance exchanged with the parlourmaid.

The whole episode in fact, including the spilled perfume, was a trick (doubtless well-rehearsed and performed many times before) to get me into the boudoir and out of my clothes!

But how could I leave, as I most certainly should have done, before my dress was ready or she chose to hand over the promised blue one? And I was surely not prepared to demean myself by thrusting her off and playing catch-as-catch-can around the furniture!

Dagmar – her given name is Dagmar, and in view of what occurred I fancy it more seemly to use this now rather than her formal title – Dagmar was by now unthreading the tapes closing the leg of my drawers. Her other hand had travelled my bare arm and was tracing the line of my jaw. 'So lovely, such beautiful boning, and your shape is divine,' she crooned.

I was breathing fast. I was in truth almost breathless despite the freedom from the constriction of my stays. And then suddenly I gasped. Flashing down from my face, the roving hand had plunged beneath the stiffened top of the corset and spilled out the entire breast which had until then still been partly covered.

She raised her head and then, looking me straight in the eye, lowered it slightly to fasten her lips over the rosy bud at the breast's tip.

I cannot describe my feelings at that instant, nor shall I try. Let me just say that all the blood in my body seemed to drain down to my toes, while at the same time each nerve-end quivered upwards and inwards to concentrate on the tiny area she feasted upon.

Dagmar's hand squeezed my breast up to offer the nipple to her sucking mouth. The four fingers of her other hand slid beneath the loosened leg of my drawers and caressed the inside of my thigh near, too near, the top.

But Lucie — oh, Lucie, the shame of it! I was responding!

The fingers of my trapped hand tensed, flexed, felt flesh and clenched. The shuddering in my loins appeared almost to reach out, to welcome those invading fingers. My most secret, private place was on fire. And in that second of awareness, dear friend, I realized to my horror that I was wet! The next moment, breast to soft breast and tongue to tongue, we were in each other's arms . . .

And after that?

Were I the shade of Monsieur Verlaine himself, Lucie, I should be at a loss to find words to describe what followed. Words indeed, specific by their nature, would always be inadequate to celebrate an experience by its nature non-specific, timeless, as indescribable in its entirety as it would be in detail.

In my particular 'Fête Galante' (to borrow one of the poet's titles), there was touching, there was holding, there was stroking and probing and smoothing and exploring. There was the glory of the lingering kiss. Above all, perhaps, there was a warmth and a caring, a desire to submerge one's priorities in the need of another.

In a state where two fingers trailed exquisitely down

the slope of skin from breast to hip can promote the wildest exaltation, there comes — remorselessly, relentlessly, inevitably — a sense of direction and of purpose, a foaming tide of excitement buoying one up, up, higher and higher towards that pinnacle of bliss when the world explodes joyously around one.

Ah, but you see — I do nothing but prove my own point about the inadequacy of words!

We reached that pinnacle together, Dagmar and I. And after the choked cries had died away and the hammering of our two hearts subsided, we lay silent for a long time on the furs, while the dusk thickened outside the long windows, the birdsong in the trees was stilled, and I tried my best to stifle the questions warring with recent memories in my mind.

What more to say? Only this perhaps: that with a man and a woman all is fierce and hard and thrusting; a love battle with victories on both sides, to prove. . .what? Strength? Superiority? Possession? While two women express only softness, tenderness, caring. One, in short, is a taking (on both sides again, for we too have our victories) and the other a giving.

Dear Lucie, it is late. The candle gutters and I must be up early. The rest can wait. Meanwhile, do not think ill of me.

And remember me, always, your friend — Annette.

PS The blue moiré dress is heaven! You shall see it on your return.

Part Three

Couples

CHAPTER EIGHTEEN

Annette de Vervialle had spent some of her share of the money given to her by Lily Leblanc on clothes. She sat sipping a bock at a sidewalk café, wearing a new jade-green day dress with a beribboned straw hat and brown ankle boots with buttons. The café was on the corner of the Rue Clauzel, in the St Georges quarter below Pigalle. Across the street there was a mercerie which had not yet reopened after the lunchtime break. Annette was waiting to see a dressmaker who worked in a backroom above the mercerie: she wanted to order something special — something that could be run up in a hurry but would be suitable for the meeting at the Ritz hotel with Dagmar and the American, Lionel Giotto..

It was a sunny day, and the tables beneath the striped awning were crowded. Idly regarding the other customers, Annette recognized a familiar figure nearby — the tall voluptuous blonde prostitute known as Milady. With a sudden desire to confide in someone, especially someone who would know a great deal more about the underworld and the police than she did, Annette made herself known.

Milady was happy enough to accept another *menthe-à-l'eau* and join her. 'My dear, of course I remember you,' she said when Annette had reminded her of the two occasions on which they had met. 'One does not, after all, encounter so many people of one's own class that one readily forgets an example that adds beauty to chic.'

Annette repressed a smile as she called over a waiter and gave the order. Milady's honey-coloured hair was swept upward to surround a ridiculously small hat crowned with fruit. She was wearing a black satin skirt with an orange-and-white striped top that hugged her tightly corseted waist and was then scooped out to reveal an immodest amount of bosom — an ensemble that conspired a little to contradict the loud-voiced 'genteel' image she was at pains to adopt.

But Annette liked her: there was a warm heart behind the affected facade. She was about to ask a question when Milady said hurriedly: 'Quick! Lower your head and turn your back to the street! That little bastard Rochard has just come out of the Rue Clauzel.'

The policeman glanced casually at the café clients and strutted on downhill toward the Rue St Lazare. It was not until he had vanished around the corner that the two women turned back to their drinks.

'How I detest that poisonous little toad!' Annette said viciously. 'He really does symbolize everything that is wrong with this man's world!'

'I agree,' Milady nodded. 'But what can you expect, with the chief he works for?'

'The. . .chief he works for?'

'Morand. The gallant Commissaire. He's the worst of all.'

'Oh,' Annette said hotly, 'I don't think you can say that. You must be thinking of someone else. Why, Bruno Morand is – '

'Is a blackmailer, an extortionist, the biggest rip-off artist walking the streets of Montmartre today,' Milady interrupted. 'Look, my dear, let me be frank. You have been seen around with him, I know. But you must be careful: it does your reputation no good at all. It is time someone told you the truth.'

'I know he receives favours from the owners of the houses,' Annette began dubiously, 'but – '

'His pay-off, yes. And money from the clients who frequent them, to ensure that he doesn't spill what he knows to the voters or the press or jealous wives. And contributions from us girls whenever he feels like leaning on us: we have to pay up if we want to stay in business. *And* hush-money from politicians to make sure he keeps his mouth shut on the subject of certain deals his job brings him into contact with.'

'Yes, but . . .' Annette bit her lip. This was a side of her lover she didn't want to know about. But she couldn't help remembering the sealed envelopes so frequently handed over, the fact that Morand never, ever had to put his hand in his pocket, not even for cab fares. And a scene in a Pigalle night-club when the Commissaire had quarrelled with two politicians out on the town with two whores – an argument which had rendered the politicians furious but which Morand won. She recalled too the fact that he was clearly an habitué of the brothels himself – and that she had once thought of him as 'a philanderer, a lecher'.

Even so, she was totally unprepared for Milady's next revelation.

'Don't imagine that you are the apple of his eye,' the blonde said. 'He's always complaining about his job, but a vice squad *flic* has more opportunity than any other married man for playing around, believe me!'

'Did you say. . .m-m-married?' Annette stammered.

'Of course married. With three children. He has a little house at Fresnes, south of the city. Why do you think he can never stay in Paris the whole night? Why do you suppose he so often has to see informers *in Montparnasse?* It's on his way home! Why do you think he will never plan ahead? Because even with a mousey little wife like Cécile Morand one can only be "kept late at the office" so many times a month.'

Annette felt as though she had been struck in the face.

A dream of future domesticity dissolved and vanished, to be replaced by a deep sense of shame at her own willingness, indeed at times her own instigation of the Commissaire's excesses. How could she have been so blind, so stupid, so tempted and yet so fooled by that very male arrogance she detested so much?

'He is just using you as a cheap bedfellow, a whore who does not have to be paid,' Milady pursued as if reading her thoughts. 'I could name at least three other girls in the same position — two of them already dumped, and the third run in tandem with yourself.'

She laid a hand on Annette's arm. 'I can see this is a shock to you. You must forgive me, but it is time, as I say, that you knew the truth.'

'No, no,' Annette said in a choked voice, trying to blink away the tears of rage. 'You are quite right. Thank you for t-t-telling me.'

Although her attention was fixed on her companion, Milady could not resist an involuntary downwards glance to satisfy herself that her breasts were sufficiently exposed as an elderly man in an ulster sauntered past the café. 'There is something, in return, that you could find out for me,' she said. 'Turkey Phiz tells me that you still see from time to time the Van den Bergh woman, the one whose house you —'

'Good heavens!' exclaimed Annette. 'Can one do nothing in this town without the whole world knowing about it? Suppose I have by chance happened upon her again, what then?'

'The Phiz says that she rides in the Bois. Is that so?'

'I believe so.'

'And that she owns a race horse?'

'I was not aware of that, but it's certainly possible. She is a rich lady.'

'We are told that this animal will be ridden for her at the big Spring meeting at Longchamp, at the end of next week.'

'We? Is this something to do with Lily Leblanc and her gang?'

Milady nodded. 'An idea of Young Benoit's. He thinks —'

'I'd like to help Lily, of course. But I wouldn't want any harm to come to the Comtesse. I wouldn't want her to suffer a loss.'

'There is no question of that. She would not be involved, even indirectly. And it has nothing to do with her horse or the race it runs in.'

'Then I don't quite see . . .?'

'All we need is information, a few details of how things are organized inside the paddock.' Milady grinned. 'None of us spend much time inside the Members' Enclosure,' she said drily. 'We don't belong to the Jockey Club either. Lily thought your friend might be able to oblige — if she's a competitor, that is.'

'You want me to ask questions and pass the answers on to you, is that it?'

'Just that,' Milady said.

'Then you had best tell me what the questions are, and I will decide whether or not I can help.'

Milady told her what the questions were — and why they were wanted. 'And you would of course be cut in on the profits if the operation was a success,' she added.

Illegal though it certainly was, the operation seemed inoffensive enough. No violence would be involved and, as Milady promised, Dagmar van den Bergh would in no way be affected. Annette agreed to do her best — spurred on perhaps, after the blonde's revelations, by the thought

191

that she would in some way be hitting back at the law.

'In any case,' she said, 'if Lily's scheme works, and if she can think up a few more like it, life should be a little easier for you in future.'

'It's a big if,' said Milady, suddenly despondent. 'The particular hell we live in is man-made. So far the only answer has been to play the game their way.'

'Very well,' Annette said passionately. 'But I agree with Lily: I refuse, absolutely, to play it lying on my back. It's better, the way she suggests, to *beat* them at their own game.'

Milady shrugged, raising her glass to her lips with a little finger delicately extended. 'For the moment,' she said, 'I have to be thankful that I have a broad back. while they're ploughing away down there, I think of my mother's cottage in the Yonne. It's on an island in the river. You can only get there by boat, and at this time of the year the meadow beneath the trees is golden with cowslips.' She sighed. 'I go there for two weeks in the middle of each October, while my mother is visiting her sister in Belleville. It's the only time I really feel alive.'

'But you should not accept that!' Annette cried. 'You are intelligent, you are attractive, you should be able to live on that island all the year round; you shouldn't be forced to live this. . .this *degrading* life just in order to eat!' She paused for breath, and then − suddenly fearful, remembering that Belleville was a slum area − asked: 'What does your mother's sister do in Belleville?'

'What do you think she does?'

'You should fight, both of you; *you should not accept it*.' Annette repeated.

The blonde put down the glass and looked her in the eye. 'Just what do you suggest we do instead?' she demanded.

Before Annette could reply, Milady rose to her feet.

Across the street, the man in the ulster had reappeared and was looking into the window of the mercerie. 'You must excuse me,' the big blonde said, returning to her haughtiest manner. 'An old friend of the family. . .you understand . . .?'

She swept off toward the mercerie.

There was a sealed envelope waiting for Annette when she returned to her lodgings, It had been delivered by a uniformed *agent* from the local police commissariat, the concierge told her.

The note inside, unsigned and lacking any endearment or expression of affection, informed her that Morand would be visiting the fair at Neuilly the following afternoon. An acquaintance there possessed a caravan, comfortably furnished, which would be vacant until late that night. He would call for her at three o'clock.

Annette found a sheet of paper, scribbled a short message, and sealed it inside another envelope. Her hand was shaking with rage as she addressed it to Morand. The message read:

> *Mademoiselle de Vervialle thanks the Commissaire for his generous invitation but regrets she has a prior engagement.*

She walked down to the Opera, took a two-horse omnibus to the Palais Royal, and crossed the river to the Quai des Orfèvres. Here she gave an urchin a coupe of sous to deliver the envelope to Morand's office, then turned to stalk all the way back home.

Morand was outside the building, waiting by the open door of a fiacre when she emerged the following morning. 'What the devil's the idea of this?' he demanded, tapping her message, which he held in one hand. 'I ask you to

193

come to the fair, thinking we could have an afternoon and evening together, and you reply by sending me this – '

'Monsieur le Commissaire,' Annette interrupted, 'I do not believe there is any service I could render you in your friend's caravan at Neuilly that could not be better supplied by your wife. Unless,' she added icily, 'you require my help choosing teddy-bears for your children.'

She turned, went back into the house, and slammed the door.

Lionel Giotto, Annette thought, was even more handsome than she remembered. His tall, blond good looks and elegant manner seemed perfectly at home in the opulent crimson and gilt décor of the Ritz tea-room.

The young American and his French contact were both installed when she arrived – nervous and a little apprehensive as she followed a flunkey across the marble hallway and between ornate classical pillars into the high-ceilinged room. They were accompanied by the fair-haired German woman who had been with the Comtesse outside No. 14, Rue de Monthyon.

Dagmar van den Bergh wore a lemon organdie dress covered with appliqué flowers; the Baroness von Zwickenheim was dressed in a severely cut black broadcloth jacket tailored to end below her hips, and an ankle-length skirt of the same material. Her hair was pinned up and she wore a silk hat with a curly brim and shiny black riding boots.

'My dear, you look divine!' the Comtesse exclaimed, extending both hands across the table loaded with silverware and patisseries on tiered cakestands. 'Let me introduce you once more – only this time correctly! – to Doctor Lionel Giotto of Boston, Massachusetts.'

The American was already on his feet, larger than life against a background of palms in tubs. 'An honour, mademoiselle,' he murmured, bending low over her proffered hand. 'I am delighted at last, thanks to our mutual friend, to rediscover you.'

He had a good voice, deep, not too much of a twang; an accent certainly, but not bizarre enough to make people stare. Strong, very white teeth. A firm, dry handshake. Annette's heart was fluttering already.

She was, however, ill at ease. She found the atmosphere oppressive. Sunlight shining through a glass roof arching above the palms made the room uncomfortably warm — an impression heightened somehow by the hushed voices of customers leaning over tables on the far side of the room, by the passage of soft-footed waiters carrying trays. Even the chandeliers were menacing.

Annette felt as though she was herself regarding the scene through a thick sheet of glass. There were undercurrents and cross currents, too, at her own table.

It might have been simply that anger and distress at the Commissaire's betrayal had left her ultra-sensitive to the nuances of behaviour, but she could have sworn that she detected an exchange of glances between Lionel and the Comtesse when the American used the phrase '*mutual* friend'. A glance implying. . .what? She had no idea, but she was certain it was there. As certain as she was that it was swiftly followed by a meaning look — a suppressed smile even? — between the two women.

Added to this was an acute awareness of her own complicity, however fleeting, in the private life of Dagmar van den Bergh. Between the flowers and beneath the organdie, she saw as clearly as if the woman had been stripped naked the generous, perfumed curves amongst which she had herself so recently, and with such abandon, wallowed and exulted.

So far as the German woman was concerned, she too felt bare beneath that challenging scrutiny. A cool nod had been the Baroness's only greeting. Now she felt that her clothes and everything else about her were being subjected to a critical and analytic examination.

Until that moment, Annette had been confident that the little dressmaker in the Rue Clauzel had provided exactly what was needed — white lace draped over a belted, high-waisted brocade skirt with a cross-over top in printed cretonne.

Now, under that penetrating, haughty gaze, she was all at once conscious that the lace was cheap; that the brocade, instead of being buttoned down one side, should have been swathed; that the violet colour was garish; that the cretonne was not only unsuitable but might be considered vulgar. The whole effect was too fussy, with too many tucks and ribbons and bows.

She felt as though she had been taken down off a shelf, favoured with a cursory glance, and then put back as being unworthy of further interest.

She settled her wide-brimmed hat more firmly on her head — at least the ostrich feathers were real — and smiled at Dagmar. There was certainly one thing that *they* had in common! Seated opposite the young man, she accepted a wafer-thin cup filled with scented tea. So far as the cakes were concerned, she permitted herself only a plain madeleine. No sticky fingers, sugar dusting the corsage or whipped cream squished from an eclair by that tiny silver fork were going to sully this particular afternoon!

Lionel Giotto noticed none of this subtle social interplay. He saw only the girl he had been longing to meet again for what seemed like several aeons of eternity. He saw a ravishing, tawny-haired beauty, the delicacy of whose petal face was sublimely offset by the feminine sweep of that feathered hat. He saw cushioned hips and a splendid bust separated by the slenderest of waists. He saw tapered ankles and tiny feet. He thought the flowers printed on the cretonne were enchanting.

For perhaps twenty minutes there was a stiff, rather stilted exchange of views – on the exhibition, the weather, the differences between life in Paris and life in Massachusetts, the advantages of Panhard and Levassor's latest horseless carriage which had been fitted with a second cylinder and could travel at no less than fifteen miles per hour.

But at last, with a significant glance at Giotto, the Comtesse rose to leave, explaining that she and the Baroness had a rendezvous with friends at the Palais de Glace. After the correct politenesses had been exchanged, Gisela von Zwickenheim took her arm in a proprietorial manner and steered her from the room without a backwards look. Annette had the impression, strange in so dominant a personality, that the German was relieved to get her away.

She settled back in her chair and helped herself to a chocolate eclair. With the handsome American, she felt at once completely at ease.

'Mademoiselle,' said he, leaning towards her with an intent expression, 'custom would normally decree that a hiatus of at least two days should separate this happy meeting and our next. An intimation, moreover, should properly have been subsumed from yourself that such a thing would be desirable. But much time has been wasted already. So forgive me, I beg of you, if I circumvent the proprieties and ask: will you do me the honour, the extra special honour, of dining with me this very night?'

Beneath the imprisoning clasp of her corset, Annette could feel her heart beating wildly. 'Nothing, Monsieur,' she said truthfully, 'would give me greater pleasure.'

197

CHAPTER NINETEEN

The dinner lasted three days. Like any young couple simultaneously transfixed by a double salvo from Cupid's quiver, Lionel and Annette lived in one another's eyes from the moment the first glass of champagne was drained.

Dinner that night was at Fouquet's, above the passing glitter of the Champs Elysées. But no sooner had that initial amazed awareness registered than the rumble of wheels, the clip-clop of hooves, the murmur of drifting crowds, even the rich, warm, winey atmosphere of the restaurant with its discreet tinkle of silver and glass, faded all of them to a distant dream — a far-off obbligato to the music of their discovery.

Drowning in the depths of his blue-eyed desire, Annette allowed herself to drift on a tide of emotion as intense as anything she had known. The backs of his hands, she saw with a pang of tenderness, were downed with fine blond hairs. She wanted suddenly, savagely, to feel those hands on her flesh.

The young American could see nothing but perfection, the idealized version of the woman he had always wanted. He saw eyes misted with promise, a bosom beneath the white shawl soft as a bird's, a wide mouth avid for kisses. In the light of a table lamp shaded by pleats of crimson silk he observed a small, pale bulge of flesh beneath the young woman's arm where stitching had come apart and a seam of the new dress had split. He found that almost unbearably endearing. . .seeing at the same time with his mind's eye the continuation of that fleshy swell to the curve of breast he so desperately wanted to handle.

Neither of them could ever remember what they ate. Of what did they talk? What subjects were discussed? Annette could not have said. She knew that she had studiously avoided any mention of Morand, any reference to the Moulin Rouge or the reason why she no longer worked there. She thought she told him she was a dancer presently seeking a rôle suitable to her talents. Perhaps she mentioned her parents, her childhood, her friend Lucie away in Brittany? She supposed he had told her about his life in Boston. But Lionel could never remember either.

They were not drunk. They drank champagne but they were not inebriated: their desire for each other was much too serious for such frivolity. But the alcohol served as a catalyst, a release, freeing them both from the restrictions imposed by a society too anxious to make its members conform to a code of behaviour, permitting them to suppress their inhibitions and react as their natures dictated.

There was never any question, once they left the restaurant, that they would separate. Lionel was unwilling to return to the Meurice, since he was already known there, and to bring in a woman with no baggage late at night would place Annette in an invidious position. She was adamant that her lodgings were too small and too unromantic. There were several Hôtels d'Angleterre in Paris: they went to the one on the Boulevard des Italiens, opposite the Olympia music-hall.

The room was comfortable, with a huge brass bedstead, a marble wash-hand stand furnished with a basin and ewer in Limoges china, and heavy floor-length curtains in dusty green velour.

An empty champagne bottle upended in an ice bucket stood on the bedside table when they awoke in the morning, but neither of them could recall drinking the contents; Lionel could not even remember ordering it. His personal horizon was bounded by the soft warm shape curled around him and the firm breast heavy against his arm.

Those were the only things that were real. For him the past night was a swirl of erotic images, an unending symphony of love orchestrated for the five senses. In memory he saw eyes limpid with desire, heard again small intimate cries of ecstasy as hot flesh convulsed at his touch and he spurted out his tribute to the beauty of his young mistress. He tongued the salt, sweet taste of perfumed skin; he smelled the musky woman-scent and the onion tang of fresh sweat.

It was not until the second night that either of them could assess the other with any semblance of objectivity. But there were other, less earthy joys in store for them first.

Emerging from the shower cubicle in one corner of the room before their hot coffee and rolls were sent up, Annette drew back the curtains and stared down into the sunlit street four floors below. 'But it's exactly like the Camille Pissaro painting of the Boulevard!' she exclaimed. And indeed, apart from the fact that the plane trees flanking the avenue were now misted with green, the scene did resemble the Impressionist masterpiece. . .the strollers crowding the sidewalks, two-deck buses and cabs jockeying for position in the roadway, domed kiosks plastered with posters for every theatrical attraction in town.

When, dewy-eyed and fresh, they came out of the hotel

and joined the crowds themselves, the street, the whole world around it, seemed to have been newly created, specially for their pleasure.

The sky above the rooftops was bluer. The sun shone more brightly. Pigeons, iridescent in their new plumage, wheeled more sharply against the sparkling shopfronts.

It was still quite early, and the horses' breath steamed in the windless air. For Lionel, the iron ring of their shoes on the cobbles, the swish and swirl of water as storekeepers hosed the pavements, the cries of a newspaper seller and a carillon chiming from a nearby church made music sweeter and more poignant than anything he had ever heard before. Even the yeasty hayseed odour of horse dung enchanted him.

Annette shared his wonder at their own good fortune and the beauty of the bustling city. 'Oh, those flowers!' she cried, passing green shelves stacked with multicoloured blooms on the street corner. 'Did you ever smell anything so divine as those roses?'

The flower-seller, an old woman wrapped in shawls, sat on a stool beneath a striped umbrella. 'Roses for the lady, Monsieur?' she croaked.

'Certainly roses for the lady!' replied the young American. 'I'll take all you have.' And then, to an errand boy with a bicycle who had been talking to the woman: 'Here, my lad — this money's for you if you deliver them to the Hotel d'Angleterre and tell the receptionist to have them sent up to Room 42.'

He paid for the flowers and hailed a cab.

The fiacre deposited them at the main entrance to the exhibition. They spent the morning admiring the scientific marvels in the pavilions behind the Eiffel Tower. Although Annette had in fact seen most of them before, looking at them with Lionel's New World eye added an extra dimension to the visit. The whirling governors of skeleton clocks beneath glass domes, the clicking brass gearwheels of rectification machines, the complex wiring of electrical apparatus, all took on additional lustre in his presence.

Coming from a country of great distances, he was naturally interested in the transport section. In the ten years since Gottlieb Daimler and Carl Benz had made horseless carriages available to a public rich enough to buy and run them, a great deal of progress had been made: Giotto spent a lot of time examining different types of motor proposed by Panhard, Peugeot, Renault and André Citroen. He was interested, too, in the model of a heavier-than-air flying machine invented in 1890 by Clément Ader, the original of which, propelled by its creator, had flown more than fifty yards unassisted. 'It will be the omnibus of the future,' he enthused as they lunched in a café overlooking the river. 'There are two brothers − Rice? Wright? − working on a similar idea in the state of Ohio, back home.'

Annette was dutifully impressed. But by the time the wine was finished she was less impressed by the marvels of science than by the thought of the feather mattress in Room 42 at the Hotel d'Angleterre.

At two o'clock Lionel suggested that it was time to take a siesta.

The roses had turned the place into a conservatory. Crimson and scarlet, yellow and white, they packed the windowsills, covered the dressing-table and spilled from the basin and ewer. The room was heavy with their exotic perfume.

'You dear man, I feel cosseted, I feel spoiled!' Annette cried as they entered − a little breathless after a rapid climb up four flights of stairs, although the thudding of their hearts was due more to anticipation than to the exertion.

'No more spoiled than I. . .to have the privilege and the pleasure of so rare and so beautiful a bloom within the reach of my hand,' said Lionel, drawing her into his embrace. For a timeless moment they stood kissing, the door still open behind them, their hungry mouths clinging, tasting, exploring.

Her lips, William Shakespeare had written three hundred years earlier, *suck forth my soul.* Journalist as he was, Lionel Giotto saw no reason to update the phrase. He could not, he thought, have expressed it better himself.

It was not until footsteps in the passageway outside — pausing, hesitating and then hurrying away — claimed his attention that he released Annette and closed the door. Wordlessly, he steered her towards the bed.

The previous night had been all fever, tumult, an explosion of desire. Today, secure in their love for each other, they could afford to make undressing a ritual. As each layer of clothing was removed, each lace unthreaded, each tape undone and button unfastened, their excitement mounted with every inch of skin exposed.

And when nothing shielded them from total nakedness but Lionel's drawers and the corset that clasped Annette's waist and thrust out her breasts, they delayed still further the ultimate exposure, teasing their passion. . .daring the tide of lust to overflow while their eyes were locked in love.

The young man's hands, tangled in the tawny riot of her unpinned hair, held her dear head fast. And then, as she lay back on the bed, he knelt beside her and allowed electric fingers to trail past the pulses fluttering like a bird's heart in her neck, down and across the satined slopes of her breasts, swiftly over the rigidly sculptured corset and finally between her thighs.

The muscles on the inside of those smooth columns

quivered, and involuntarily she parted them slightly. But his roving fingertips bypassed the furred chalice between them — as they had scrupulously avoided the quivering buds tipping the breasts above — and circled on down to caress her calves.

Annette's own fingers, locked over her lover's hips, clenched. She was breathing very fast now. Her eyes, freed from his burning gaze, homed on the ivory linen of his drawers, where a darkening patch at the apex of the pyramid jutting stiffly from his loins testified to the urgency of his desire for her.

Abruptly she changed her grip, hooked her fingers over the waistband of the garment, and peeled it down to his knees in one decisive movement. Released from the constriction, his upstanding member sprang into view and remained poised above her, a shaft ready to be thrust home. She cradled the soft pouch of flesh beneath it. 'My dearest,' she whispered, 'a part of me is still concealed. . .and I want you to see and to have *all* of me!'

She removed her hands and rolled quickly over onto her face.

Lionel needed no second invitation. As fast as he could, he began with trembling fingers to unlace the corset.

When at last she could struggle out of it, she lay prone once more, arms crossed above her head so that her breasts were provocatively raised. 'Lionel,' she murmured, 'I adore you. Come to me, my dearest, *now!*'

'At once,' he said. 'But first . . .' He leaped from the bed and plucked the most exquisite, the most exotic long-stemmed yellow bloom from the ewer. Satisfying himself that there were no thorns to lacerate her flawless skin, he laid the flower head between her breasts. He stood looking down at the whole splendid length of her naked body.

He leaned over her then, and, spreading her legs tenderly apart, paid tribute with his lips to that other rose whose petals, already dewed with moisture, had opened to reveal the palpitating stamen within. 'No flower,' he said, lowering himself to lie beside her, 'was ever so entrancingly fashioned, or so delicately perfumed, as the one you wear between your thighs.'

Annette gazed at him through slitted eyes, a half smile twitching her mouth. 'Monsieur is gallant,' she said. 'But what, after all, is a flower without a stem?'

And, reaching for the fleshy stalk projecting from his loins, she pulled him over and into her.

'I must go home; I really must go back,' Annette said. It was dusk and the street lamps in the boulevard below cast lozenges of light on the ceiling.

'But why?' asked Lionel. 'You are not happy here? There is something wrong with the bed? You don't love me any more?'

'No, silly!' She smiled fondly, tracing the line of his jaw with her fingertips. 'You don't understand. For a woman it is different. I have no change of clothes, no creams and ointments, not even the wherewithal to wash my teeth! I will not be long, I promise. And I do promise to come back!'

'Very well, if you must. I will come with you.'

'No!' she said vehemently, panicking suddenly. The shabby room on the top floor of the house in the Rue Halévy. . .the clutter she had left, dressing, undressing and re-dressing for the momentous rendezvous at the Ritz. . .the possibility — horrors! — that Morand might be waiting in the street outside. Lionel must be kept away from that side of her life at all costs.

'No?' he repeated, raising himself on one elbow and staring at her through the gloom. 'I don't understand. I cannot allow you to cross the city alone, after dark. Where do you live, anyway?'

Annette levered herself off the bed and crossed the room. She opened a window. Four of the yellow lozenges on the ceiling elongated and swung toward the opposite wall. 'In my profession,' she said over her shoulder, 'one is always crossing the city alone after dark. I am quite used to it, I assure you. In less than an hour we can meet for an apéritif at the Café de la Paix.'

'I cannot permit it,' he said stubbornly. 'Even an hour without you would be intolerable.'

For a moment she said nothing. Over the muffled rumble of traffic a fluttering of wings was audible as pigeons settled themselves for the night in the eaves above the window. Lionel admired the gracefully interacting curves of shoulder and breast and waist and hip, golden in the reflected light, as she leaned over the sill.

'I cannot explain,' Annette said at last, looking down into the street below. 'You. . .me. . .this room. Even the exhibition. I – '

'I can't hear you.' Swiftly, he left the bed and crossed the room, leaning beside her with an arm around her bare shoulders.

'I was saying that since I met you, since we both. . .I mean the two of us together is something wonderful, marvellous, for me. It is as though there was a completely new me, quite separate from the old one. A new me of which you are an essential part, as I am of you. And. . .well, it's just that I don't want the new in any way whatever mixed up with the old. I'm frightened, Lionel: life has become so good, so true, that I dare not take the slightest risk of anything spoiling it. Which could happen if the two overlap. Do you see what I mean? Or does it sound just foolish, a woman's silly whim?'

He left the question unanswered, gently lifting the dark mass of her hair with both hands and planting a kiss on the nape of her neck.

'Just the same,' she said, twisting her head to smile at him, 'I do have to get out of here and fetch some fresh clothes!'

'We shall compromise,' he decided. 'The Place Vendôme and the Rue Royale are no more than a block away. We will both get out of here and hurry down there, and I will buy you new clothes.'

'They will all be closed, the expensive shops there,' Annette said.

'What, Worth? Paquin? Poiret? In the year of the exhibition?'

'Certainly. It must be after seven already.'

'Then I shall hammer on the doors until they re-open!'

'You'll get us locked up!' Annette said, repressing a shudder of memory.

The couturiers' showrooms were indeed closed and shuttered and dark, but they found a department store near the Opera that was still open. Giotto bought a small valise, and into this they packed two dresses, a peignoir, a silk nightgown, some underclothes and a selection of toilet articles, for all of which, at his own insistence, he paid.

Once the valise was safely back in their hotel, they took a cab to the Rue de la Boétie and dined Chez Lucien. At eleven o'clock, they were on the Trocadero landing stage, waiting for a boat to take them downriver to the late-night fair at Neuilly, beyond the Bois de Bologne.

Here, on the northwestern outskirts of the city, a full spectrum of the capital's night life glittered from midnight to dawn.

Here at *La Fête à Neu-Neu*, after the skating, the theatre and the music-hall, after Le Véfour, Maxim's and the private balls in the mansions along the Champs Elysées, fashionable Paris could be seen showing itself to be seen. In the wavering illumination of hissing

naphtha flares, victorias, dogcarts, broughams, coupés
– perhaps even a landau full of cocottes or Liane de
Lancy in an *Americaine* drawn by two trotters – formed
a double line moving slowly on the fringes of the crowd
thronging sideshows and stalls.

Costly perfume from the Rue de la Paix spiced the feral
stench of wild beasts in their cages and the smell of grilled
sausages and roasted chestnuts. Among shouting barkers
and the wheeze of steam organs, the hoi-polloi divided
their attention between the shrieking occupants of merry-
go-rounds and the fabled creatures in their carriages on
the roadway. It was of course not chic for 'one' actually
to 'descend' at Neuilly – to rub shoulders with 'them'?
What a thought! – although one's escort might leap
down to impress and make his way to Marseille's
wrestling booth, where odds were laid against any
amateur who dared take on The Terror from Martinique
or Battling Bertrand or Black Monsieur Beaucaire (and
where, oddly enough, the playboy often beat the
professional, for Marseille was a good businessman and
knew how to keep a client).

It was gay, it was exciting. Lionel and Annette danced
to a hurdy-gurdy, tasted Genuine American Ice Cream
supplied by an Italian with a concession at the US pavilion
on the Quai des Nations, screamed with the rest of the
world on a switchback. They swallowed raw herrings
from Holland and watched three Bengal tigers leap
through a hoop of fire. They even held hands among
giant spiders and skeletons during a ride on The Ghost
Train.

Annette won a blue plush teddy-bear after three
successive bouts at a shooting booth. Lionel was
fascinated to see an imported Daimler-Benz cabriolet
parked behind a row of gypsy caravans. On the roadway,
an excited seller of sweetmeats told them, the Comte de

Dion himself had passed, steering his latest model.

But finally — the thought seized them simultaneously — the world of manufactured entertainment, of bright lights and contrasts and the marvels of men, came in a poor second best to that other private world of which they themselves were the sole architects and arbiters. Nothing at the exhibition or the fair was as exciting as the thought of the feather bed surrounded by roses at the Hotel d' Angleterre!

'The boat is too slow,' Lionel said. 'I'll find a cab and we will drive there. Perhaps you would like to give that animal to a child?'

'No, no,' Annette said, hugging the blue bear to her. 'I'll find a home for him myself: there's someone I know that I'd like to send him to.'

'Whatever you say.' Lionel darted out among the slow moving cabs and carriages clogging the roadway, his alert gaze having spotted a homeward-bound fiacre with no fare.

The plush teddy was perched among the roses for the rest of the night, watching their lovemaking with his shiny black boot-button eyes.

After his Japanese experience, after his encounters with Nellie, the Comtesse and her challenging friend — in all of which the arcane pleasures of the flesh had taken precedence over even the most rudimentary spiritual considerations — Lionel discovered in his relationship with Annette a sublime contentment mated with excitement such as he had never felt before. For the first time in his life, concepts that he had always dismissed as the blatherings of an elder, blinkered generation, related to his own existence, to life as actually lived.

The idea, for instance, that physical love was only valid when it involved the meeting of two souls as well as two bodies. The belief that the sexual act only reached its apogee when it was the expression of one human being's love for another. These things, he now realized, were true. . .not just abstractions mouthed by the moralists.

At his age – he was not yet thirty – he was not prepared to reject entirely the joys of the casual encounter, the tingling elation of curiosity satisfied, of alien hands on his flesh. But the extra dimension added when love was involved, he had to admit, could in no way be quantified.

The fourth-floor bedroom of the Hotel d'Angleterre became the laboratory where – under strictly uncontrolled conditions! – such theories were tested and evaluated.

Dreamlike in its slow development, the remainder of the night they had spent at the Neuilly fair brought to the young lovers an enchantment that left them wordless with delight and wonder.

At first, with the windows wide open to the balmy night air, Lionel was content to kneel entranced on the floor and watch the successive revelations, each more exciting than the last, as his love peeled off her clothes in the light reflected from the street lamps below.

The hollow of a shoulder, the pale glimpse of a thigh, a shapely leg golden in the tawny illumination etched themselves into his awareness as first the new dress, then a camisole top and finally the cobweb sheath of silk stockings fell beside the bed.

She turned away then, and the superb twin curves of her bottom rose gloriously into view as she bent forwards to undo the tapes and slid the white drawers down over her hips and thighs. After that it was the turn of the corset.

This was a new one, bought with part of the proceeds of her 'arrangement' with Lily Leblanc. It was of oyster-coloured satin, with whaleboned busks, and its advantage was that those busks hooked together in front, so that a slight loosening of the laces behind, easily effected by the wearer, at once allowed the two halves of the foundation to be parted and the garment discarded.

The corset was at Annette's feet. Lionel gazed spellbound once more at the long nude beauty of his lady. Sculpted by the yellow light, the infinitely subtle convexities of flesh moulded one into the other from shoulder to wrist, from hip to knee, and from the hip itself with incomparable elegance back into the taut scoop of a waist that was as pliant as it was trim. From the depthless shadow between her splendid breasts, warm tints of amber and ochre swept down over the silky swell of her belly, past a deliciously dimpled navel, to that furry triangle separating her thighs where the entrance to her secret treasure lay concealed.

Lost in awe and admiration as he was, it was only when she unpinned her hair and let it tumble over her shoulders that the young man remembered more would be expected of him than mere visual approval. At the same time, naked himself, he became aware of a tightness, almost a pain, an ache that clamoured to be released in that part of him that was pointing like a rigidly extended finger at the object of his desire.

He rose lithely to his feet, picked her up, and laid her gently down on the bed.

Their coupling this time had a timeless quality about it. Wet as they were with anticipation, the portals to that shrine consecrated to his adoration slid open easily to let him in. Embedded smoothly in her flesh, Lionel started a gentle rocking movement, matched by an elusive, artful shifting of her hips, that floated them both away on a tide of sensation which, rising steadily, still threatened never to overflow.

Thus buoyed up by their shared ecstasy, they drifted, half sleeping and half waking, into that mystic haven where tension and release have no further meaning, and only being counts. When they awoke late in the morning, they were still clasped in each other's arms.

It was some hours later — a few francs to a conspiratorial chambermaid had ensured that they would remain undisturbed — that Annette decided to broaden the scope of their activities.

Perhaps as a result of the wanton excesses imposed by the life-style of Bruno Morand, maybe because she was naturally adventurous and that abandoned facet of her personality had remained hidden until the Commissaire exposed it, she determined that romantic love, delirious though it might be, must at times make way for lesser, lighter pursuits. There were, after all, a lot of games yet to be played.

In the middle of the afternoon, Lionel found himself lying flat on his back on the bed, with Annette standing naked above him, a narrow, graceful foot planted on each side of his hips. He was staring, fascinated, at the auburn hairs shielding the furrow between her thighs, at a foreshortened view of the belly curving above that, and the twin globes of breasts jutting from her rib cage, when she bent her knees and lowered herself slowly towards his male stem which, gently quivering, was now arrowed in the direction of the ceiling.

Parting the pink lips nestling in the heart of that furrow with a licked forefinger, she positioned herself in such a way that the engorged head of his manly pride eased itself between them. . .and then slid its whole hot length into her as she finally sat, straddling his hips.

Lionel caught his breath as she began to move, flexing her pelvis, rising and falling again in those invisible stirrups while he lay in a trance of delight, watching enraptured as her mouth fell half open and the changing expressions on her face settled into a single sightless gaze of pure lust.

She rose him like a steed with her hands on her hips, a slight smile twisting her lips when he reached up both hands to caress her stiffened nipples.

As the exquisite movement continued, the turbulent blood coursing through Lionel's veins seemed to flood toward the centre of his being; the sensation transmitted by each nerve end concentrated its force in the fleshy spike on which his love was impaled. He thought he would burst with sheer joy, simply staring at her.

He arched his hips up off the bed to meet her thrusts, but she shook her head, gently removed his hands from her breasts and leaned forwards to stretch his arms above his head. 'Lie still,' she commanded. 'I don't want you to move; it's my turn to ride.'

The up-and-down motion quickened. What had started, as it were, as a leisurely walk, accelerated into a trot that jolted the supine American's hips, transformed itself into a canter. . .and finally ended in a veritable gallop.

The bed-springs creaked in protest as the nude beauty thrashed to and fro.

Beneath her, Lionel — forbidden to make his normal, muscular response — found the whole of his vigour centred on the reaction of his vibrating nerve. This inner and passive answer to stimulus, rather than the natural exterior reply, converged the entire apparatus of his sensory perceptions on the part of him enshrined within his lover's loins. When the pumping of her hips reached a crescendo, and the rhythm she had established faltered and became sporadic as she gasped out a hoarse release, he fountained up into her the whole gushing proof of the rampant desire held in check for so long.

She collapsed face down across him, and it was many minutes before their breathing subsided to a normal rate. A confused noise from outside the open window finally tempted them from the bed.

Annette slipped into her new peignoir and leaned over the sill. There was some kind of parade marching along the Boulevard below. Poorly dressed men, some of them carrying placards and banners, walked behind a uniformed brass band playing martial music. The sidewalks were crowded with onlookers, children ran and skipped beside the marchers, a line of police waved impatient coachmen and cabbies to the side of the road so that the procession could pass. 'It's a demonstration by factory workers, I think,' Annette called over her shoulder. 'They complain that some of the money spent on the exhibition should have been channelled their way. Why don't you come and look?'

Lionel was buttoning himself into a shirt. He looked. . .not at the parade below but at the shining surface of Annette's peignoir where it was tightened over her backside, and the cleft between the two fleshy hemispheres into which the heavy silk had dropped.

The temptation was too much for him. The desire to pry apart those two sumptuous globes was too strong. Already his cavalier, exhausted though he had been after the recent demands on his patience, was stirring and eager once more to remount. But this time a different general would be in command!

With a swift movement, Lionel lifted the hem of the peignoir and draped it over the small of her back. From her bottom downwards, she was nude and defenceless, while that part of her outside the room remained normal and decently clothed! Apart from a sibilant intake of breath when the cool air fanned her naked skin, she made no move.

215

Overcome with a surge of lustful desire such as he had seldom experienced, Lionel clenched trembling fingers in the curves of flesh flanking the fork of her thighs and dragged them apart. Annette gasped and the nerves of her bottom quivered as he dug vigorous thumbs into the brown-haired lips that were now revealed, and parted them too.

He stood immediately behind her, thrusting his hips suddenly forwards so that the hard projection already fully extended from his groin stabbed in through the still-wet portals of her citadel.

She squealed, wriggling her own hips until he became fully embedded, the whole length of his staff lapped in her hot embrace.

And this time, rather than employing a full stroke in and out, he stayed stock still, contracting and expanding the muscles of his most precious asset to establish a subtle sexual rhythm in time with Annette's responsive inner contractions.

He stretched forwards across her back and looked down into the crowded street.

To an outside observer, they were no more than a couple of hotel guests, leaning out of a fourth floor window to watch the animated scene on the Boulevard. In fact, like the heroine of Flaubert's *Madame Bovary*, the lady was being serviced, secretly, splendidly and salaciously, by her lover from behind!

CHAPTER TWENTY

'Where are we going tonight?' Annette asked.

'Nowhere,' said Lionel.

'Nowhere?'

'We shall stay here. Enough of this gallivanting around Paris,' he smiled. 'For once we are to remain at home and enjoy each other's company!'

Annette drew aside the sheet to reveal his lean, muscular body. She reached out a hand to touch that part of him which had provided so compelling a reason for the length of their stay in the room. She laid her head in the hollow of his shoulder, the tawny hair spilled over his chest in wild profusion. 'So far as enjoyment is concerned,' she said dreamily, 'we seem to have been favoured already! We have been very. . .active! In such situations, a lady can become hungry.'

'But of course. Naturally we shall dine here.'

'Lionel!' She propped herself up on one elbow, the fingers of her free hand teasing through the springy hairs sheathing his loins. 'There is no restaurant in the hotel. They only provide breakfasts. You know that.'

'What of it? We shall send out for food.' Despite recent forays resulting in a considerable expenditure of energy his cavalier was again stirring with interest, anxious to remount and continue the campaign.

An hour had elapsed since they watched the procession pass, and the light outside had thickened into dusk.

Mantled with a faint blush of pink, Annette's skin shone through the gloom with the sheen of silk. He sat up and leaned across her.

With a sly, conspiratorial smile, she cupped the breast nearest to him and raised it towards his eager mouth. He lowered the lips, sipping gently at the darker bud crowning the mound of flesh.

Her fingers tightened then on his manly pride, already lengthening, stiffening, coaxing him, pulling him closer to her, over her, into her.

Lionel sank with a wordless exclamation between her spread thighs, allowing the spearhead of his sensibility to be engulfed in her warm wet embrace.

As they climaxed together fifteen blissful minutes later, he felt that he had never been so happy, so content in his whole life. This beauty, this adorable, exquisitely fashioned creature who had so many times already told him that she loved him, was entirely his! His treasure, his love, his mistress and his friend! He had enjoyed her three times in this one afternoon. . .and he could hardly wait for a fourth opportunity to present itself! Satiated only for the moment, he allowed his mind to wander down endless corridors of years blazing with the glory of this physical completeness while the young woman beneath him became his fiancée, his wife, the mother of his children. . .but always and for ever his partner and accomplice in the world of sex.

Another hour passed before he levered himself off the bed, shrugged into a bathrobe, and trod down the creaking staircase to the small first-floor reception hall, where he gave the boot-boy a twenty-franc gold piece and sent him down the street to the Café de la Paix with orders to bring them back a hot meal.

In that centenary year, dinner at Maxim's among the rich and the notorious had increased to five francs a head.

218

The lobster soup, roast wild duck and peach mousse that the boy brought back from the Café de la Paix cost, with the champagne, seventeen francs and seventy-three centimes, but Lionel considered the extravagance worth every sou. He pocketed two francs, bestowed the twenty-seven centime balance on the grateful lad, and prepared to serve his naked lady with all the aplomb of an international maître d'hôtel.

There were of course several culinary games to be played before an order was sent downstairs for coffee. Cherry sauce garnishing the duck to be licked from Annette's deliciously dimpled navel, part of the mousse — still chilled — used to cool her lover's ardour, and other, more recondite pleasures. But it was not until the dishes had been cleared away and they were preparing, just for the sake of variety, to go to bed that Lionel's lustful imagination reached its peak.

Its peak for that day, that is.

Annette had gone first into what passed as a bathroom. There was an elementary form of shower, or douche, worked by tugging on a chain, and what was known as a sitz-bath — a square porcelain tub three feet deep with a shelved bottom designed so that the bather could sit upright with the hot water reaching to his chest and his feet lowered into the rectangular well beneath.

The bedroom windows and the ornate mirror behind the wash-hand stand were misted with steam when Lionel decided to join her. Droplets of condensation pimpled the vulcanized rubber shower curtain. He thrust it aside and walked into the cubicle, naked and trembling once more with desire.

She was sitting in the tub with her back to him. The hair was pinned up beneath a shower cap. Above the stark white rim of the porcelain, the subtle pink curve of her spine, the flawless taper of her neck as she bent forwards over an outsize sponge, filled him with a tenderness that threatened to choke him. He stole up behind her.

Annette shivered with anticipation, feeling the current of cool air as he approached fan her heated skin. She did not turn her head.

'My dearest,' she murmured faintly. And then: 'Oh, Lionel. . .I think, yes, I can sense something hot touching my back!'

'And I,' replied the young man with uncharacteristic banality, 'can sense the world's most beautiful back against my hot something.' He was in a state of excitement too fervent to seek fine phrases.

He placed his hands on her wet shoulders and then, leaning over her, swept them down through damp hollows, up over the moist swells of flesh below, past the tightening buds and under the breasts lapped by the soap-frothed surface of the water.

Hammocking those breasts in his two hands, he drew them gently upwards and back, obliging the girl to straighten up and then lean back against the rim of the bath. Her head dropped back farther still. Her mouth opened. And suddenly, there between her wet lips, was the swollen head of that portion of her lover's body which had given her such incommensurate joy. She opened her mouth wider. Her tongue flicked a warm welcome to the invader.

Lionel gasped. Involuntarily, his hips and loins began to sway, an easy, dreamlike rhythm that slid his proudest possession half-in, half-out, of the opening so lovingly offered.

Bent almost double now, he plunged his hands beneath the surface of the water, smoothed sensitive fingers over a soft swell of belly, and tangled them in the fronds of hair floating below. He dove his hands between the curves of Annette's thighs, prising them apart, then tenderly parted the outer lips of her secret shrine, the inner, until his questing fingertips could stimulate the ridged surface of the hypersensitive innermost bud with a sliding submarine caress.

For timeless moments they remained like that — a complex element fashioned from skin and flesh, muscle and mind, twin parts of one whole moving in effortless counterpoint.

Steam rising from the surface of the water welling around their locked bodies dewed the ceiling and ran in rivulets down the shower curtain.

And then, suddenly, Annette jerked into motion. She released the young man, sat upright, and then stood, turning to face him. Swirls of water, stirred into turbulent action, lapped over the rim of the tub and splashed to the floor. 'Come to me,' she commanded huskily. 'I want you. Here. Now.'

Following the direction indicated by his arrowing shaft, Lionel stepped into the bath. She held out her arms and they melted into a steamy embrace.

Her skin, shining with moisture, was slippery to the touch, soaped and oiled so that the rotundities of flesh — of breast and buttock, of hip and thigh — shifted and slid easily beneath his roving hands. While she cradled the nape of his neck in both her own hands and tilted back her head to respond to his kiss, Lionel's fingers, delicate as a sculptor's, smoothed over each swell, burrowed into hollows and probed the cavities.

Abruptly Annette turned, hot water swirling around her knees, and presented her back to him. She stood astride, leaning slightly forwards to support herself with outstretched hands planted against the wall. He waded in close, wrapped his arms around her body so that he could cup her wet breasts in his crossed hands, and allowed his spearing pride to dock between the girl's parted thighs.

It took only one hand, removed swiftly from the wall to dart below, for Annette to reach beneath her, seize this bursting stem and lodge it accurately within the space expressly designed to receive it.

For some while, only laboured breathing and the suck and slap of water were audible in the cubicle as the two lovers played their to and fro, reciprocating game.

But then Lionel locked his hands over her hips, dragging her backwards while he lowered himself to the step beneath the surface.

Seated on this porcelain shelf with the water above his belly, he continued to support Annette's weight at arm's length, positioning her carefully above that part of him which had been temporarily removed from its resting place during the manoeuvre.

Bending his arms slowly, he lowered her in turn, down towards the water, towards the engorged pink head of his maleness just visible breaking the foamy surface.

Annette shuddered with pleasure as the lips of her pussy, gaping already from its previous entry, closed over his rigid stalk.

He moved her up and down in a transport of delight, catching his breath each time the scalding clasp of her inner flesh, hotter even, it seemed, than the water in the tub, swallowed his whole hard length. His hands remained on her hips, his lips tasted the salt skin over her spine.

And then yet again there was a sudden change. Fishlike, the girl eeled from his grasp, sending a tidal wave crashing to the floor as she twisted completely around, squatting over his knees this time to face him, the upstanding staff re-locating as easily as a key in an oiled lock.

For perhaps two more minutes she rode him. . .and then, with an elbow on each side of the tub, she leaned back and away raising her legs to range one each side of his waist. She smiled slyly, rotating her hips, flexing the inner muscles of her belly so that even deep within her he was aware of a multiple caress.

The sight was too much for the young American. Breasts bobbing, buoyed up by the water. . .the creased curve of her wet belly. . .the lewd spread of her thighs. . .above all the vision of his own stout stem buried amongst floating hair, his finger parting the lips swallowing it to find the ultra-sensitive bud inside. . .all of these things, some shockingly vivid, some veiled by the opacity of the water, sent the blood thundering through his body and raised him to such a pitch of excitement that he feared he would burst.

He jerked, choking out some endearment. At the same time the lower half of Annette's frame convulsed. The ridged muscles within her clamped ferociously around him. She uttered a high, wailing cry as she was shaken by her release. Her arms flailed, showering water. One hand caught a length of chain, pulling the rubber bung free of the drain-hole in the bottom of the bath.

As the water gurgled down and away, Lionel's tribute to his love, triggered by her own galvanic reaction, gushed suddenly upwards and inwards in a paroxysm of delight.

'Nothing would please me better than to stay right here,' said Lionel the following morning. 'But, alas, I must leave you, at least for a couple of days because I have work to do.'

'And I have work to look for,' Annette said. 'Are you still investigating Paris low-life for your newspaper?'

He nodded. 'I have to meet this policeman, Morand, who has kindly agreed to show me around. He's a bit of a dull fellow, but I suspect he may have hidden depths.'

'I wouldn't be surprised!' Annette said viciously, recovering from the first shock of hearing her ex-lover's name pronounced by her present one.

Lionel looked at her curiously. 'You sound. . .Do you know him?'

'No!' she said. 'Not at all. No, I certainly do not!' She began throwing clothes and toilet articles into the new valise.

'Do you have a telephone, where you live?' he asked.

'Good gracious, no! This is not America, you know.'

'Then promise me you will call me at the Meurice. The day after tomorrow. About six. Or, if you cannot find a telephone, leave a message at the reception desk.' He smiled fondly. 'We have to meet again, my dearest. We must. And soon.'

She returned the smile. 'I promise.'

'Next time,' he told her, 'we shall talk about future plans!' He took her head in both hands and gazed into her eyes. 'I love you,' he said.

They left the hotel. On her way home, Annette stopped off at a stationer's shop and bought brown paper, string, and a small cardboard box. She took the blue teddy-bear she had won at the Neuilly fair from her valise, wrapped it up, and then went to a post office to mail the package to Commissaire Bruno Morand, care of the *Brigade des Moeurs*, at the Quai des Orfèvres.

There was no message with the parcel.

CHAPTER TWENTY-ONE

The man known as Turkey Phiz ducked out through the back door of the Red Rooster, ran past the outside privy and jumped up onto one of the galvanized trashcans ranged along the wall at the end of the yard. Panting heavily, he hauled himself to the top of the wall and jumped down into an alley on the far side. He continued to run.

The policeman, Morand, had just come into the Rooster with a foreigner, and the pickpocket could not afford to be seen there today. Three wallets, a gold pen and a couple of fob watches, recently handed over by his confederates, were stowed in his capacious pockets, along with a solid silver cigarette case he had lifted himself off a German tourist in the Gare St Lazare. Worse, the foreigner was the one whose gold hunter had been dipped while he was being questioned by the damned flatfoot in the exhibition.

The sooner he handed the spoils over to Lily Leblanc, swelling the already generous 'float' they had amassed, the better!

Turkey Phiz emerged breathless from the alley, dodged through the horse-drawn traffic circling the Place Blanche and laboured up the hill towards the Moulin de la Galette, where Lily would be waiting.

In the Red Rooster, apparently oblivious of the silence which had fallen the moment he entered, Bruno Morand swaggered up to the bar. 'A fine day, Mamma,' he said, glancing over his shoulder at the sunlit lane outside. 'Summer is going to be early this year. To celebrate it, I'll have a double *fine à l'eau*, with an absinthe for my friend here.'

The big woman behind the bar served the drinks without comment.

'A real thieves' kitchen, this,' Morand said to Lionel Giotto without troubling to lower his voice. 'More than half these rascals in here are permanently on the wrong side of the law.' He stared around the crowded room. 'What are they plotting today, Mamma? A Footpads' Union? A scheme to lift the gold reserves of the Banque de France? Some kind of blackmail plot with the help of their doxies?' He laughed boisterously.

The owner of the Red Rooster was swabbing the bar with a damp cloth. 'My clients pay with good money for what they consume,' she said. 'I don't concern myself with their private lives or their morals. That's none of my business.'

'Spoken like a true businesswoman,' Morand said. He drained his glass and set it on the counter. 'Talking of which, we ourselves have a little matter to discuss. Perhaps it would be best if we went upstairs?'

He nodded to the American, murmured 'Give me two minutes', and lifted the flap to follow the woman through the door behind the bar.

Embarrassed, Lionel concentrated his attention on the fiery aniseed drink, aware of the sullen, low-voiced muttering which swelled into a growl of suppressed menace the moment the Commissaire disappeared. It was in this very bar that he had caught that fleeting glance of Annette while he was still searching for her. What could she have been doing in such a place? He must remember, as a matter of interest, to ask.

What, for that matter, had he been doing himself? He was taking notes for a descriptive article on lower Montmartre, in premises recommended by Morand, alone at that time, so that he could savour the atmosphere of the place with no police around, see the inmates in their natural habitat. But it certainly couldn't be the natural habitat of the girl he had then known as the Comtesse van den Bergh! She had, he recalled, collected an envelope from the dark girl he had met after Aristide Bruant's performance. A prostitute, that one, or at any rate an ex-prostitute. What could she have for Annette? Maybe she was an ex-dancer, too, and the envelope contained an introduction to an impresario who could provide work?

Well, she wouldn't have to run herself into the ground any more in search of dancing jobs when he got her back to the United States: Giotto wives were not expected to work!

Morand was coming back down the stairs. . .and oddly enough he, too, was handling an envelope, stuffing it into an inside pocket. Lionel doubted very much that it was an introduction to someone who could offer him work as a dancer.

He felt happier at the next stop on Morand's daily round — a gloomy tavern near the Bourse, panelled in dark wood, with oaken tables and brass-buttoned leather chairs. But despite the funereal aspect of the place there was an air of purpose among the clientele — mainly whiskered, sober-looking men with starched collars — and the low hum of conversation was sober too, and serious.

'As bad as the rabble at the Rooster,' the Commissaire confided, 'but higher up the scale, if you follow me.'

Lionel looked surprised. He didn't follow.

'Counterfeiters, forgers, confidence tricksters of one

kind or another, half of them,' Morand explained. 'The other half are clerks from the Bourse, selling them secret information about movements in the stock market, proposed mergers, fiscal decisions and that sort of thing.'

Lionel frowned. 'But I cannot see why coiners of false money – ?'

'Oh, Lord,' the Commissaire interrupted, 'don't run away with the idea counterfeiters only forge money! Much the greater part of their trade has to do with documents: stocks, bonds, promissory notes, certificates of one kind or another. But they are a pretty dull lot today. I'll just have a word with the *patron*, then I'll take you to a brasserie where the fur really flies! The place where the radicals, the politicos, the agitators and the anarchists congregate to shout their abuse! You'll find plenty of good copy there. Throw a bomb at you as soon as look at you, some of those fellows would.'

They had left the tavern and were waiting on the corner of the Rue de Richelieu for a cab when Lionel saw a liveried carriage draw up on the far side of the street, and two ladies, handed out by the coachman, walk into an imposing mansion with a flower-decked courtyard.

'My goodness,' he exclaimed, 'what a coincidence!'

'Coincidence? What is? What do you mean?'

'Nothing really. Just a surprise.' He indicated the carriage pulling away from the kerb as the coachman whipped up the horses. 'Two people I happen to know went into that house. A friend called Annette de Vervialle and the Comtesse van den Bergh.'

'Annette de Vervialle!' Morand repeated. 'You know that hussy?'

'I know her, certainly. I am not sure that I like – '

'Keep away from her if you want to keep clean,' Morand said venomously.

Lionel stared at him.

'You're in the right company if you want to know about low life, I'll admit,' Morand grated. 'But I'd keep away from her if I were you. She's a real bad lot, that one.'

'We cannot be talking about the same person, Commissaire. The lady I mean is Mademoiselle Annette de Vervialle. A dancer. I believe she once starred at the Moulin Rouge. A. . .very well-shaped person with auburn hair.'

'There's no mistake. She was once a hoofer in the back row, yes. But she got thrown out because she was on the make. On the game, too, as it happens, until we netted her in one of the vice squad clean-ups.'

'What do you mean?' Lionel said heatedly. 'This lady is a friend of mine, and I protest most violently at the implications of – '

'A friend you say? Then I'd suggest, Monsieur, that your sights are set rather low for a man of your station.' The Commissaire's voice grew more vindictive with every phrase. 'She may do her best to hide it, with all her la-di-da airs and graces, but when you come down to it she's no more than a cheap prostitute with pretensions to – '

'Stop! How dare you say that? I don't believe it for one moment!' Lionel cried.

'You don't believe what? That the girl's a common tart?'

'I don't believe any of it. Especially that she's a. . .prostitute.'

Morand's demeanour had become almost aggressive, but now suddenly he cooled down. 'Well that, as it happens, I can prove,' he said calmly.

'I challenge you to do so!' Lionel shouted. 'And I warn you, there will be action taken for defamation if – '

'Very well,' Morand cut in, 'we shall go to the

Commissariat of the VIIIth Arondissement and you will see for yourself.'

The cab ride passed in frosty silence.

In the square outside the police station, a party of children, supervised by a governess, chattered and shrieked in the dappled sunlight beneath the trees. Two uniformed *agents* snapped to attention and saluted as Morand took the steps leading to the entrance two at a time.

Inside the charge room, a bulky, red-faced man with side whiskers was talking to the desk sergeant. He wore a loud check suit, a hard hat with a curly brim and highly polished black boots. '*Bonjour, Monsieur le Commissaire*,' the two men said in unison.

Morand nodded. He turned and said to Lionel: 'Inspector Rochard, my assistant. I don't think you have met before. Rochard, this is Doctor Giotto, the American writer I told you about.'

Lionel inclined his head, wondering if he was supposed to shake the Inspector's hand. He was too angry to worry about it.

'Doctor Giotto doubts my word concerning the reputation of one of our fancy ladies,' Morand said. 'The one calling herself de Vervialle.'

'What, that little vixen?' Rochard exploded. 'Why, she's one of the worst, if you ask me!'

Before Lionel could say anything, Morand turned to the desk. 'Sergeant, we want the day book for, let me see, yes. . .April 14th, the day the exhibition opened. Charge sheets on the night shift.'

The sergeant climbed down from his stool and opened a wooden cupboard, one of six ranged against the flaking plaster wall. He took a heavy leather-bound ledger from a shelf inside and carried it to a table beneath the window. He opened the book and rifled through the thick pages until he located the right date. Morand leaned over his shoulder, scanning the lines of spiky handwriting. 'There!' The Commissaire's index finger stabbed down on an entry at the foot of the long page. 'Among the catch netted by Dulac's team.' He turned to Lionel. 'Here. See for yourself.'

Lionel didn't want to look. But the clerkish desk sergeant on the April 14th night shift had a scholarly copperplate hand. Among the Berthes and Jacquis and Lilys and Fifis, the name Annette leaped out at him like a beacon.

Annette de Vervialle. Fifty francs.

The young American was stunned. He couldn't believe it. He raised his eyes from the book and looked out of the grimy window. Sunlight still slanted through the trees in the square; the children were still playing. The world outside had not changed.

'Bring the card,' Rochard told the sergeant.

'Why fifty for her and only twenty or thirty for the others?' Lionel asked dully. It was all he could think of to say.

'She was disorderly,' Rochard said. 'She was kept in the cells all night.'

'*Disorderly?* Mademoiselle de Vervialle?'

The inspector held out his hand. The sergeant, who had opened a box file on his desk, handed him a slip of pasteboard.

'De Vervialle, Annette, known as,' the policeman read out. 'Real name Durand. Father, Armand Durand, a silversmith, deceased. Mother, Marie-Thérèse, laundrywoman, maiden name Fournier, deceased. Arrested along with other prostitutes in the Rue Rudolphe Laporte. Charged with, one, open soliciting on the street; two. . .but here, you can read it for yourself.' He passed the card to Lionel.

Dazedly, he read the damning words, the testimony of the arresting officers. *Operating from unlicensed premises. . .loitering in a darkened doorway. . .a lewd display of her body to passers-by. . .abusive and obstructive in the charge room . . .*

No, he could not believe it! Yet there it was in black and white, in the official records. There could be no mistake.

Or could there?

Could the whole thing be a trick? Some kind of forgery, a set-up concocted by the three policemen? Impossible. He was only here by chance, as the result of an argument after he had happened to see Annette in the street. Nobody could possibly have known he would ever come to this sleazy precinct house, and there was no way Morand could have contacted the other two during the short trip from the Rue de Richelieu. In any case, what would be the point?

Shaken to the core by the police revelations, he found certain situations, certain phrases, rising unbidden to the turbulent surface of his memory.

He had himself seen her amongst the low-life customers of the Red Rooster. He knew that she knew the ex-prostitute, Lily.

He could hear the voice. *A new me, separate from the old one. . .I dare not take the risk of anything spoiling it* — that was when she refused to allow him to escort her home or even reveal her address. Was there a ponce, a *maquereau* waiting there?

Most damning of all: *in my profession, one is always crossing the city alone after dark.*

He had thought she meant her profession as a dancer.

The woman he had dreamed of as his future wife!

'I am extremely sorry, Doctor,' Morand began suavely, 'if this has been a shock to you. But I thought it best . . .'

He left the sentence unfinished. The American had turned on his heel and walked blindly from the room without a word. They saw him run down the steps, cross the square, and vanish down a side street on the far side.

A little girl in a straw hat, standing with a hoop by the railings, turned to the governess and asked: 'Mademoiselle, why was that gentleman crying?'

In the charge room, Morand and Rochard exchanged glances. To each in his own way it was essential that Annette de Vervialle be discredited. For the Inspector, it was simply a matter of revenge after the double affront to his male pride. Morand's case was stronger. Not only had the little bitch refused point-blank to sleep with him any more; she was also a witness to the fact that he was on the take, that he received regular payoffs from brothel keepers and the owners of bars and drinking dens all over town. Worse, on at least one occasion she had seen him put the bite on a senator who wanted the details of his extra-marital activities kept secret.

How fortunate for both of them, he thought, that the recent archives of this station held documents that could be interpreted in more than one way.

Annette de Vervialle, approaching the Hotel Meurice at five minutes to six o'clock, threaded her way through the crowds thronging the pavement with a light heart. She was wearing a new dress, the evening was warm, the sky above the boulevard's mansard roofs still blue. She was happy, humming one of Monsieur Offenbach's latest airs as she ran up the steps beneath the hotel's glass entrance canopy.

A night and two whole days without Lionel had seemed an eternity. But now she was going to see him again and everything would be all right.

'I am sorry, Mademoiselle,' the receptionist behind the

desk informed her, 'but Doctor Giotto checked out two hours ago.'

'Checked *out*?' She was dumbfounded. 'But why? Where did he go? I do not understand.'

'I am afraid I cannot say, Mademoiselle. The Doctor did not leave a forwarding address. However . . .' The man turned to the rows of pigeonholes behind him, then looked back over his shoulder. 'Would you be Mademoiselle de Vervialle?'

Annette nodded, her throat suddenly and unaccountably dry.

'In that case, I have a message for you.' The receptionist handed her a sealed envelope franked with the hotel crest.

She sank into an armchair on the far side of the busy lobby and tore open the flap with trembling fingers. The unsigned message read:

In view of her professional activities, Dr Lionel Giotto feels that he can no longer with decency permit himself to monopolize Mademoiselle Annette Durand's valuable time.

Part Four

Merry-Go-Round

CHAPTER TWENTY-TWO

Shocked and dismayed more than he could tell by the revelations of Commissaire Morand and his assistant, Lionel Giotto plunged himself into the low life of the capital. It was after all, he told himself, necessary as authentic background to his articles.

He had used the argument to justify his libidinous adventures before, but this time there was an added, a more personal inducement: if it was acceptable for the woman he had once considered fit to share his name to be part of the Paris *demi-monde*, why should he too not share at least a taste of the seedy life she had chosen?

The thinking was woolly and the reasoning specious, but the hurt was deep and it was compounded each time he endeavoured to put Annette out of his mind by memories which seemed to do nothing but confirm Morand and Rochard's estimation of the girl. Why, for instance, had she been at the house in the Avenue Kléber, masquerading as its mistress? How was it that, for a person of her age, she had such a fund of sexual expertise, such an overwhelming sense of abandon? It did not occur to him that this could be a natural adventurousness, stimulated by their mutual attraction, and he never thought of querying Morand's original premise: he wouldn't know where to begin.

His slumming-on-the-rebound took him first to such notorious places of assignation as the *promenoir* of the

Folies and the Moulin Rouge garden, the *brasseries des filles* in the Boulevard Poissonière and the café-concerts among the trees off the Champs Elysées.

He discovered several more Montmartre hotels, some almost respectable, some sleazy, in the company of the more stunning among the 800 women permitted to promenade in the folies. He even essayed a second night with voluptuous, warm-hearted Nellie. But this time her caresses seemed mechanical, the hot coupling of their bodies no more than the satisfaction of an appetite.

Brief encounters with brasserie girls left him unsatisfied.

A quick survey of the women seated in the garden of the Moulin Rouge, some of them graceless trollops not yet eighteen years old, left him with nothing but an acute pang of loss, remembering the beauty who once pirouetted within the *Bal*.

Dancing at a riverside guingette outside the Neuilly fair, he found himself with an Armenian slut who slung her belly against him like a sack of ripe corn, tempted him to a gipsy caravan with lewd promises, and refused to accept money two hours later when he left limp and exhausted. Penetrating deep within the coarse thatch covering her loins, rolled like a ship at sea between her big, loose breasts, he forgot for a space of time his anguish in the exertions of lust. It was only later, waiting for a boat to take him upriver, that he realized why she had refused money: there would have been none to give her; his pockets had been rifled by a confederate while he was clenched in her fiery embrace.

He was living a wild life. It was gay, it was exciting in a way, it filled the long hours of the day and night. But it was not enough. Not enough to replace Annette de Vervialle and the dream future she represented for him. Lionel's spirits flagged. He thought of returning home and handing over the journalistic job to a junior.

Then, one night, a chance acquaintance from the American Consulate said to him: 'You're wasting your time, friend, prospecting among the burlesque queens at the Folies and the pick-ups one finds at Neuilly. Do you never go to Maxim's?'

Giotto shook his head.

'Good God, man, that's the only place if you want to live! Why the women there . . .' The diplomat shook his own head, at a loss for words.

'I thought they all. . .well, belonged to someone. That is . . .'

'Even if they did, just seeing them would be worth whole nights abed with these other janes. But their protectors are not in town all the time. Some of them are always ready for a little extra-mural activity . . .You want to go there between eight and ten.' He laid a white-gloved finger alongside his nose. 'And if you want your card marked, if you want a table among the rich and the infamous, a place where you can join the fun, a fifty-franc note into the hand of Ugo is a wise precaution.'

'Ugo?'

'The senior Maitre D. If Ugo is happy, Gustave Cornuché, the manager, will see you right. You'll be well looked after.'

'I shall go tomorrow,' Lionel promised.

Maxim's, a later generation would say, was jumping. The place, decorated in the latest Art Nouveau style, where every drooping curve suggests the anatomy of a woman, was all scintillating crystal reflected in kidney-shaped mirrors. Lily flowers and acanthus leaves cut from brass twined over the rich mahogany panelling the walls. The atmosphere was heavy with the fragrance of wine cooking and expensive cigars.

Cornuché advised against the main dining room. That

was for the rich and staid. He installed the American at one end of the more intimate, more fashionable 'omnibus' — so called because the facing banquettes, with their velvet, crushed-strawberry upholstery, were arranged on either side of a long central gangway. Here, just through the bar at the entrance, Lionel was astonished to see the victims lampooned by France's celebrated cartoonists and caricaturists — suddenly endowed with three dimensions, fleshed out with bones and sinews and facile smiles.

He saw Jean Lorrain, the famous journalist who aped the foppish manners of Oscar Wilde, sculptor Falguière dining the curvaceous Cléo de Mérode, even Otéro with her smouldering eyes and the notorious twelve-string pearl choker. He saw Caran d'Ache, with a huge sketch pad propped up on the table, dashing off a charcoal portrait of a girl whose black hair hung down to her waist. He saw Gilda Darthy and Arlette Dorgère and a dozen other exquisitely painted courtesans and stars of the music-hall with daringly exposed bosoms and jewel-encrusted dresses that sheathed them like the armour of a medieval knight. And alone in a corner, half reclining on a chaise longue beneath a potted palm, he saw the incomparable Liane de Pougy.

Lionel's heart was thudding behind the starched front of his dress shirt. He thought he had never seen a human being of such rarefied beauty. She looked as delicate, as though she might snap as easily, as the stem of a Lalique glass. Lorrain, he remembered, had written once that her figure was so perfectly sculptured that it drew the attention away from the flawless symmetry of her features.

But Lorrain himself had now moved. He was sitting, with several other men, at Caroline Otéro's table. The Spanish dancer, big teeth dazzling, magnificent eyes flashing, was finishing her third plate of duck *à la Rouennaise*, wiping up the remains of the thick dark blood sauce with a chunk of bread. Lionel recalled that Colette had described her as 'selfish as well as greedy' – an egoist whose self-indulgence extended from the acquisition of jewels to gluttony, from the condescension with which she treated her lovers to the pleasure she took in her art. She would dance as much for love as for money. That was why her tempestuous temperament was tolerated, because her explosive performances – for her own enjoyment rather than the audience's – were unique.

It was clear that something of the kind was expected now, for the admirers clustered around her were clamouring excitedly. Boisterous laughter drowned the hum of conversation and the discreet tinkle of cutlery from the other tables in the omnibus. Someone shouted an encouragement.

Otéro spooned up three scoops of chocolate ice cream, swallowed a large cupful of coffee, and rose abruptly to her feet.

There was a burst of applause. Waiters rushed forward to whisk the dishes from the table. A man dressed in a gipsy costume hurried in from the dining room carrying a Spanish guitar.

The dancer leaped onto the table top, fixing a pair of castanets to her thumbs. She was wearing a heavy, flared brocade skirt in crimson, with a low-cut corsage so closely patterned with jewels that the basic colour was masked by flashes of fire beneath the glittering chandeliers.

Otéro stamped her heel three separate times, shouting: '*Ha!. . .Ha!. . .Ha!*' in three explosive exclamations. The guitarist fingered an arpeggio. Men standing around the table called '*Olé*!' And she whirled at once into a violent, foot-tapping, finger-snapping fandango, one arm snaked above and behind her head, the hand of the other cocked insolently on one hip.

Customers crowded in from the dining room. One or two dandies and their disdainful cocottes ostentatiously left. Others stood on their own tables to watch. Liane de Pougy ordered a glass of seltzer.

Otéro's splendid teeth flashed; her head was tilted back and her brilliant eyes half closed. She was singing with the throb of the music now, increasing the tempo, the castanets chattering around the threshing of her hips. Her familiars started a rhythmic clapping in counterpoint to the clack of her heels.

The brocade skirt was unfastened and tossed aside. The crowd yelled. The dancing grew wilder, more passionate. After ten minutes she paused, snatching up a sauce-stained table napkin to mop her face, neck and moist armpits. . .and then — applause, whistles and well-bred cheers — she was off again with a drumroll of the heels, her fine lawn petticoat clinging to her sweat-drenched hips, the swaying furrow of her bare back and the muscles of her waist rippling over those powerful loins. The strumming of the guitar rose to a crescendo.

Lionel had remained seated, fascinated by the savage performance but with half his attention still covertly drawn by the statuesque pose of Liane de Pougy.

The difference between the two beautiful women could scarcely have been more pronounced. Liane de Pougy, still elegantly draped over her chaise longue, had moved nothing but her head since Otéro left her seat. Occasionally she allowed herself a languid glance around the rest of the room. Once, Lionel thought, just for an instant, their eyes met — the courtesan's arched eyebrow raised a supercilious eighth of an inch, one corner of the mouth lifted in an infinitesimal half-smile. But then she was gazing past him, at an expensively dressed couple sweeping in from the bar.

Cornuché was standing by his side.

'In view of Monsieur's earlier and discreet inquiries,' he murmured below the racket from Otéro's table, 'there is a possibility, no more than that, that an introduction could be effected with Madame de Pougy . . .'

'*Madame de Pougy?*' Lionel's heart beat crazily. 'You mean that she is. . .*disponible?*'

'*Disponible, je ne sais pas. Mais accessible, oui,*' Cornuché replied. 'Available, I'm not sure. But approachable, yes.'

'How should such an approach be made?' The American's throat was dry. He looked hungrily towards the chaise longue, but Liane de Pougy was displaying an intense interest in the leaves of the potted palm. The quizzical half-smile, nevertheless, was definitely in place. 'You would not find me ungrateful if you could arrange it,' he said.

'I will do my best,' Cornuché said, palming the folded note he was offered. 'In the case, however, of a positive reply, there are certain points − if Monsieur will permit me − to be remembered.'

'Of course,' Lionel said. 'Go ahead. I don't know the rules.'

The manager coughed, twirling the waxed ends of his moustache. His brilliantined head, the dark hair parted in the centre, was bent low. 'Madame de Pougy's current . . .companion. . .the Arch-Duke, is absent for three days in Vienna,' he said in a low voice. 'If she were to agree, it would be on the strict understanding that any. . .liaison . . .should encompass the remainder of tonight and those two other days, no less. And of course no more.'

'No problem. *I should be so lucky!*' Lionel added in American.

'It would of course be impossible for Madame to receive you in the apartment – ah – reserved for the Arch-Duke. My advice would be to choose the Chabernais. It is comfortable and discreet. Madame Kelly is an admirable hostess.'

'The Chabanais. Thank you. I will not forget.'

'And finally, I have to inform Monsieur that it is considered not at all chic to mention the subject of money.'

'Not to mention . . .? But then how can I . . .?'

'Monsieur may rest assured that Madame will make things quite clear in her own inimitable way,' Cornuché said.

Three minutes later the young American, overcome with delight, was brushing with his lips the hand of the most desired woman in all of Paris.

The reception hall of the Chabanais, most luxurious of the city's houses of assignation, was flamboyant in its opulence. Antique furniture islanded the white fur rugs strewing the floor; black marble fauns flanked a carved unicorn which had once graced a Neapolitan roundabout; rich woods inlaid with gilt arabesques reflected the light from glittering candelabra.

Madame Kelly was a stouter version of Madame Renée in the Rue de Monthyon, with red hair piled on top of her head in a bun. Diamonds winked from heavy gold rings on all four fingers of her left hand and two on her right. 'Sometimes,' Liane said, handing her ermine cape to a discreetly gowned receptionist, 'I like to relax in the cabin – but not, I think, tonight.'

'The cabin?' Lionel queried.

'A *retiro* fashioned to resemble the stateroom of an ocean liner. The walls, hung with canvas, carry ropes and pulleys holding up sails which act as curtains. There are fishnets and glass floats, and the bed is a huge hammock — so that the slightest movement therein reproduces the rolling motion of a ship. It is amusing. . .but more to the taste, perhaps, of those intimate for a long time. You and I, *cher ami*, are after all but novices one with the other!'

'Madame,' said Lionel gallantly, 'out of all the words recorded in every dictionary, novice is the very last I would choose to apply to yourself.'

She smiled, expecting the compliment. 'Monsieur is chivalrous.' And then tucking jewelled fingers under his arm: 'You are not by chance English?'

He shook his head. 'American.'

'Ah. Then you will not be attracted by what we here call "The English Vice". A pity in a way. Madame Kelly prides herself on offering below what she terms "the prettiest torture chamber in France". Is that not so, Madame?'

'So the dominatrices and their slaves tell me,' the red-haired woman smiled, revealing a lot more gold in her mouth. 'Now what would be your pleasure tonight?'

The courtesan tilted an imperious chin. 'We shall take the Raphael Room. If it is available of course.'

'For you, Liane, it is always available.' Madame Kelly snapped her fingers. 'Séverine: take Monsieur and Madame upstairs.'

The darkened chamber, carpeted in black and gold, was hung with leaf-patterned drapes woven in imitation of the quattrocento master's background to his world-famous portrait of *La Fornarina* — The Baker's Daughter. The enormous bed, of ginger-wood inlaid with Renaissance motifs in ivory, sported a headboard carved in the shape of a Palladian facade. Above this was a painted copy of La Fornarina herself, holding out one naked breast and gazing down at the ecstatic occupants with her fathomless Machiavellian smile.

Lionel's hands were already trembling as he feasted his eyes on the famous courtesan's statuesque figure reflected in the huge mirror opposite this bed. Words of admiration and adoration choked in his throat as he started towards her.

She held him off with a stately gloved hand. 'Not too fast, my friend. It requires a refined hors-d'oeuvre to honour the delicacies that may follow!'

The hors-d'oeuvre was refined indeed. He had been so dazzled by the total effect of Liane de Pougy, so overcome by the realization that this magnificent symbol of femininity, the playmate of arch-dukes and kings and the princes of commerce, was his for three whole days that he had somehow neglected the details of her actual appearance, overlooking the parts, as it were, in favour of the whole.

She was of medium height, with a superbly upright carriage, a long straight nose and chiselled, curling lips of infinite promise. A halo of very dark hair, shorter than was customary, framed her heart-shaped face.

Her taffeta dress was corn-coloured, encrusted with precious stones around the corsage, with enormous leg-of-mutton sleeves that narrowed to a tight wrist. The hem of the voluminous panelled skirt was raised in front to reveal a heavy wine-red organdie underskirt patterned with appliqué flowers in rhinestones.

Privileged to remove her wide velvet hat with its decorations of fruit and then unpin her hair, Lionel felt himself palpitating with desire as he cautiously unhooked the back of the dress. The wide expanse of satiny flesh exposed by her low-cut neckline, the smooth swelling slopes whose tips were only just concealed by the jewelled material, promised that the pampered, perfumed body beneath this finery would be more marvellous even than he had imagined. The hard thrust of his virility against the tight striped trousers he wore below his black frock-coat was already becoming uncomfortable.

She turned towards him, raising both arms above her head as she stretched luxuriously. The movement displaced her breasts, and one purplish sun rose above a horizon already fiery with gems. 'And now,' she said, 'a quick bath and we can start exploring one another's secrets.' She let her arms fall. The sun sank. She vanished into the steamy fragrance of the *salle de bains*.

'I shall expect to see you unclothed when I return,' she called.

She herself was wearing no more than a flimsy kimono when she did return — a wisp of black silk embroidered on the back with a golden horse in the rampant pose. He was standing by the bed's Palladian headboard. 'My goodness,' she said, 'His Highness down there is certainly on his mark, set, and ready to go! Let us hope that he is a devotee of the marathon rather than a mere sprinter!'

'He runs to order,' Lionel said. 'Whatever his trainer demands, he will do his best to satisfy.'

'Splendid. An admirable arrangement. On second thoughts, nevertheless — Madame Kelly should be sending up champagne shortly; Bollinger '88, I trust — might it not be wiser to invest in a trial run first?'

'My feeling exactly,' said Lionel. His heart was beating so fast, he could scarcely get the words out.

She lowered herself then to the huge bed and stretched languorously the whole length of her supple body. The edges of the kimono fell apart, and he saw with a thrill of pure delight the incomparable sweep of her tapered thighs, a tiny, firm, scooped-out waist, taut high-set breasts that in their small perfection were as delicate and tempting as those of a virgin. Between her thighs the ebony fur had been cut short and then shaved to the form of a heart, whose tip pointed invitingly to those twin portals whose opening allowed access to the hot clasp of the Venus who was queen of the temple within.

She reached for him, wrapping cool fingers around his stiffened part, and he cast himself down beside her. Already, between pink lips half parted in anticipation, a single pearl of moisture gleamed, more perfect in its lustre and symmetry than any jewel on the clothes she had cast off. In tribute to the matchless fashioning of such a gem, he lowered his head to her loins and introduced the tip of his tongue to the tender bud sprouting beneath it.

Through his impassioned kissing flowed the entire flood of his devotion to the ideal of womanhood that she represented. But soon the sighs and moans of pleasure that he heard above his head changed to a more questioning note.

He heard her say softly — in the tone of friendly raillery she used throughout their association — 'The stable doors are open my friend; it is warm within. Perhaps your cavalier would like now to canter inside, to slam, if you like, his sword into a suitable scabbard? Meanwhile, there are other lips up here that require your attention.'

Lionel needed no further invitation. In a trice he had her clasped in his arms, his lips smothering with a hundred, a thousand kisses her neck, her mouth, her deliciously pointed little breasts. 'My princess,' he gasped hoarsely, 'you are so absolutely, so uniquely . . .I never thought . . .How could I ever . . .?'

She closed his mouth with a reproving finger. 'The time for talking, *cher ami*' she told him, 'is afterwards!'

She was, he sensed at once, incredibly expert, each

movement of every muscle coordinated in a choreography that seemed both to stimulate and be stimulated by the wordless murmurations it provoked.

The brush of one silken leg across the hairs on his calf, the sudden thrust of a warm belly against his hip, the manipulations of those practised hands over his secret parts – pumping him up always almost to the point of explosion but never, ever crossing the hairs-breadth gap that would be one stroke too far – all these ministrations lifted the young American to such a frenzy of sensual awareness, such a pitch of pure excitement, that when at last her fingers guided him inside the warm haven of her body, it was as though the last barriers blocking the entry to paradise had been forced and now there was nowhere to go but on.

The long, shared voyage of physical union that followed left them stranded, after a tempest of mutual ecstasy, on the calm, quiet shore of satisfied desire.

It was after a servant had knocked and deposited an ice bucket carrying a magnum of champagne that she said to him: 'That was incomparable! What a good lover you are. I am pleased now that Cornuché had the wit to present you.'

Lionel was too happy, too satisfied and gratified to make any coherent reply.

But before she had finished her second glass of champagne, she was up again, throwing an elegant leg across him and then straddling his hips as he lay on his back, staring up the subtle planes of belly and bosom to her perfectly formed breasts and the provocative mouth he could see between them.

The short upper lip lifted, the mouth smiled. 'We were talking of athletics,' she said. 'Now perhaps it is my turn to – shall we say? – hold the reins. For I have decided that the sport this time shall move into the equestrian sphere. Like the *Amazones* in the Bois, I shall make you my personal steed and ride you to death!'

It was as she seized his already rigid part and moved it towards her own welcoming clasp that he noticed for the first time her slender feet − drawn up beside his hips in those non-existent stirrups he seemed to have worn ever since he arrived in Paris.

She wore emerald rings on her toes!

Seeing his astonished glance as she rose and fell in those invisible stirrups, she laughed aloud, a honeyed sound as mellow as her speech. 'My rings? They are what you Americans call my trademark, *n'est-ce pas?* But I only wear them when I am in bed and happy.'

He frowned. 'But. . .there are only nine? The middle toe on your left foot lacks an emerald.'

'I know,' she sighed. 'Losing that one was a tragedy. I am always hoping that some friend will be kind enough to find me another.'

Arching his hips to meet her thrusts, Lionel nodded. He knew now what Cornuché had meant when he said that Liane would 'make things quite clear in her own inimitable way'.

CHAPTER TWENTY-THREE

Outrage, disillusion, a sense of betrayal, and despair warred for precedence in Annette de Vervialle's mind once she had digested the implications of Lionel's cold, impersonal rejection.

There was no place for doubt. The fact that he had deliberately used her baptismal name rather than the one he knew her by was itself an indication that he had seen the damning material on file at the police station of the VIIIth Arrondissement. There was nowhere else he could have stumbled on the name Durand.

No doubt either about who must have shown it to him.

Instead of erasing the misleading and untrue entries in the vice squad files, instead of destroying altogether her dossier as he had once promised, Morand — out of rage and spite and wounded pride, no doubt — had used them to break up her relationship with Lionel Giotto. That he had believed the 'evidence' was obvious: the use of the phrase 'professional activities' in his note proved that.

How had the Commissaire known that there was a relationship to destroy? That, too, was easy enough to divine. It was natural enough, as the two men were in a sense working together, that the American might have mentioned the girl who occupied so much of his thoughts. Natural, given the policeman's egocentric character, that he would vindictively deny to another what was no longer available to him.

Explanation of Lionel's behaviour this might be, but it was not an excuse. The hurt, the fact that she had been condemned with no opportunity to defend herself, ran deep.

She walked out of the Meurice and took the first side road she came to, wandering through a network of lanes that led towards the river, not caring where she went until she found herself unexpectedly in front of the main entrance to the exhibition. The sun had set and the lights glittering on each side of the main avenue sparkled like jewels through the tears filling her eyes. The thoroughfare was crowded. There was movement and noise and a distant blare of music in there. Anything was better than being left alone with her bitterness and the pain of memory. She paid the entrance fee and walked through Binet's flamboyant arch.

For a while she meandered this way and that, oblivious to the raucous sideshows, the gaping crowds, the click and ticking of machines jerking forever in their glass display cases on each side of the long cool alleys traversing the scientific pavilions. Then, aware suddenly that despite her distress she was ravenously hungry, she walked out into the shining night and headed for a riverside stall selling hot sausages and salad rolls.

'Annette! What a marvellous surprise! My dearest, how are you?' The soft voice came from a park bench she had just passed.

She swung around. Already on her feet, Lucie Clément stood there with her arms held wide.

Annette burst into tears and ran into her friend's embrace.

Thirty minutes later, when she had poured out the whole sad story and Lucie had been properly sympathetic, she ended: 'And almost the worst part of it is that I *still* have no work; I have been too busy day-dreaming about impossible futures to bother about it. And now the money from this. . .well, this rather dubious affair I told you about. . .is coming to an end, and I don't know what to do.'

'But you should contact Lily Leblanc again,' Lucie said. 'She has something much more important in mind it seems. Maybe you could help.'

Annette stared at her. 'But. . .I never mentioned Lily's name to you! How could you have known . . .?'

Lucie smiled.

'Wait a minute!' Annette exclaimed – they were eating bacon rolls and drinking coffee in the Danish pavilion – '*Wait* a minute! You're a midinette; you work for Landolff. Do you mean to tell me. . .are you saying that you are one of the girls who. . .one of the girls who smuggled out those beautiful dresses for us to wear for Lily's first venture into the field of crime?'

Lucie nodded.

'But that means. . .Lucy said they had to have a lever, they had to know something, well, discreditable about the girls before they could persuade them to "borrow" the clothes. Blackmail them, in fact.'

'That's right.'

'Oh, Lucie. My dear friend! Does that mean that you too – ?'

The pretty midinette gestured helplessly. 'Landolff does not pay a fortune. Life becomes dearer and dearer. It was only occasionally. And at least one can pick and choose. One is not on the street.'

'Then where . . .? How do you . . .?' Despite the fact that she was shocked, even outraged, by a disclosure that ran so much counter to her own convictions, Annette was intrigued. She had seen enough, heard enough and learned enough while she was with Morand not to draw too definite a line, not to be too hasty to condemn, to catalogue people into compartments such as the good, the bad and the merely stupid.

'I go to Maxim's,' Lucie said, 'when I need to. Are you shocked? Do you hate me?'

'No,' Annette said decisively. 'Only sad that you have to.' She paused. 'But. . .Maxim's? I thought the *grandes horizontales*. . .I mean I thought only the famous courtesans and the men who kept them went there. I didn't think you could use the place. . .what I should say is I believed only couples . . .' She stopped, confused.

'You mean you didn't think it could be used as a pick-up joint?' Lucie smiled. 'Well of course it can't in the normal way. But there are always a few gentlemen hoping to nab one of the cocottes on an off day. . .and who will happily look elsewhere when they find they cannot. You won't get a seat in the omnibus, of course, But there's a back room. Or one can always have a drink in the bar, sit there at a table in the entrance if one goes early enough.'

Lucie finished her coffee and set the cup down carefully in its saucer. 'As it happens,' she said casually, 'I was going there myself tonight. Why don't you come with me?'

'Oh, Lucie, I couldn't. It's not my . . .No, I couldn't, really.'

'Why not?' Lucie said fiercely. 'After what's happened to you, after the way you've been treated, who do you owe anything to? Who are you trying to fool? After all, you can always say no. And it looks better with two. There's this fellow I'm meeting who has a friend –'

Annette shook her head. 'You've heard me go on often enough,' she said. 'You know how I feel about women who are forced to earn. . .no offence to you, dearest, of course. . .but since my own convictions are –'

'What about women who are forced to impersonate

ladies of rank so that they can steal trinkets?' Lucie interrupted hotly. 'No offence to you, dearest, of course.'

The shaft went home. Annette bit her lip. Her eyes filled again with tears.

'I'm sorry,' Lucie said. 'Look, let us not quarrel.' She laid gloved fingers on her friend's arm. 'Life is already too difficult. And we are in the same boat, after all. One way or another. At least come and have a drink with us. You are not committing yourself to anything. You can leave whenever you want to. And Maxim's is amusing, even if one is just watching.'

'No, Lucie,' Annette said firmly. 'I really cannot.'

The two girls found a bar table from which they could see the strollers on the sidewalk and the traffic in the Rue Royale as well as observe the fabulous creatures and their dandyfied escorts who started to come in around ten o'clock to compete for places in the omnibus.

Annette was excited in spite of herself. 'Oh, Lucie — *look* at that dress!' she breathed. 'It must be from Worth or Paquin. Can all those stones be real? . . .Isn't that the deputy who is supposed to be having an affaire with the wife of — Now I swear that must be Polaire: the little one with the beehive hair. They say she has a fifteen-and-a-half-inch waist! Can you *imagine* the corset!'

Lucie's friend was an industrialist from Lyon. The man with him was English. He was introduced as Hector Champney, a photographer. He was a tall, sandy fellow, prematurely balding, with a heavy moustache and prominent blue eyes. He was in Paris, he said, on a pioneer assignment: to take aerial pictures of the exhibition from a Montgolfier hot-air balloon. There was in addition the possibility of a contract with an American newspaper, illustrating the articles some special correspondent would be writing.

Annette liked him well enough. He was polite, with a high, drawling delivery that made her laugh when he tried to communicate with the waiter in his halting, villainously accented French. The industrialist was a thickset man of fifty, with a pink face and a complacent expression, very sure of himself behind gold-rimmed pince-nez. She thought she would feel more comfortable if honey-haired Lucie — her friend Lucie, taking *money* from this man! — if Lucie would spirit away her Lucullus, with his twitchy fingers and his calculating stare.

But would she then be expected to remain with the Englishman? Certainly not. Lucie had said she could leave whenever she wanted. She was under no obligation to this lanky, awkwardly moving foreigner with his braying laugh. He was, nevertheless, interesting when he was talking about his work. Or the joys of travel by dirigible. He had become quite lyrical, praising the new perspective on life provided by a viewpoint 3,000, 5,000 feet above the rooftops, when Lucie suddenly exclaimed: 'Look! Oh, *look!* There's Liane de Pougy. . .without her Arch-Duke for once. And, my goodness, what a handsome substitute she found!'

Annette glanced up. The courtesan was sweeping haughtily into the omnibus on the arm of her escort. The handsome substitute was Lionel Giotto.

At that moment he turned his head and saw her.

He registered an instant's indecision and then, raising his straw hat above his head, he nodded coldly, murmuring in a low voice that only she could hear: 'Good hunting. . .Mademoiselle Durand.'

To distinguish herself from the other single girls in the bar, Annette had refused champagne and was drinking white wine and seltzer. Now she almost choked with mortification into her tall glass — and the American had been welcomed by Cornuché, was being ceremoniously ushered together with his fancy woman to an omnibus table, before she could think of any reply.

For some minutes, so sharp was the bitterness and the hurt and the insult that seemed to have turned her stomach into a knot of pain, she was unaware of the conversation around her. Then she saw the industrialist was on his feet, pulling back Lucie's chair so that she could extricate herself and squeeze between the closely packed tables.

'Dearest, thank you for joining us,' she said to Annette. She was already a little drunk. 'Go home whenever you want.' And then, giggling: 'Don't do anything I wouldn't do!'

'Don't expect me to do anything you *would* do!' Annette flashed as the couple walked out into the night. But she didn't think Lucie heard.

'What was all that about?' Champney asked. 'I say, look here, do you speak English? I find this local lingo frightfully tricky.'

'A little,' Annette said. 'It was useful. There were so many English customers when I. . .when I worked at the Moulin Rouge.'

'The Moulin Rouge! Did you, by gad! Well, that's splendid. We'll stick to that then, if you don't mind.' He paused, brushing the ends of the sandy moustache outwards with the back of one hand. 'Now look, I can see you're an awfully nice girl, top drawer an' all that. Don't want to put a bally foot wrong, y'know. But François has taken your chum to a club where I'm not a member, so we can't tag along. No reason, just the same, why we shouldn't paint the jolly old town on our own, what! What I mean. . .how about tanking up and then having a bite together? Are you game?'

'Pardon?'

Champney gulped. 'Will you have dinner with me, and allow me to buy you a proper drink?'

Annette was about to refuse, to excuse herself and go home alone, when she suddenly thought: why not? He's harmless enough. If people insist on casting me as. . .if the whole world persists in treating me as if I were. . .Yes! Why the devil not? She said: 'Thank you. I will be very happy drinking with you a proper drink. And perhaps later dinner.'

'Spoken like a brick! Café de la Paix?'

'The Café de la Paix shall be very nice,' Annette said.

The Café de la Paix was indeed very nice. It was very crowded too. The audience streaming from Garnier's great domed and golden opera house on the far side of the *place* were happy with their *Tosca*. Inside and on the canopied sidewalk, the famous meeting place was bubbling with gaiety. After her third glass of champagne, Annette was sufficiently mollified and mellowed to start playing devious games with herself, games in which a certain American was always the loser. She owed it, she told herself tipsily, to her woman's pride. And because contempt is the unforgivable sin to a pretty woman, she played dirty.

She ordered and ate exactly the same meal that Lionel had paid the boot-boy to bring to their room at the Hotel d'Angleterre — the lobster soup, the duck *à la Rouennaise*, the peach mousse, everything. And when, sometime after midnight, Champney had begun in his coltish, diffident and slightly naive fashion to hint at a more intimate way of finishing the evening, she stopped him with a finger against his lips.

'Monsieur Champney,' she said unsteadily, 'I have to tell you that I do not accept money from men . . .However, if you are wanting to terminate —

258

terminate? No, to end is perhaps better! — to end this most pleasant encounter in a way friendly and warming, then I am telling you that across the street is an hôtel both comfortable and accommodating. It is called, most suitably, the Hôtel d'Angleterre. And there is a certain room on the fourth floor, they tell me, that may be especially — how do you say? — rewardful.'

In this way, she thought hazily, she would prove to the world that she was no whore, she would in turn strike a contemptuous blow against the man who loved her so little that he had basely condemned her without calling for all the evidence, and she would raise the standard of woman's right to choose.

Also she would save herself the trouble and expense of finding a cab and persuading the coachman to take her home to the Rue Halévy.

Love with Hector Champney — it had to be admitted — was different.

There was no chance here for those long, wild flights of abandon launched — provoked and nourished almost against her better nature — by the sensual transports stimulated by Bruno Morand and Lionel Giotto.

The Englishman, to be sure, had an unexpectedly athletic figure. He was also surprisingly well equipped and quite outstandingly virile. He was attentive, even adoring. But his attentions were paid on a different time scale to that of her two former lovers.

His clothes had been flung aside before Annette had finished untying the tapes on her drawers and camisole.

Clearly there was no place in his romantic *schema* for that blissfully dawning awareness of emerging beauty, that titillating, breath-stopping sense of imagination surpassed, as each fleshly treasure is rumoured, hinted at and finally revealed with the removal of each successive layer of clothing designed to display what it conceals.

If he had played football, Hector Champney would undoubtedly have been a centreforward.

'Here, let's have a go at that,' he offered as she was about to unclasp the small metal grips joining the busks of her corset. 'Strong fingers, don't y'know. Have to, hauling on those deuced balloon ropes.' Before she could answer, the constricting garment had been wrenched off and tossed aside and what remained jerked down to her ankles or pulled over her head.

'That's better!' the Englishman approved. 'My, what a spiffing shape you are! Better get down to it, what, before the sands run out of the bally hourglass!'

He picked her up and laid her on the bed. . .that same bed on which she had with Lionel passed so many ecstatic hours.

The muscled fingers which parted her thighs were in fact gentler than she expected. What followed was beyond any expectations she might have harboured, good or bad.

Lowering himself between her spread legs, Champney clamped his two hands over her breasts, bunched his slim hips and thrust forwards.

Annette experienced a sudden blare of sensation, much as a traveller, unaware of the route, suffers an abrupt blockage of the ears, a momentary numbness, when an express train plunges into a tunnel.

The shaft of flesh penetrating her shared locomotive qualities with the knights of the iron road. It was steel-hard, it moved fast, it pistoned in and out with relentless energy, and the engineer in charge was a man of determination and courage.

The hands covering her breasts rotated them as if they were the control levers of a tramway car. Between them she felt the coarse hairs covering Champney's chest scrape her skin. The blundering of his hips was bruising her.

And then suddenly, with a manic heave and a hot, convulsive spurting within, it was all over. He groaned once, collapsed across her, and then pulled free to run for the shower cubicle.

Two minutes later he was back with a towel wrapped around his waist. 'By Jove, that was good!' he enthused. And then, aware that a partner had been involved in the transaction: 'Better now, eh? Did you a bit of good, I expect? Nothing like it, if you ask me.'

Annette had not moved. She lay spreadeagled on the bed, her breasts tinged pink where they had been manhandled. 'Thank you, yes,' she said faintly. 'That was. . .impressive.'

He nodded. 'Needed it meself. What I like, you're a good girl. No footling around playing hankie-pankie. Straight for the goal, hole in one, an' all that. That's my aim in life: decide what you want to do. Do it. No messing about, if you know what I mean.'

'I didn't get much chance to find out,' she murmured. (Later, when Lucie asked her if the Englishman was a good lover, she was to reply: 'To be honest, I didn't really notice.')

Champney was burbling on. 'What's that you say? Never mind. Do you know, believe it or not, there are some chappies take ages over this. Love, I mean. Go on for hours and hours. Fact. Sister of a fellow in my house at school told me. Must be hell for their wives; poor dears would be quite worn out. Some chaps never think of other people.'

'You think love should be — how do you say? — sweet and short?'

'Short and sweet actually. Good Lord, yes. Any man who's fit should be able to manage it in three or four minutes. Five at the most. Anything longer shows lack of concentration. In any case. . .Haw!' — he uttered his braying laugh — 'Wasting time delays the starting pistol for numbers two and three, what!'

'You were thinking of. . .more?' Annette asked.

'What do you think, old thing? 'Course there'll be more. Fellow can't leave a stunner like you in midfield after only one shot at goal! Called to the colours, do your bally duty an' all that. I mean, my old nurse used to tell me when I was a nipper, "Hector," she'd say, "always remember – *you must think of other people*."' He chuckled. 'In any case, there's always the old saw: third time lucky, and so forth. French even have a saying with much the same message, don't they?'

Annette sighed. '*Jamais deux sans trois*,' she said dismally. 'Never two times without a third.'

Bruised and a little breathless, Annette contrived to start some kind of conversation going between the second wrestling bout and the third. She managed this because she was astute enough to question Hector Champney about his hobby.

'Ballooning?' he replied enthusiastically. 'Oh, my Lord, yes! Nothing like it. But you have to do it to know it, if you follow me. Take you up one day, if you feel like a treat.'

'I should like that very much,' Annette said. 'Tell me – after you have. . .lifted off, is it called?. . .after that, can you put the balloon down again wherever you want? Or do you have to wait until the wind shall stop or something?'

'Good Lord no! Fully under control. Guy ropes, heat control, ballast control. Just like driving an omnibus. Whip up the horses, rein them in. Put the bally thing down on a tennis court.'

'You could,' she said carefully, 'if you were taking your photographs above the city, you could perhaps place the balloon down, say, in an area like the paddock at the Longchamps racecourse?'

'Easy as winking. But why would I – ?'

'And take it up into the air again a few minutes later? If you wanted?'

'Yes, of course. But why would I want? Wouldn't mind drifting in low to get a different view of the nags and the ladies' hats, but I can't see the point in a touchdown. Not there. I mean, not quite the thing – especially if it was in the middle of a meeting.'

'Not even for a wager, a bet?' Annette said craftily.

She had very special reasons for asking these questions. The Spring Meeting, due to start in a few days time, was held at Longchamp, in the Bois de Boulogne. She had promised Milady to find out certain things about the organization, was in fact calling on Dagmar van den Bergh the very next day in order to keep that promise. And it had occurred to her as soon as this absurd Englishman started to boast about his damned balloon that he could be made use of to help Milady and Lily Leblanc with their 'not very illegal' plan. But she had to know, and she reckoned this was the best way to find out. She had always heard that it was a point of honour with a particular class of Englishman never to refuse this kind of challenge.

She had not been misinformed. Champney's eyes gleamed. 'A wager,' he repeated. 'A jolly old dare! Well, of course, that'd be different. You – er – you don't happen to know anyone foolish enough to suggest such a thing? I mean, did you actually have some chap in mind?'

'I might have. I know a man who is a gambler, a man who will wager money on anything, however bizarre,' Annette said untruthfully.

'Sounds exactly my kind of cove,' Champney said. 'But

I have to tell you, the favourite'd be six to one on. Very short odds indeed. I mean, dammit, your friend would lose.'

'Maybe that is the chance he likes to take,' she smiled.

'Whatever you say. He'd be on to something better if I was using hydrogen as an inflater. People say it's the coming thing in dirigibles. Very rum. For me the old Montgolfier's far more precise, much more manoeuvrable. Once you get the hang of it, of course. But then I've always been a hot-air man.'

Annette forbore to comment. Observing — she could hardly miss the manifestation — the lower part of Champney's body, she realized that it was seconds out of the ring: the third round was about to commence.

He had been sitting on the edge of the bed. Now, as he stretched out beside her and rolled her onto her back, she had to admit, awaiting the onslaught, that there was something awesome about the man. They had, after all, been in the hotel less than an hour.

The only lucky thing about the third time was that it was the last.

CHAPTER TWENTY-FOUR

Last night it had been Lucie. Now, ashamed as she would have been to admit it had she been aware enough of her surroundings, it was Annette who was, as they say, the 'worse' for alcohol.

What could be admitted was that the fault was not her own: it was entirely that of Dagmar van den Bergh. And that of her German friend Gisela.

Champagne *coupes* – a generous dash of brandy and a few drops of angostura bitters added to the best that the house of Krug could produce – had helped, indeed accelerated her along the downward path.

The two women, especially Gisela, had been the most assiduous of hostesses, never leaving their guest with an empty glass. By the time that Annette – oh, so casually, she thought – had obtained the information about the Longchamp meeting that she required, the chandeliers in the first-floor sitting room in the Avenue Kléber were spiralling giddily around her head. Except – and this was most odd! – she was not in fact in the sitting *room* but sitting on the floor of Dagmar's boudoir upstairs.

She had no clothes on!

'A bath, *liebchen*, is what you must have,' the German woman said solicitously. 'Then you will so much more comfortable feel.'

Annette remembered hazily that she had, quite unaccountably, broken down after the fourth drink and

265

confided her distress at Lionel's betrayal to the two *Amazones*. She knew they had laughed immoderately when she described the lovemaking of the Englishman, Hector Champney.

Why would she even have mentioned him?

Because as soon as they had seen her body, Dagmar had exclaimed: 'My God, *chérie*! What happened? Have you been attacked by apaches?' And she had replied: 'No, no. Nothing so interesting. I have been made love to by one of our British neighbours!'

As soon as they had seen her body? Then she must already have been undressed! How did that happen?

Memory supplied no answer. She did not even remember getting into this delicious warm bath with its steamy fragrance and the heady caress of its perfumed foam.

But she was aware, sensuously, deliriously aware, of the hands — four hands! — smoothing soap, lovely, sliding, slippery, sleepy, sloopy *soap* all over the discoloured patches on her body where the balloonist's roving fingers had clenched. She leaned back, sighing with contentment. What joy to be caressed instead of grabbed! What bliss to feel the weight of the breasts cradled, fondled instead of squashed! How splendid to have the skin gentled, softly kneaded, so lovingly massaged all over between the lacy webs of froth!

She heard voices; she felt movement and the streaming of water down her belly. And then she was wrapped in a huge warm white towel, laid on the white fur covering Dagmar's bed. . .but the hands, all four of them, had not ceased their caring ministrations! Still they coaxed, they pleaded, they smoothed. . .and now, once she was dry and the towel had gone (when did that happen?), they even started to explore. Her skin had been loved to a tingling, all-over awareness. She opened her eyes. And stared at four naked breasts, two on each side. The smaller, firmer pair with the rosy tips hardened belonged to Dagmar; the fuller, only *slightly* pear-shaped, to her friend.

When had they taken their clothes off?

She shook her head. No, no, this must not happen again. Not with two of them! Not even with Dagmar. It was not right. . .but the invading hands had already brought to life the high, wild singing in the head, the voluptuous, easy, unstoppable sense of abandon awakened in her by Morand and Lionel. Those champagne bubbles were drifting down towards her loins again.

Hands shaped the curve of her waist and moulded her breasts. A slight pressure rotated her belly. Two voices crooned. There were dove-soft fingers at her eyes, her mouth, in her ears. . .and, dear God, tangled in the tawny hair downing her shrine, easing apart the portals, touching the tenderest part of her secret place . . .

Annette jerked suddenly, uttering a hoarse gasp as her breath jetted out. She opened her mouth to protest, but it was immediately filled with the tip of a breast. Involuntarily, she sucked. And then the voices were clear and urgent. '*Ach, ja!* The finger here. So! . . .Move, my sweet one . . .Feel me. Now I am inside . . .Here! . . . Here!'

And Dagmar: 'Oh, your flesh! Your skin! Your hair! . . .Oh, you lovely! . . .Yes, with the tongue, the fingers, the lips . . .Oh, *YES!*'

She was in a world of sweet, warm touching, where lips and tongues, bellies and breasts, hands and mouths combined in a single, indivisible, caring whole — a long poem of sensation in which each separate stanza led with inexorable finesse towards the final explosive couplet.

And the long, shuddering waves of joy.

* * *

'You certainly mix those drinks skilfully,' Dagmar said when Annette had left the house in the Avenue Kléber. 'My goodness, I thought the spasms would never stop! She really is a natural, that one.'

'Everything is easy if you know how to begin,' Gisela said. And then, with a secret smile: 'Also perhaps there is a little extra something to add zest to the alcohol. But I agree — that curvy bundle of flesh is. . .rewarding. You think maybe we should continue the initiation, turn her completely and have her, how do you say, join the club?'

Dagmar shook her head. 'I know you too well. You lose interest once the curiosity is satisfied. A conquest once conquered is. . .well, no longer a conquest! You would be tired of her in a week. Besides, there is something I like about the girl. I feel sorry for her. I think that young American treated her abominably.'

'*Ja, ja.*' The German girl nodded. 'How funny it should be the same one — the one we take to the bawdy house to corrupt. My first experiment with the drinks!'

'And funnier still.' Dagmar said reminiscently, 'that she herself should have been in the bordel that same night with her vulgar policeman. Life is full of ironies.'

'I hear that he has been seen around with the de Pougy creature. The American, I mean.'

'Yes. Gabrielle Dorziat was walking her Borzois and she saw them come out of Cartier's together. Ghislaine de la Rochelléraut told me they were at Maxim's three nights in succession. But the Arch-Duke returns today, so I imagine that will be the end of that.

Gisela laughed. 'So! This is why the young stud agrees to a return engagement with us tonight! A quarrel with a mistress equals lust unsatisfied equals one *horizontale* equals two *Amazones*, no?'

'It was not even a quarrel,' Dagmar said. 'He believed what he was told, walked out on her without giving her a chance to explain, left his hotel and moved in with some Embassy crony who lives in an unfashionable street in the VIIth Arrondissement. Then the de Pougy. And now he thinks maybe a social call will result in a second exciting threesome!'

'Men!' said Gisela von Zwickenheim.

'Yes, men. I believe nevertheless that this couple are right for each other and that they should be together again,' Dagmar said. 'And I am beginning to wonder,' she added thoughtfully, 'whether it might not be a good thing in fact to corrupt the good Doctor Giotto a little further, only not perhaps in the way he expects. I think that young man needs to be taught a lesson.'

Annette found Milady at the café on the corner of the Rue Clauzel. The big, top-heavy blonde was wearing a candy-striped dress in two shades of green, with a very full skirt and not a great deal of top — what there was supporting an immodest amount of pink bosom. She was drinking an iced lemon drink through a straw, which permitted her to keep both eyes fixed on the men passing by while she slaked her thirst.

She embraced Annette warmly, then became suddenly businesslike and efficient with a notebook and pencil when Annette announced that she had answers to all the questions about Longchamp relayed from Lily.

'What could be more important, I think,' Annette said when her recital was finished, 'is this mad Englishman I met. If he was played right, Lily could change the whole of the second part of her plan.'

'Lead me to him!' Milady carolled. 'I specialize in mad English. What is so mad about him anyway?

'He is a photographer. But the important thing about

269

him, so far as Lily is concerned, is that he is mad about balloons. A balloonatic, in fact!'

Milady frowned. 'That's insane enough, I agree. But I fail to see what it could have to do with Lily's racecourse project.'

Annette told her what, in her estimation, it could have to do with the project.

'*Zut!*' Milady exclaimed. 'You could have something there, I agree. But how would we get *him* to agree?'

'Through his other lunacy. He is an inveterate gambler; he will wager money on anything, accept any dare. His part in the plan could be presented — through a third party of course — as just that: a dare. He'd get paid off with a percentage of the proceeds, although so far as he was concerned he would just be winning his bet.'

'Ve-ry in-genious,' Milady approved. 'We must tell Lily at once. But how do we keep our fingers on this man? How do we make sure that he will be available when we need him?'

'The wager, when it is made, will attend to that. But he will have to be cossetted along, taken care of, brought into the circle as it were, before that is sprung on him.' Annette coughed, blushed, and then stammered a little as she said: 'He is a. . .sociable man. He is alone, he is a stranger, and he likes to find new friends. I know where he is staying. I wondered if perhaps. . .I mean I thought that maybe. . .if you were to exercise your charms, he would be so happy to find himself with a beautiful . . .' Her voice died away.

Milady laughed. 'I imagine he has money? . . .Yes? . . .Then, my dear, you can safely leave that side of it to me. I suppose you have been to bed with him? What is he like, this madman?'

'Like a bull,' said Annette. 'Only it's not the ground he paws.' She blushed again. 'Actually in one way he's

270

remarkable — and really rather nice. And at least it does not take long!'

'Meet me here tomorrow,' Milady drawled, 'and point me in the direction of the quarry. Meanwhile I shall sound out the others.' After a brief pause, she picked a thread from the sleeve of her dress and added: 'Oh, by the way, even if they don't like the plan — which I'm sure they will — but even if they don't, I suppose there's no reason, after all, why your aeronaut shouldn't come down to earth and enjoy a little female company, eh? So make sure, *chérie*, that you do not forget that address . . .'

CHAPTER TWENTY-FIVE

Lily Leblanc's project was basically simple. In its essence it was no more than a plan to relieve the racecourse authorities of a very large sum of money that belonged, theoretically, to the government. Without causing injury to anyone.

Several years before, Anton Oller, brother of the Moulin Rouge director Joseph, had invented the system of on-course totalizator betting known as the *Pari-Mutuel*. It made a great deal of money for the professionals of the turf, for some members of the public, and for the state, which pocketed a large percentage of the profits as tax. At that time the division was actually made at the racecourse, and a proportion of the money taken was set aside for delivery under armed guard to the Ministry of Finance coffers. Lily aimed to divert this shipment before it left Longchamp.

The booty was expected to be considerable. The first day of the Spring Meeting, during the centenary *Exposition Universelle*, would attract a huge crowd. *Le Tout Paris*, everybody who was anybody, would be there in their finery, and so would large numbers of the public, both French and foreign. The betting would be heavy.

Annette de Vervialle had been asked to supply a general description of the course organization and police procedure, with details of the various types of ticket, pass or badge identifying stewards, trainers, lads or racecourse personnel who needed to gain entry to the paddock or that part of the main grandstand where the *Pari-Mutuel* offices were located.

Once Turkey Phiz and his associates had burgled the right premises to collect an example of each, Pierre the Penman would forge enough copies to enable the whole gang to infiltrate the interior of the course. The plan then was to converge on the betting offices, menace the clerks and tellers, and take off with the government money *before* it was handed over to the armed guards.

The difficulty had always been the getaway. The thefts could not take place until some time after the final race. The crowd would still be leaving stands and enclosures, blocking all the exits. Alarms would be sounded immediately the loss was discovered.

A provisional plan involved the use of motor cars borrowed from the notorious Anarchist band led by Bonnot. They would happily assist any escapade they considered anti-authority. But there were objections to this. The 'Anars' would have to be told of the project. They must be allotted a percentage of the take. And there was always the risk of a leak, of Jo the Terror and his professional gangsters muscling in to hijack the loot.

The difficulties seemed insurmountable. Lily was at the point of abandoning the whole thing. . .until she was told about Hector Champney and his Montgolfier balloon. This, she realized at once, could be the answer to all their problems.

Because once they knew of the raid, police, security men and racecourse officials would naturally expect the robbers to take flight. . .away from the meeting, out of the Bois. They would fan outwards themselves, throwing a cordon around the whole area, hoping to trap the thieves before they got away.

But what if the thieves were running in the other

direction? What if they ran to the *interior* of the course, to the paddock, the most enclosed part of the whole complex?

And what if, at that very moment, a hot-air balloon should arrive and lift them off, spiriting them away, up and over the crowds, the cordon, the Bois, away to who knows where?

What, in fact, if they should *literally* take flight?

'It's perfect,' Lily enthused. 'There's enough room in those basket gondolas for a couple of us, plus the swag. And the rest can chuck their badges and melt away with the racegoers, to meet us later for the share-out. A nice, quiet country place, I think!'

Pierre the Penman nodded. They were sitting around a table in the Red Rooster. 'He may be insane, your mad balloonist,' he said to Annette, 'but it's the kind of insanity, if we pull it off, that's going to look suspiciously like genius!'

Three days with the delectable Liane de Pougy had left Lionel Giotto with a depleted bank account, a physical awareness that rendered every nerve in his body avid for sensation, and an unquenchable thirst for female flesh. Approaching the house in the Avenue Kléber, he could actually feel his skin tingling with desire.

But if he had been expecting an immediate repeat performance of the scene enacted some time previously at No. 14 Rue de Monthyon, he was − initially at least − to be disappointed. His memories of that night were certainly hazy. Yet he retained a distinct impression that the powerful, strong-limbed German had permitted him to make love, indeed had virtually insisted that he make love, to Dagmar. . .with some stupid, egotistical idea that she herself could do better, was it not? Well, he would be only too happy to prove the contrary. . .again! If he could satisfy the famous and demanding Liane de Pougy (she had been most flattering, in transports of delight), then there was little doubt that his reputation as a lover would have nothing to fear from any muscular Brünnhilde whose appetites outran her expertise.

The only reason Dagmar was a member of the Amazonian cult, in any case, must be because she had yet to find the right man. Well, once the Teutonic intruder had been disposed of — he was handing his hat and gloves to the Comtesse's footman now — he would make it his business to demonstrate the qualities the right man should have. And the lady would have no trouble at all finding him, quite literally, at hand!

Such boastful thoughts were of course a form of subconscious defence against the pain he still felt at the loss of his Annette, though Lionel himself would have been the last to admit the depth of his chagrin. Pride in his prowess, in the versatility of his approach, was uppermost in his mind as he bounded up the stairs to the first-floor sitting room.

Dagmar and her friend were dressed very formally in street attire. Each wore buttoned ankle boots with a long skirt and a tailored jacket that flared out over the hips — Dagmar's in lime green lightweight cloth, the Baroness dressed in a heavier material that was gunmetal grey. A tall silk hat and a riding crop lay on a glass-topped table just inside the double doors.

The two women sat together on an upholstered settee that the American thought of as a davenport; he himself was offered a wingback chair on the far side of an enormous flower arrangement filling the empty grate beneath the ornate marble chimneypiece.

He had thought that any conversation would be based on an acceptance of the stage their relationship had reached at the end of that wild night in the Rue de

Monthyon. In fact it, too, was formal, stilted, entirely superficial. They talked of the exhibition, the weather, the Spring Meeting at Longchamp, the differences between restaurants in Paris, Boston and Berlin. He was asked his opinion of French bloodstock compared with that of the 'blue grass' region of Kentucky. Every attempt he made to steer the conversation the way he wanted was sidestepped or politely blocked. It was as though he was meeting them both for the first time. Even when a query about his low-life articles gave him the chance to introduce the subject of brothels, Dagmar dismissed it with a supercilious 'Oh, really?' – and at once switched to an appreciation of the literary merits of Zola.

Believing that the road to the boudoir would be open and any talk an unimportant prologue to the act, Lionel had made no more than a formal request that he might be permitted to call on the Comtesse. After a time it became clear, if the social customs were to be observed, that he must either take his leave or invite the two of them out to dinner.

Gritting his teeth with frustration, he chose the latter course.

'We should be delighted,' said Dagmar. 'How very kind. Where do you suggest? Maxim's?'

He flicked a swift glance in her direction, but she was smiling sweetly and the expression on her face was totally innocent. 'Well, no, actually,' he said, feeling a little awkward just the same. 'I thought maybe the Grand Véfour, or even Chez-Luigi. . .I guess those would be more, well, kind of suitable.'

'You think maybe Maxim's is too *demi-monde* for us?' Gisela inquired. 'Many people go there who are very. . . well-known.'

'Er. . .yes. I am aware of that.' Lionel said. He cleared his throat. 'Nevertheless –'

'My dear Doctor, we are entirely in your hands,' Dagmar cut in.

It was strange — Lionel reflected as the Comtesse's coachman drove them to the Grand Véfour — but despite the fact that the three of them had been intimate, more than intimate, as close in every sense of the word as human beings could get, he nevertheless felt tonight that instead of a trio they were very much two and one. In an obscure way — well, not so obscure really — he felt rejected, an outsider. Several times he surprised a sly smile on one face or the other: it was as though they shared some secret from which he was excluded.

And yet it was a civilized enough dinner party. They drank champagne, an excellent burgundy, brandy with the coffee. Conversation became gayer, more light-hearted. They laughed together. But there was still no sign, no indication, not the slightest hint that the fire consuming his loins every time he allowed his eyes to rest on their voluptuous bodies would ever be quenched.

The change did not come until they returned to the Avenue Kléber.

'Very well, take off your clothes,' Dagmar said tersely as soon as they had mounted the stairs to the sitting room.

Lionel gaped at her. In the coach they had been joking about the habits of tourists in the capital. It was jolly, but quite impersonal, like the dinner preceding it. And now, suddenly . . .?

'Come along, take them off,' the Comtesse repeated. 'You have been ogling the two of us for hours. Now is the time to do something about it!'

Quite bewildered, he reached up to his necktie. Seemingly of their own accord, his fingers began unravelling the knot. They stood side by side watching him, two elegant ladies in trim tailored jackets and long straight skirts. He allowed his own jacket to slide off his arms and drop to the floor beside the necktie. He fumbled with the suspenders holding up his trousers, unbuttoning the waistband. They continued to watch, their faces expressionless. When he was wearing nothing but his knee-length woollen drawers and his socks, he stammered: 'B-but what about . . .? I mean, why don't you . . .? Are you not going to –'

'What we do or do not do is entirely our own affair,' the Baroness interrupted. 'For the moment, since you have vainly been trying to force yourself upon us all evening, all we wish is to see what you have to offer.'

Together with Dagmar she strode forwards until they stood one on either side of the half-dressed American. He licked his lips, feeling at a disadvantage, unaccountably diminished, even a little absurd in the company of these women in their street attire. Yet the ache in that part of him expressly fashioned for their pleasure remained as fierce as ever. Held against his belly by the pressure of the tight-fitting wool garment, his upspeared staff formed an unmistakable outline. A small patch of moisture darkened the material at the upper end of the bulge.

He felt gloved knuckles against his skin as each of the women hooked fingers into the waistband of his drawers. . .and then dragged them suddenly down to his knees, so that the column of his desire sprang free with the dependencies below, and arrowed out from his loins.

'My goodness, here's a big strong servant more eager even than his master!' the Baroness exclaimed. 'Here, you'd better come this way and sit between us before the lower classes get out of hand!' Holding his honourable member between finger and thumb, she led him stumbling to the davenport.

He kicked off the encumbering garment and sat with one of them on either side, his quivering stem launched upwards from between his thighs. He had never felt more naked in his life.

Gisela and Dagmar turned towards him. Each put an arm around his waist. 'As my friend says, the steed looks hungrier than the horseman,' Dagmar observed. 'Even so, the master's strength must be kept up. So eat, therefore. Drink.'

Already slightly tipsy, and nonplussed by the totally unexpected turn of events, Lionel tried to refuse politely, but his hostesses were adamant. There was champagne on a side table, along with a plateful of almond-flavoured macaroons. 'Do what you're told,' the Baroness insisted. And she poured him a glass of wine and stuffed one of the small pastries into his mouth.

As he obediently chewed, swallowed, and drank, the arms around his waist tightened. The flesh below his ribs was massaged, kneaded. Each of the women drank some champagne — though neither, he noticed, took a macaroon — and then their free hands returned to him. One, Dagmar's, started lazily to tease his nipples. The skintight leather sheathing the Baroness's fingers crept up the inside of one naked thigh and then gently cradled the fleshy sac below his throbbing pride.

He reached out his own hands, but his wrists were slapped away from the clothing he would disarrange and he was told sternly to keep them to himself.

The subtle manipulations of Dagmar's gloved fingers had aroused a sensitivity, a thrill in Lionel's nipples that he did not know existed. Gisela's hand was now clasped around his upstanding part, rising and falling as rhythmically as the connecting rods of a locomotive. The arms circling his waist had tightened further so that two hands could smooth and rotate the flesh of his belly. Every nerve in his frame seemed ready to explode into ecstasy.

And then, as his breath was choking in his throat, Gisela said abruptly: 'That's enough. Stand up now and walk over to the door.'

He stared at her, amazed. 'But surely . . .?'

'Do what I say.' The voice was crisp, commanding. 'Hold that in your hand. Take it over there. Face the doors. . .and don't dare turn around until we tell you to.'

Bemusedly, his whole body still quivering, he complied.

Behind him as he faced the cream and gold panels he heard small sounds: the rustle of silk, a sudden snap of elastic, soft exhalations of breath, an exclamation, quickly suppressed. Something that sounded like a shoe dropped to the floor.

'All right,' Dagmar called. 'You may turn around now.'

He turned, still absently grasping his most private part.

He gasped. They were both stark naked, stretched out on a chaise longue, wrapped in a passionate embrace, mouths clinging together, cheeks hollowed, hands roving over buttock and breast.

As he watched, fascinated, the Baroness's fingers buried themselves between Dagmar's thighs. The Comtesse groaned through the slavering kiss. Her hips arched up off the upholstery to meet the invading digits. Her own hands vanished between the generous cheeks of Gisela's bottom. Shuddering, the two bodies rolled from the chaise longue to the floor, threshing among discarded clothes.

Lionel's head was spinning. Suddenly he felt very drunk. He fell to his knees. Some time later one of the women called him. He joined them on a white bearskin rug, a sudden fusing of three selves.

His palms supported the soft loose weight of breasts; his fingers clenched on flesh, tangled in moist hair, trailed through hot wet sliding furrows. There was a hand between his legs; lips sucked at him and tongues licked; below his belly he was expertly milked.

Then he was on his back with cool thighs clamped on his head. His mouth opened and he tongued a throbbing crevice. The belly crushed down on his chest contracted and spasmed. Somebody cried out. Another voice crooned something unintelligible and he heard dimly the slap of flesh on flesh. Lips closed over him exquisitely.

He was trembling, almost on the point of climactic release. Desperately, he tried to roll over and seize the hips nearest to him, so that he could force apart a pair of legs and plunge between them. But strong hands seized his shoulders and pulled him backwards. He found himself sprawling on the floor at one side of the rug.

The two nude women were on their feet. As Lionel struggled to sit upright, Dagmar lowered herself into an easy chair. She lay back panting, with her arms draped over the sides and her legs, stretched out straight, parted.

Her mouth, the lips glistening, was half open. Her perfect breasts rose and fell with her breathing. Some inner trembling fluttered the shallow curve of her belly above the chestnut triangle that furred her groin. Among the springy twists of hair a thin pink slit gleamed.

Gisela pulled the American to his feet. 'Go on,' she murmured. 'She can use you now.'

Lionel needed no second invitation. He caught his breath, consumed with delight at the thought, and moved forwards to lean over her. But once again he was thwarted. The Baroness seized his arm roughly and hauled him back. 'No, no,' she cried. 'Not like that! Down on your knees, man. . .and kiss her!'

Kneeling in front of the armchair, he looked once more at the delectable body of the Comtesse so invitingly spread before him. And then, hunched between her legs, he lowered his head to pay wordless tribute to her beauty.

As lips closed over lips and the tip of his tongue worried the taut little bud standing sentry at the entrance to her shrine, her hips jerked in delight and her legs rose to hook over his shoulders. At the same time he felt nails rake down the sensitive skin of his spine and the pressure of a heavy body crammed against him. The Baroness was kneeling behind him, her breasts squashed against his back.

Her arms wrapped around his waist and her strong hands grasped his rigid part, pulling, stretching, squeezing, compressing.

For some minutes the three of them worked in harmony, moving together as precisely and effortlessly as the mechanism of a Swiss watch. Then Dagmar's deep, hoarse breathing quickened and her loins began to shudder. The play of Gisela's hot breath on Lionel's neck became erratic. And he himself felt the whole impetus of his desire narrow and then concentrate on that part of him being so expertly manoeuvred.

The wave rose within him. He could do nothing to stop it.

It broke, with a thundering in his ears, as Dagmar uttered a wild cry and her threshing hips slammed again and again against the brocade covering the seat of the chair. He fountained the proof of his maleness into the Baroness's waiting hands.

Ten minutes later – he was still lying exhausted with his head resting against one arm of the chair – the Comtesse hooked up a speaking tube at one side of the chimney piece and said: 'And now I think it is time for you to go, my good Doctor. My coachman will be at the entrance door in ten minutes.'

He stared at her, still puzzled, amazed. The Baroness gathered up the discarded female clothes and left the room without a word.

Lionel shook his head, struggling to his feet. 'I don't. . .I mean I am not. . .I don't quite understand,' he mumbled.

The Comtesse smiled. There was something in it of Gisela von Zwickenheim's conspiratorial smirk. 'You were not meant to, *mon ami*,' she said. 'At least not at first. The evening was organized by way of a little lesson — to demonstrate that things are not always exactly what they seem. Or indeed what some people seem to expect!' She paused with the door half-open, her exquisite figure pale against the dark landing beyond. 'And the lesson,' she added, 'although you may think otherwise, is not yet over . . .'

From the window of the boudoir on the floor above, Gisela von Zwickenheim watched the carriage rumble out of the courtyard, beneath the arch and into the Avenue Kléber. 'Astonishing,' she said as Dagmar walked into the room, 'what a few grains of hashish will do!'

It was eight o'clock the following morning that Inspector Rochard, together with two uniformed *agents*, knocked on the door of the apartment where Lionel was staying. They were armed with a search warrant and a sworn complaint.

He was still half-asleep, his mind hazed by an unaccustomed torpor, when Rochard discovered a small gold snuff-box, two diamond rings, and a miniature casket in Chelsea porcelain, the property of Dagmar, Comtesse van den Bergh, in the pockets of the suit he had worn the night before.

Violently protesting his innocence, the American was arrested and taken to the local Commissariat of Police.

CHAPTER TWENTY-SIX

By ten o'clock in the morning on the opening day of the Longchamp Spring Meeting, clouds which had covered the sky during the night had blown away to the east and the course was bathed in sunshine.

Along the rides crossing and recrossing the Bois de Boulogne, early racegoers streamed towards the stands and terraces in cabs, carriages, motor cars, bicycles and on foot. Soon after midday the official reception marquees were crammed with politicians and presidents, *mondaines* and *demi-mondaines* in extravagant hats, and members of Montesquiou's horsey aristocracy mingling with check-suited breeders, trainers and other experts of the turf. Reutlinger and Amar set up their photographic apparatus, hoping to immortalize for posterity the allure of the fashionable world bedecking the ladies' enclosure. At the back of the royal box, Leopold II of Belgium drank champagne with someone who bore a remarkable resemblance to the dancer, Cléo de Mérode.

Ten miles to the north-east, in the suburb of Le Bourget, Hector Champney opened a picnic hamper and offered a salmon sandwich to Milady. On the far side of the meadow where the photographer's hired coachman had deposed them, a crew in workmen's overalls laid out the envelope and readied the guy ropes of the Montgolfier balloon.

'What beats me, old girl,' Champney said, 'is why your

mysterious friend insists that I bring her down at that precise time. Surely the bet is on whether or not I can position the damned balloon accurately in a small space? What does the exact time matter?'

The big blonde shook her head. 'What he is challenging you to do is manoeuvre the balloon *across Paris* accurately enough to land at an exact time,' she said. 'Time is more important, almost, than place.'

'Very rum,' Champney shrugged, pouring her a glass of Chablis. 'All the same, I'd have preferred to thrash out the details with him myself, meet the fellow face to face. No reflection on you, of course.'

'Impossible. He must remain anonymous. If it was known that he was prepared to wager such a large sum, it would. . .compromise his position. A man in his place cannot be seen as a gambler.'

'What place?'

'In. . .in the church,' Milady improvized wildly.

Champney crowed with laughter. 'I have a bet with a bally Bishop!' he cried delightedly. 'I say, what a jape! Good thing the old boy wasn't laying out the shekels on my performance last night, what! That would have had him counting his bidets, eh?' He exploded again with mirth, digging her in the ribs with one elbow.

Milady sighed, pushing herself back into a sitting position and mopping the spilled wine from her flowered skirt with a handkerchief. She was still sore from last night. But at least, as Annette had told her, the sessions were mercifully short. 'Talking of time,' she said, 'don't you think you ought to be supervizing those men? You don't want to risk a delayed start, in case the wind drops.'

He fished a watch from his pocket and sprang open the lid. 'By Jove, no' he said. 'Mind you, it's a nice little westerly. Should hold until dusk. Breeze could be a mite stiffer up there, too.' He glanced at the white clouds sailing across the blue sky. 'But you are absolutely right, of course. Absolutely. Better safe than sorry, what! I'll nip across and take a last-minute look at those burners.'

He rose to his feet and lumbered away through the long grass.

Milady sighed again, this time with relief. She poured herself another glass of Chablis.

'A mistake,' said the Comtesse van den Bergh. 'An unfortunate, a most regrettable mistake. The whole thing, you see, was a misunderstanding. My friend, the Baroness von Zwickenheim, was playing a little joke — the details are unimportant — but, alas, she forgot to let me into the secret! And since she happened to be absent when I discovered the loss — what I assumed to be the loss — then naturally I . . .'

She allowed her voice to die away. The desk sergeant looked sceptical. 'If Madame the Comtesse is absolutely sure . . .' he began dubiously.

'Of course I am sure. Doctor Giotto is a friend. He is completely innocent of any evil intention. I withdraw the complaint. Unreservedly. It is terrible that he has already spent twenty-four hours in a cell. If only I had known . . .'

The sergeant sighed. 'In that case. . .' he said. For thirty seconds the charge room was silent except for the squeak of his nib as he made an entry in his ledger.

'But it wasn't a mistake, was it?' Giotto asked as they drove away from the Commissariat in Dagmar van den Bergh's coach. 'You planted that stuff on me, didn't you, when I was under the weather?'

'Perhaps.'

'Might I ask why? Because that was no little joke. Not in my book.'

She did not answer him directly. 'It is instructive sometimes,' said she, 'to see how easy it is unwittingly to find oneself on the wrong side of the law. To discover how a set of so-called facts, wrongly interpreted, can lead to a totally erroneous conclusion.'

He was silent for a moment. And then he said: 'I see. You are drawing a parallel. This was in effect the final part of what you chose to call your "lesson"?'

'Let us just say that appearances can be deceptive. No evidence, however damning, should be accepted without an explanation being asked for. Let us say that *both* sides of any dispute must always be heard.'

And then he really did see.

'Three times a week,' Dagmar said inconsequentially as the carriage turned into the Avenue Kléber, 'the Orient Express leaves Paris for Vienna, Bucharest and Constantinople. Tomorrow the train will be stopping also at Strasbourg, in Alsace.' She handed him a sealed envelope. 'Here are tickets and reservations for a first-class sleeper. At Strasbourg an Englishman, a Monsieur Hector Champney, will board your Pullman and take the next compartment to yours, together with his companion. I understand that he may be obliged to stay away from France for a while, but he will nevertheless be happy to arrange for any photographs to be taken that you may require to illustrate your articles.'

She called out to the coachman. The carriage drew up behind a cab rank 200 yards from her house. 'I have to leave you here,' she told the American. 'I have a horse running at Longchamp later today. But I have one more thing to say to you.'

Smiling, Dagmar van den Bergh turned to lay gloved fingers on the back of his hand. 'I advise you to take that train, for a third person will be joining it at Strasbourg – a person I dare think you may find even more interesting than Monsieur Champney and his photographic apparatus!'

'But how do you *know* all this?' Annette demanded fifteen minutes later as the carriage rolled down the Avenue de Ranelagh toward the Porte de Passy and the Bois. 'How can you know about Lily Leblanc and the robbery she plans? And the Englishman and his balloon? About this supposed wager and the escape from the course?' She shook her head. 'How?'

The Comtesse suppressed a smile. The girl had been waiting outside the Trocadero as instructed in her note, and now they were on their way to the course. 'No mystery, *ma chère*,' Dagmar said. 'Most of it you told me yourself! And the rest I picked up from a woman I. . .chanced. . .to meet. Someone who is known, I understand, as Milady.'

'*I* told you? *Myself*?' Annette was dumbfounded. 'But how? When? Where?'

'The other night, in my house. After you had plied me with such a multitude of questions – oh, so casually, as you thought! – about the arrangements at Longchamp. Naturally I wanted to know why. You told me.'

'But I don't remember anything about it!' Annette cried.

'Well, there I am afraid I have to admit that Gisela was a little naughty with the drinks, so you mustn't blame yourself.'

'And you've done all this, bought train tickets, arranged everything, even spoken to' – Annette gulped – 'to the American? Knowing what was going on? Why did you do it?'

'Because, *chérie*, I have a fondness for you and wish you well.'

289

'And you told nobody! I don't know what to say. I – '

'Let us just say,' the Comtesse explained, 'that it pleases me to strike a small blow for women in a man's world.'

The meeting was a success. In the big race, The Exhibition Gold Cup, the favourite fell and the first past the post was an outsider, Cherry Ripe, owned by the Comtesse van den Bergh, herself a noted equestrienne. The other drama was saved for later.

Throughout the afternoon the members of Lily Leblanc's band had drifted inconspicuously towards the *Pari-Mutuel* offices. By the time the tapes were raised to start the last race they were in their allotted positions – Suzy Half-Pint and Jacqui the Jerker as lookouts near the rear entrance, Fat Berthe by the paddock gate, Turkey Phiz keeping an eye open for the law. Lily herself had decided to organize the spearhead group actually holding up the tellers. She would be with Pierre the Penman, masquerading as a racecourse official, Young Benoit, and Battling Bertrand, one of the wrestlers from Marseille's booth at the Neuilly fair. Bertrand and two apache friends, equipped with German army Mauser pistols supplied by confederates in Montmartre, would provide the necessary 'weight' to convince the PMU officials that it would be in their best interests to relinquish the sacks destined for the Treasurey.

The final race was over, the horses had been withdrawn from the winner's enclosure, the last lucky gamblers were being paid off at the ticket windows when a low murmur of surprise swept through the crowds heading for the gates. A Montgolfier balloon, gay with gold and purple stripes, had floated into sight above the treetops of the Bois. It drifted across the sky, losing height rapidly. When it was hovering low down above the finishing straight, the onlookers could see that there were two people in the basket gondola: a man and a tall woman with blonde hair piled on top of her head. The man appeared to be aiming the leather bellows of a large plate camera at the colourful throng scattered like flowers across the greensward below.

Soon he lowered the apparatus beneath the wicker rim of the gondola and busied himself with the ropes and ballast and burners under the inflated envelope of the balloon.

The subdued roar of the burners grew louder as the Montgolfier sank towards the trampled turf of the paddock.

At the same time a stout woman by the paddock gate began signalling like a tictac clerk to a red-faced man standing outside a door that led to offices beneath the grandstand. The man opened the door and shouted something inside.

By the exit from the PMU suite, Pierre the Penman, wearing his official's badge and Owner's Enclosure ribbons, knocked three times on the door and then ran to the building's side entrance. An armoured two-horse van stood in the yard outside with a sergeant and two gendarmes in attendance. Pierre beckoned the NCO, 'Very heavy betting today,' he said. 'A great deal of money wagered. They're a trifle behind, making the count. The chief teller says could you give them another ten minutes?'

'Very well,' the sergeant agreed. 'It's going to take us an age getting through this lot anyway.' He gestured towards the noisy crowd streaming homewards beyond the iron gates.

Pierre nodded. He went back inside and closed the door.

Once the shutters had been banged down over the ticket windows, an unnatural quiet had reigned in the PMU offices. This could have been because the tellers — who would normally have been joking together as they prepared to go home — were all locked, bound and gagged, in their strongroom. It could have been because Lily and her henchmen, having mastered the personnel without the use of violence and secured their booty, were anxious to do nothing that might attract attention. It was in truth because a third and unexpected factor had been added to the drama.

During the last race, Turkey Phiz had seen three or four toughs from the Montmartre gang led by Big René and Jo the Terror mingling with the crowd outside the windows. Had there been a leak? Were the strongarm men there to hijack the money once Lily had taken it? Or had they been sent simply to observe, to identify any pigeons that might be ripe for the plucking? Impossible to say. But in any case their appearance imposed a radical change of plan. For if they were to see a number of petty crooks from their own *milieu*, all of them wearing official badges or rosettes, their suspicions would at once be aroused and Lily's chances of getting away with her plan reduced to nil.

It was vital therefore that as many of her confederates as possible should discard these false identities and make themselves scarce. This in turn meant that the planned rush to the paddock, with everyone carrying stolen sacks of money to the balloon, would have to be abandoned.

It was Pierre the Penman who devised the alternative.

Two people only, the pair least likely to attract attention, would go to the paddock. Instead of the chained Treasury money-bags originally envisaged, they would carry with them as much gold and banknotes as could be stuffed into their clothing and whatever handbags, reticules and small valises a person might believably have with them at a racecourse.

Lily herself would be the first of these. The second —
although her rôle initially had been simply to wait in the
paddock as a liaison with Hector Champney — would
be Annette de Vervialle.

This would drastically reduce the amount of the take.
But it would greatly increase their chances of success.

Turkey Phiz, the professional bag-snatcher, had
acquired a leather attaché case, a capacious canvas
rucksack, and a couple of large lady's handbags. Into
these, about their persons, and in the purses they already
carried, the two women packed everything they could
from the ripped-open sacks. Bertrand and his friends
agreed to take whatever they wanted from what remained.
Pierre and the other members of the gang thought it more
prudent to leave empty-handed and meet Lily later for
the share-out in accordance with the original plan.

The robbers' task was made easier by the fact that the
PMU tellers had already divided the money into
banknotes of different denominations and small pouches
each containing one hundred gold Louis. But it was as
much as they could do to secrete the coins and packets
of larger notes in the ten minutes extra time gained by
Pierre when Turkey Phiz announced the touchdown of
Champney's balloon.

Once out of the grandstand building, Annette and Lily
ran for the paddock. Pierre, Young Benoit, the Phiz,
Berthe and the other girls dropped their badges into litter
bins and made for the exit gates.

Alarm bells shrilled when the two women were still fifty
yards from the balloon, which was hovering two or three
feet from the ground. Racecourse police and officials,
eager to find out why a *dirigible* was landing on their
territory, swarmed towards the paddock. At the same
time four rough-looking men jumped the rails and ran,
shouting, after Annette and Lily.

But by the time they were within reach, the runaways had scrambled aboard the basket gondola and the balloon, with burners roaring, was rising above the treetops surrounding the racecourse.

'Strasbourg, did you say?' Hector Champney stared over the rim of the basket at the patchwork of woods and fields drifting past 3,000 feet below the Montgolfier. 'That's a rum place to rendezvous! Neither Frog nor Boche, what! But we should make the outskirts by dusk all right: this little westerly's a real pippin, don't y'know.'

'It had to be Strasbourg because of the train,' Annette explained.

'Yes. Well. I can't see, all the same, why we have to be *on* the bally train. I mean, I've taken me pictures of the exhibition. Got some good ones too of the jolly old nags, thanks to the bet I just won.' He patted the pockets of his Norfolk jacket, where the money given to him by Lily was stowed. 'But even though I'm at a loose end now, why should I have to go all the way to *Vienna* just so that I can yak to this writer chappie on the old iron road?'

'Because it could be dangerous in France, that's why,' Annette said.

'Dangerous?'

'You're harbouring a desperate gang of international criminals,' she explained with a smile. 'Or that's what the newspapers will say. A confederate helping them to escape, you know.'

Champney stared at her. '*Criminals?* She's not serious, eh?'

And then, as he saw from their faces that she was, the eyes crinkled, the moustache bristled, the big teeth showed, and he uttered a great hoot of laughter. 'Haw!

Putting one over on the rozzers, eh? I say, what a jape! What did you do? Rob a bank?'

'Not quite,' Lily said. 'We helped ourselves to a little money that didn't belong to anyone. Nobody got hurt.'

'Hector with a band of lady cut-throats!' Champney crowed. 'Footpads of the fair sex, by gad!' It was clear that he regarded the whole thing as some kind of schoolboy prank.

'No newspapers are going to call *you* an international criminal,' Milady said to Lily. 'Only the tellers would have seen you, and they wouldn't have the faintest who you are. The same goes for the others.'

'No,' Annette agreed. 'But they'd know the balloon, wouldn't they?' She gestured towards the gaudy gold and purple stripes bellying above them.

'H. Champney, Esquire, on the Wanted list, by gum! That'd be a turn-up for the books. I can just see the guv'nor's face. Haw!' Again the sharp bark of laughter. 'And you mean to tell me that part of the ill-gotten gains . . .?' He patted his pockets once more.

'No,no,' Lily assured him hurriedly. 'You don't need to worry. You won that fair and square on a wager.'

'I do wish I'd met the old bishop, just the same,' Champney complained. 'Do him a bit of good, breathing the pure air up here, what! That much nearer his lord and master an' all that.'

Lily burst out laughing. 'He's a card, that one!' she choked. The laughter turned into a fit of coughing. She held a blue-veined hand to her mouth. When the fit was over she gasped: 'He's dead right, though. Up here, even after this short time, I feel the difference.'

The wind whistled through the ropes suspending the gondola. A long way below, wisps of cloud floated above tree-covered hills.

'What are you going to do with your cut?' Milady asked Lily.

'I'm going to Switzerland until this damned cough is better. Got me a beau too — a nice young man I met in Montmartre. He's an actuary and he's going to make the money earn more money. Or so he says.'

'An actuary?' Annette echoed. 'Not a tall, fair fellow, wears a curly-brimmed hat? Not. . .Paul Duclos?'

'That's right.' Lily looked astonished. 'You know him?'

'I did. Once.' The arguments she had with him over the rights of women seemed a very long time ago. 'He is nice,' she said warmly. 'I hope you will be happy.'

'I shall do my best,' Lily said. 'And you?'

'Like Monsieur Champney,' Annette said demurely, 'I have to meet a man on a railway train!'

'And Milady?'

'Actually, dear, I plan to get married, don't you know,' the big blonde drawled. She squeezed the balloonist's arm. 'Isn't that right, Hector?'

'Oh, by Jove yes, absolutely!' the Englishman shouted. 'Or something very like it, haw!'

CHAPTER TWENTY-SEVEN

The reconciliation was tearful. But the bitterness and wounds — from shame on Lionel's side, from offended pride on Annette's — were quickly submerged in a tide of mutual joy. By the time the Orient Express pulled out from beneath the glass canopy of Strasbourg station and rolled over the long bridge crossing the Rhine, the wonder of rediscovery had filled their minds.

So strong was the desire to touch, to hold, to reassure, to comfort even, that for long minutes after Annette's timid knock on the compartment door and the explosive embrace that followed it, the two of them were seized by a curious, paradoxical prudery, an unwillingness to transgress the borders of intimacy that had encircled them so closely before. It was as though everything that had happened, each abandon, every wild physical adventure, had been wiped from the slate and they were meeting again for the first time. They stood clasped together, separated by layers of material, lost now with only the light of desire in each pair of eyes to guide them.

It was Lionel who finally broke the embrace to hand her gently to the seat beneath by the pullman window. 'I think,' he said shakily, 'that we could both do with a drink. To fortify as well as to forget!'

The small private salon was luxuriously equipped. Pleated silk shades masked the bracket lamps projecting from a wall panelled in mahogany with an ivory and ginger-wood inlay. The curtains were fashioned in dark crimson brocade threaded with gold. Soft, deep-buttoned leather upholstered swivel chairs on either side of a sandalwood table. The brasswork was polished to a dazzling shine.

Lionel returned from the adjoining washroom with an ice bucket containing a magnum of champagne and a small three-legged stand. He wedged the bucket into the stand, unwrapped foil and wire, and eased out the cork.

The subdued report acted like a starter's pistol, freeing them from blocks on an athletic track. They both began to talk at once.

'If only you knew how much I blamed myself . . .'

'If only you knew how stupid I've been . . .'

'I should surely have realized . . .'

'I behaved in the most absurd . . .'

'I know I should have tried . . .'

'If only you could . . .'

'If only . . .'

They broke out laughing together. Lionel raised her tenderly from her seat and put his arms around her. He kissed her.

And the evening caught fire.

She responded passionately, hands laced behind his head, breasts and belly pushed against him. His hands moved, one to cup the warm swell of a breast, the other to clench her buttocks, pressing her more firmly to the hard ridge of desire already thrusting out the stuff of his trousers.

At last, as their tongues temporarily ceased their jousting and the lovers had to draw breath, she dropped her hands and leaned back in his embrace with shining eyes. 'Lionel, Lionel!' she breathed. 'My Lionel. Oh, my dearest!'

He looked deep into those eyes, his own mirroring the

love and desire his searching gaze found there. Very slowly, fingers working sight unseen, he started to unfasten the row of buttons curving out over the front of the short, waisted jacket she wore on top of her dress.

The dress was damson-coloured, fashionably tight-skirted with a fringe at ankle height and panniers of contrasting material draped over the hips. The jacket (she had bought new clothes in Strasbourg, waiting for the train) was black, with a tiny, close-fitting ermine collar. Against the furred caress of this white choker, the column of her neck, her perfect jaw-line, the blush of her cheeks, glowed with a sensual vitality that hinted subtly at the delights of the pliant body concealed below.

The jacket was undone. He stared with wonder at satin-smooth slopes of flesh cradled by the low-cut neckline of the dress. In the shallow valley between them lay a single teardrop ruby supported on a gold chain. 'A farewell present,' she told him, suddenly defensive. 'From Dagmar.'

He touched the taut damson curves thrust out by the constriction of her corset, pressing them up so that flesh bulged out over the ruched white lace bordering the neckline. 'There are finer jewels,' he whispered huskily, 'within the reach of a determined man!' He pushed harder, so that the rosy tips of these breasts, hardened now with excitement, spilled into view above the lace. He lowered his head.

A shudder of sensation thrilled through the upper half of Annette's body as his lips closed hotly over one of the erect buds. She drew a deep and shaky breath when the tip of his tongue explored the puckered skin surrounding it.

For a small eternity they stood there, rocked slightly by the motion of the train. Black smoke from the locomotive whipped past the window. A field, a farm, a wooded hill slid past and then veered back into sight as the express rounded a curve.

Her knees were suddenly weak. 'Undress me, Lionel,' she murmured, fondling the back of his head. 'I want you to have all of me.'

He straightened, smiling his love into her eyes. For an instant, fleetingly, he experienced a pang of indecision, of doubt. He was afraid he might tarnish the splendour of the moment by clumsiness or fumbling. But his fingers, living a life of their own, were already at work, unhooking, unlacing, loosening tapes, feeding buttons through buttonholes. The open jacket, pushed back, slid down her arms to the deep-pile carpet flooring the compartment. Like Venus rising, she emerged from the dress, her camisole was no more, silk drawers unsheathed her thighs, slipping smoothly down past hose and garters.

She stood, wearing nothing but a deep-red corset fringed with black, dark stockings and tight black boots buttoned over the ankle.

Lionel was electrified by the sight. Amid the rich furnishings of the luxury train, the half-naked young woman was the incarnation of his every dream. With a languorous smile, she raised her arms to unpin her tawny hair, lifting at the same time those swelling breasts whose memory had haunted his imagination for so long.

Alternations of colour and texture in that confined space fired the young man's passion to fever heat. A glossy tumble of hair that framed the heart shape of her petal face. Smooth shoulders and the provocative soft tilt of nude breasts above the rigid clasp of a corset whose reinforced satin and whalebone drew in the waist. Below that, the billow of womanly hips and a slope of belly sweeping into the hairy triangle that separated her alabaster thighs. And then flesh gleaming through the thin web of stockings, and the tight leather boots. The contrasts, against the ornate décor of a compartment on the Orient Express, made her seem, paradoxically, more naked than any woman he had ever seen.

He moved towards her, hands reaching for the laces securing her corset, but she shook her head. 'No, no. Not now. It takes too long.' She was breathing hard and her voice was tremulous. 'I can't wait, Lionel, I can't!'

The bed and its covers were folded up into the compartment wall. She sank down onto the oriental-style tapestry covering the seat.

He was already tearing off his own clothes, hurling aside shirt, tie, jacket, trousers and undergarments in his haste to project himself on the divine creature sprawled so invitingly before him, his aching stem — for too long corseted itself by the restriction of clothes — speared before him like a lance.

Half sitting, half lying, Annette slumped against the seat's backrest, her buttocks on the front edge of the cushion. She bent her legs and drew up her knees, hooking her forearms behind them to keep them raised and expose her secret parts to his burning gaze.

Lionel dropped down to kneel between those spread thighs.

He stared, fascinated as always, at this most intimate revelation. And once again the contrasts underlined the explicit invitation: smooth skin of the inner thigh against a furrowed curl of hair; pink lips gaping pale around a darker red bud; a wrinkle of tight flesh separating the wide curves of her bottom.

Her head was bent forward so that her chin rested on her chest. She looked at him through half-closed eyes, looked between her mounded breasts, over the crimson corset and the slack bulge of belly, at his face poised between her parted legs and above her shamelessly offered shrine. 'I missed you, Lionel,' she said throatily.

For a second more he gazed into her eyes. And then with a choked cry he lowered his head to her loins.

The moment his open mouth touched her warm wet flesh, the moment his lips caressed those other lips and his probing tongue tipped the surface of the sentinel within, he was lost in a world of heightened sensation. Apologies for his lack of faith, gratitude for the rediscovery of his love, proud offering and humble acceptance all fused with the expression of physical joy in his passionate tribute to the young woman whose belly heaved beneath him.

Annette moaned softly, shifting her hips. She released her legs, draping them over his shoulders and crossing the ankles in the small of his back so that she could use her hands to press his head more firmly to her burning loins.

The train slowed, obeying a signal, and shuddered almost to a halt in a country station. It was dusk and the gas lamps along the platform were lit. The wide uncurtained window of the Pullman, and the erotic tableau visible behind it, slid slowly past the astonished regard of passengers waiting for a local train. Neither of the lovers was aware of the unexpected audience.

It was not until the locomotive bellowed and the express, with a sudden jerk and a clutter of couplings, accelerated away that Lionel — his own loins so bursting with desire that he could no longer contain himself — separated himself to rise unsteadily to his feet.

Panting hoarsely, he laid the unresisting girl along the seat, thrust apart her thighs and cast himself down between them. She uttered a single gasp as his cavalier, requiring no guiding hand on the rein now, galloped home. And then there was just a series of soft cries, mounting to a passionate crescendo as their plunging bodies hurled them into a mutual release — too long delayed — with explosive force.

They lay still curled together, exhausted but blissfully happy, when they heard the ringing bell. In the corridor outside the locked compartment, a white-coated steward shouted: 'First service! First service! Dinner is now being served in the restaurant car. Please take your places for the first service!'

They dined in the restaurant car. The second service. 'They will bring it in here, if you prefer,' Lionel offered. 'I have only to ring the bell summoning the conductor.'

Annette shook her head. She was pinning up her hair. 'Let us sit among the public,' she said. 'I shall leave off my drawers and so must you. Then we can touch each other beneath the starched tablecloth and nobody will know!'

The Orient Express roared through the densely wooded hills of the Black Forest and crossed a bridge spanning a stream at Ulm that was in fact the Danube at the beginning of its 1,776-mile journey to the Black Sea. Threading its way through the industrial complex on the outskirts of Augsburg, the great train arrowed along the moonlit tracks towards Munich.

In the dining car, Annette and Lionel faced each other across an immaculately laid table, their faces glowing in the subdued light from a softly shaded lamp. Around them was a murmur of voices and the jingle of cutlery and glass as the express traversed a set of points or rounded a curve. Waiters in mess jackets glided between the tables bearing fine wines and silver trays loaded with exquisitely cooked food. The reunited lovers didn't see the waiters, were not aware of what they ate, and heard no voices. Even a bray of laughter from Hector Champney at the far end of the coach passed unnoticed.

Lozenges of yellow light reflected from the Pullman windows raced along rock walls, undulated over fields beside the permanent way and slid past the sheds at wayside stations. It was only when the train was halted because of work on the line that Annette glanced through the double glass. She saw a two-horse dray piled high with hay bales waiting at a level crossing; shining levers in a signal cabin; and in the distance a necklace of bright lights strung along the gantries and walkways of a foundry blowing flames into the night. She looked back across the winking wine glasses, the silver chafing dish, trying to decipher the expression on his shadowed face. 'Just where, my dearest, are we going?' she asked.

Lionel smiled, strong teeth glimmering in the diffuse light. 'In theory, just to Vienna,' he replied. 'But I fancy we should stay with the train the whole way, following the Danube past Linz, Vienna, Budapest, and then on through the Carpathians to Bucharest and the Black Sea. Then Istanbul, perhaps Athens, and a boat that will take us to America. And a church.'

She touched him beneath the table. 'Oh, Lionel!' she breathed.

Back in the private club compartment, he manoeuvred the cork from a second bottle of champagne which had appeared in the ice-bucket. It was time now for the delights of love to be savoured, for the wine of passion to be sipped rather than gulped.

With time stretched limitless ahead, the first frenzy of their coupling and its explosive release behind them, they could afford to linger, to taste, to sample, to admire.

Undressing, no longer a frantic rejection of unwanted obstacles, could once more become a ritual. Lionel unsheathed her slowly from her dress, pausing between

304

each tape, each hook, every button, to marvel at the smoothness of a shoulder revealed, the curve of her back, to press a kiss into the crease of an elbow. When her breasts were again bared he could not resist paying an extended tribute to each roseate tip with his lips and teeth and tongue.

He unfastened and drew off her boots, rolled down the stockings and stripped away the drawers. Then, at last, it was time for the crimson and black corset. Three glasses of champagne later, with the yards of lacing gently unthreaded through the eyeholes and the edges of the busk unclipped, he held her naked in his arms and breathed in the warm, musky scent of her womanhood.

Intoxicated more by this heady perfume than by the fumes of wine, he laid her down on the bed, which had been made up by the conductor and lowered into place while they dined.

His head was spinning; he was giddy with desire. He feasted his eyes on the long, alluring length of her body – tawny hair spread fanlike on the pillow, the delicate face smiling mistily up at him, arms raised to lift those tender breasts, a supple waist still ridged with weals from the corset's embrace, and then the soft shallow dome of a belly that plunged between two perfect thighs under a coverlet of springy hair.

Slowly, with trembling fingers, Lionel began to remove his own clothes. She lay silently watching him, only reaching out a hand to tweak down the drawers when his trousers had gone, so that his male part jerked stiffly into view.

She took the rigid stem in one hand, massaging it slowly with forefinger and thumb. 'I do declare,' she said, 'that is has grown bigger even than it was before we dined!'

'It will continue to do so,' he said hoarsely, 'so long

as you look at me like that. And so long as you keep doing this!'

Annette squirmed her body on the bed. Her hips rose slightly and her legs parted to show a gleam of pink pouting through the tawny fur. 'I think I would like you beside me now,' she murmured.

He lay down at once and took her in his arms.

For a long time then there was touching and caring, a period of stroking and exploring, of probing and searching, of old acquaintances renewed and unexpected surprises; a reflective period of fingers and mouths on skin that was creased and skin that was bursting smooth, of the hot, wet sliding caress and the cool, dry grasp of pulsing flesh. A period, nevertheless, when the breath quickened with each passing second, the two hearts thudded, and excitement welled up inexorably to the moment when contemplation gave way to action.

When at long, thrilling last he was over her – although it was not so much that he rolled on top as that she slid insidiously beneath – the junction of their bodies was as exact as the thrust of a finger into the perfect glove.

The thunder of the distant locomotive, the rumbling of wheels, the hiss of steam and the creak of wood as the curtains swung into the compartment and the train leaned into a curve, formed a dreamlike obbligato to the tumultuous orchestration of their mutual desire. Their dual rhythm mocked the relentless advance of the express. And when at last the world spun away and white light engulfed them both in a shuddering, spurting spasm of shared release, it was the onwards, roaring rush of the engine that lulled them to sleep.

They woke later to the echo of martyred springs and a loud thumping noise that shivered the wall separating them from the next compartment. 'What the devil is that?' Lionel cried, starting up in bed.

'Monsieur Champney, I think, making love to his lady,' Annette replied sleepily, burrowing her face in his shoulder. And then, mimicking the Englishman: 'Or something very like it, haw!'

Later still, Lionel woke again. Through the uncurtained window, curling away towards the head of a long valley, the front of the train was visible with reflected flames from the locomotive's furnace flickering on the underside of smoke billowing from the funnel. Two minutes later they ran out onto a plain and he could see the snow-capped crests of the Kaisergebirge, unbelievably white against a navy-blue sky.

He reached for the warm, pliant body nestled beside him. Annette snuggled closer, muttering something in her sleep. He was close to slumber himself but the urge to love, stronger than any automatic compulsion of his brain and nerves, spurred him on.

Her fingers closed over his male part, effecting an instant transition from limpness to rigidity. His own hands then moved of their own volition. . .and in his half-conscious mind a parallel grew between the rhythms of the train and the voluptuous stirring of the bodies in the bed.

The express steamed across the marshes separating two lakes near Fürstenfeldbruck (Lionel's hands dabbled in the damp fur nested between Annette's thighs). Crossing the plateau south-east of Munich, the locomotive panted up the grades leading to the high ground south of Bernau (he cupped a breast, shifting the soft mound of flesh until the taut bud topping it peaked). Light spilled from the moonlit Chemsee dappled the compartment's pale ceiling, tinged now with red from flames that streamed above chimneys marking the new petroleum refinery outside Linz (a fire within the American was stoked suddenly to white heat, and he rose in the bed).

The rumble of wheels, the racing of his pulse and the beat of the heart beneath his hand were one. In the distance a whistle shrilled.

Lionel was kneeling. With a strangled endearment, he spreadeagled the girl below him, forcing apart her thighs so that he could drive into her. He felt her legs lock around his back. She cried aloud, swallowing his maleness in the hot clasp of that secret throat which lay behind the lips smiling from her loins.

The thundering rush of the luxury express echoed the turbulent surge of blood through their veins. The train plunged into a tunnel, forging onwards into the darkness, into the light.

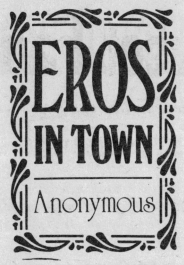

Sweet Fanny

The erotic education of a Regency maid

Faye Rossignol

*'From the time I was sixteen until the age
of thirty-two I "spread the gentlemen's
relish" as the saying goes. In short, I was
a Lady of Pleasure.'*

*Fanny, now the Comtesse de C———, looks
back on a lifetime of pleasure, of
experiment in the myriad Arts of Love.
In letters to her granddaughter and
namesake, she recounts the erotic education
of a young girl at the hands of a mysterious
Comte – whose philosophy of life carries
hedonism to voluptuous extremes – and his
partners in every kind of sin. There is little
the young Fanny does not experience – and
relate in exquisite detail to the recipient of
her remarkably revealing memoirs.*

More Erotic Fiction from Headline:

EROS IN THE FAR EAST
Anonymous

Recuperating from a dampening experience at the
hands of one of London's most demanding ladies, the
ever-dauntless Andy resolves to titil.ate his palate with
foreign pleasures: namely a return passage to Siam.
After a riotously libidinous ocean crossing, he finds
himself in southern Africa, sampling a warm welcome
from its delightfully unabashed natives.

Meanwhile, herself escaping an unsavoury encounter in
the English lakes, his lovely cousin Sophia sets sail for
Panama and thence to the intriguing islands of Hawaii –
and a series of bizarrely erotic tribal initiations which
challenge the limits of even her sensuous imagination!

After a string of energetically abandoned frolics, Andy
and Sophia fetch up in the stately city of Singapore, a
city which holds all the dangerously piquant pleasures of
the mysterious East, and an adventure more outrageous
than any our plucky pair have yet encountered. . .

Follow Andy and Sophia's other erotic exploits:
EROS IN THE COUNTRY   EROS IN TOWN
EROS IN THE NEW WORLD   EROS ON THE GRAND TOUR

FICTION/EROTICA   0 7472 3449 3   £3.50

A selection of bestsellers from Headline

FICTION

A WOMAN ALONE	Malcolm Ross	£4.99 □
BRED TO WIN	William Kinsolving	£4.99 □
MISTRESS OF GREEN TREE MILL	Elisabeth McNeill	£4.50 □
SHADES OF FORTUNE	Stephen Birmingham	£4.99 □
RETURN OF THE SWALLOW	Frances Anne Bond	£4.99 □
THE SERVANTS OF TWILIGHT	Dean R Koontz	£4.99 □
WHITE LIES	Christopher Hyde	£4.99 □
PEACEMAKER	Robert & Frank Holt	£4.99 □

NON-FICTION

FIRST CONTACT	Ben Bova & Byron Preiss (eds)	£5.99 □
NEWTON'S MADNESS	Harold L Klawans	£4.99 □

SCIENCE FICTION AND FANTASY

HYPERION	Dan Simmons	£4.99 □
SHADOW REALM	Marc Alexander	£4.99 □
Wells of Ythan 3		

All Headline books are available at your local bookshop or newsagent, or can be ordered direct from the publisher. Just tick the titles you want and fill in the form below. Prices and availability subject to change without notice.

Headline Book Publishing PLC, Cash Sales Department, PO Box 11, Falmouth, Cornwall, TR10 9EN, England.

Please enclose a cheque or postal order to the value of the cover price and allow the following for postage and packing:
UK: 80p for the first book and 20p for each additional book ordered up to a maximum charge of £2.00
BFPO: 80p for the first book and 20p for each additional book
OVERSEAS & EIRE: £1.50 for the first book, £1.00 for the second book and 30p for each subsequent book.

Name ....

Address ....

....

....